Praise for *Lola Dances*

"Sometimes I would be able to have more words in English to describe a book, cause I really want to transfer to you the joy and the emotion I felt reading it. Lola Dances is not a simple book. It's a powerful novel, and it's strong but real."

Elisa Rolle

"… a sultry saga that takes you on a journey of dark secrets, murder and the forbidden…Victor J. Banis weaves a complex story with some tantalizing surprises; Terry's loneliness gives a tug to your heartstrings, and a feeling of indignation for his loss of innocence. Lola Dances is a most intriguing odyssey."

Chocolate Minx, Literary Nymphs Reviews

"I was impressed with the way the setting was effortlessly fused into the story. Banis portrays well the tension between Lola, whom everybody is in love with, and Terry, whose best hope is to stay under the radar."

Vashtan, Speak Its Name

"*Lola Dances* is a suspenseful, gripping and heart-wrenching story, rich with historical details and believable characters. I enjoyed the growth of Terry's character as he matures from a shy boy living in a harsh and violent environment, to a self-confident performer, to a young man who knows what he wants out of life and love."

Nancy, Outlaw Reviews

Notable among Victor J. Banis's other work:

The Why Not
The Man From C.A.M.P.
Angel Land
Longhorns
The Deadly Mysteries
   Deadly Nightshade
   Deadly Wrong
   Deadly Dreams
   Deadly Slumber
   Deadly Silence

For a more extensive listing, see Victor's page at Goodreads.

http://www.goodreads.com/author/show/119291.
Victor_J_Banis

Lola Dances

Victor J. Banis

ROCKY RIDGE BOOKS

ISBN-13 978-1-62622-028-7

Copyright © Victor J. Banis 2008, renewed 2015
Cover art by Shobana Appavu
Interior Layout by P.D. Singer

First edition 2008 MLR Press
Second Edition 2015 Rocky Ridge Books

Published by:
Rocky Ridge Books
PO Box 6922
Broomfield, CO 80021
www.RockyRidgeBooks.comPrinted in the United States of America

For all the "sissies" out there everywhere.

"Never let the fact that they're doing it wrong stop you from doing it right."

Jake Barnes, *The Opening of Misty Beethoven*

Part I

The Bowery

Chapter One

"Sissy."

"Hey, little girlie."

"Guess what I've got for you."

Terry Murphy was used to it. He went past the loading dock every day to get to the theater for his dance lessons. They were always hanging around there, never fewer than two of them and more often four or five, and always quick to taunt him. He pushed his glasses up on his nose and ignored them.

At first he'd been afraid they might physically assault him, and he'd had to resist the urge to run from them. Some instinct told him that would be a mistake, that it would only empower them, encourage them to follow through with threats that were, as yet, only implied.

It wasn't that he lacked courage. But even if he had thought, even for a moment, of standing up to them, what chance would he have had? They were young, some of them probably younger even than he was, at least in years, but they were far older than he was in other ways. They were all of them as tall and as burly as any grown man, hard-muscled from loading and unloading the drays that came and went at all hours of the day and night. He was five foot five inches in his stocking feet, slim, skinny really. He was muscular enough, in a wiry, dancer's way but it wasn't fighting-muscular.

Anyway, it wouldn't have mattered how tall he was or how muscular. He wasn't the sort for fisticuffs. He had learned that early

Victor J. Banis

on, at the Mission School. He'd always been smaller than the other
boys his age and it hadn't taken the bullies long to discover him.

Once, when he was little and working in the washroom, he
had found one of the girls' uniforms, fallen behind a rinse tub and
left unnoticed. On some whim he hadn't paused to analyze, he'd
put the blouse and jumper on—and had been found in them by
a couple of the older boys. The story had quickly spread around
school, and made him the center of an attention he would rather
not have known.

He had quickly learned the strength of passivity. He couldn't
outfight them, or outrun them or stay clear of them. What he
could do, he soon discovered, was spoil their fun. The pleasure
of just punching on him had paled quickly for them, especially
since no matter how often or how brutally they did it, he flat out
refused to cry or, as they demanded repeatedly, to "say uncle."
He simply would not give them that satisfaction. Even if they
had killed him—and once or twice he thought they might—they
couldn't get that out of him.

There wasn't a lot of fun for them, as it turned out, in punching someone who responded so passively, and it hadn't been long
before they found better candidates for their torture. After that,
they had mostly simply ignored him and Terry had conspired with
them in that by getting very skilled at "fading into the woodwork."

At first, he had been convinced that these toughs at the loading dock, too, would eventually take their fists to him, until they
lost their enthusiasm for a victim who refused to participate in
their sport, and the prospect dismayed him. At the same time,
though, there was something about these hooligans that fascinated him in a way those other boys hadn't, though he couldn't
have put into words what it was.

The truth was he could have avoided them. Though it would
have been several blocks out of his way, he could have reached
the theater from the alley on the opposite side, and he wouldn't
have had to encounter them at all. But that, some stubborn part
of him insisted, would have been a victory of some sort for them,
too much like crying uncle.

∾ 2 ⌒

Sometimes when he saw them, though, stealing glances at them because he tried to pretend he was not aware of them, he was assailed by a strange kind of lightheadedness, a dizziness almost, that came over him out of nowhere.

They were ruffians, crude, boorish, unwashed. Sometimes, even at a distance, he actually thought he could smell them: the grease on their hair, the stains on their too-seldom-laundered clothes, the sweat of their too-seldom-bathed bodies.

He couldn't, of course. They were never close enough for that. It was just some trick of his imagination. They never ventured more than a foot or so from the loading dock. They sat playing cards or knelt, dice snickering on the ground between them. Still, it seemed as if there was a scent that emanated from them, that filled his nostrils like the odd spices that wafted from the shops in the Jewish quarter when he walked that way. Odd and yet strangely familiar, reminiscent of something he couldn't possibly have known.

But where did it come from, that peculiar sense of familiarity with these young men, of some proximity, even, that was not of a physical sort? What caused it? What was it about those thick-muscled arms and legs, those stubbled chins, already showing men's beards, the hair some of them already sported on their chests, while his chin was as smooth as porcelain, his body all but hairless?

His voice, too, was hardly changed from what it had been when he was a boy. When he sang, it was in a woman's voice, not a man's. But why did those man-deep baritone voices with which they jeered at him make his head swim, give him that strange fluttering feeling in the pit of his stomach, at the same time it—and they—frightened him? None of which he had experienced with those earlier bullies.

What had changed, then, in the years since he—and his tormentors—had passed through puberty? That something was different here, he was stone certain.

He had a strange feeling that if he had even paused to smile at them, to stroll over to where they were, they'd have run from him just as he had sometimes wanted to run from them.

He couldn't think why that should be true, though. It was ridiculous to think that these street toughs could possibly be afraid of him, of anything he could do; but somewhere inside himself, he believed it. There was something overdone in their bravado, something concealed within it of an opposite nature.

It had given him courage, that peculiar conviction, not the stand-up-to-them kind of courage, but the stoical, go by and pretend he hadn't seen or heard them kind. He did that now, looking straight ahead, his chin tilted upward. He ignored the titters that followed him, though his senses as he passed by them were so preternaturally heightened that he heard them clearly enough, was aware of them not just as a group, but each of them singly. He could have sketched them if he'd been an artist, recognized each voice for its individual timbre, as a mother was said to know by instinct the cry of her child out of an entire crowd of children. He couldn't prevent himself from blushing, though, as they shouted and jeered him—something that he did all too easily and that was one of the banes of his existence; but he doubted they would notice that.

His face the color of rose petals, he let himself in the stage door, hurrying. He was late. The girls were already in the rehearsal hall, the pianist banging out a facsimile of a can-can, slippered feet making a swishing noise on the wooden floor. The professor stood in the open doorway, watching Terry run down the corridor.

"So good of you to join us, Master Murphy," he said. "I hope we're not interfering with your social life."

"I'm sorry," Terry said breathlessly, hurrying past him to the dressing room. "The manager was late. I can't leave the bar until he gets there."

"That, Master Murphy," the Professor said, "is not my problem. My problem is a dance class that I run for all my students, and that I cannot hold up for one of them who refuses to be on time."

Terry didn't waste the breath arguing. He stripped quickly, donned the dance cup, the tights, the slippers. He left his glasses in the dressing room—he saw everything through a myopic haze without them, but it was too hard to keep them on when he danced and he couldn't afford to have them go flying off and get broken—and hurried back to the hall. He did not even take time to do the customary warm up stretches, though he knew he was flirting with disaster dancing without warming up.

Flirting with disaster. That, he thought, pretty well described his life, didn't it?

Afterward, when the girls had gone, he stayed to practice. His body ached, the predictable penalty for skipping his warm up. There was a pull in his groin that would be an actual cramp in no time, and the Professor had been particularly punishing today. The muscles in his shoulders felt as if he'd been tortured on the rack.

He stretched at the barre to loosen up, and worked some more on the jeté. He almost got it right, but he landed badly, nearly twisting his ankle. He dropped to his knees instead to spare it, and found the Professor watching him from the doorway, unsmiling.

"I think, Master Murphy," he said, "perhaps dance is not your métier. Not classical ballet, at any rate, though if you had arrived in time for the can-can..." He shrugged and left that thought unfinished. It was hardly a compliment, in any case. The girls danced the can-can.

"I'll get it," Terry said, getting up and brushing the stage dust off his tights. "Anyway, so long as I'm willing to pay for the lessons..."

"You pay half what the girls pay," the Professor said, "and cost me twice as much work. And, you're two weeks behind in your fees, might I remind you?"

"I'll get your money," Terry promised. "And I'll practice more. I really want to be a dancer. And I will one day. I know I will."

The Professor regarded him solemnly for a moment longer. Then, with another dismissive shrug, he turned away. "Be sure the stage door is locked when you go out," he said as he departed. "The watchman's not here until ten."

The dressing room was empty. Terry stripped wearily and paused for a moment to look critically at himself in the mirror that ran the length of the dressing room. His jet-black hair fell in damp ringlets about his face, making it look even paler than it was. It seemed to him as if he could see the bones through his skin, like a baby bird's.

He had lost weight, too. Even working half the night as he did, rushing from one end of the Bowery to the other, cleaning three different bars for old man McGuirk, it was all he could do to make ends meet. Most of it went for that dingy room with its one tiny window and its soot-covered walls, and what his landlady called, rather grandly in his opinion, "dinner"—all that watery soup, with bread that was always stale and occasionally moldy, and on Sundays, beef ribs that were mostly ribs with the occasional bit of fat or gristle still attached.

One meal a day. He had hope sometimes of being able to supplement that with something more filling, from one of the street vendors, maybe. Even an apple from the apple cart would have been a delight. They always looked so red and shiny, they might have been made of wax, and every time he passed the cart, saw them sitting in their crimson loveliness, he could imagine the taste, the crunch as he bit into one, and the sweet juices running down his chin—but by the time he had paid the Professor's fees, and too frequently replaced the quickly worn through dance shoes, he was lucky if he was left with a penny or two to spare, if that, and the growl that these days never quite left his belly.

Of course, hunger was no stranger to the neighborhood. Others, little children, even, ate what rotten food they could find on the streets and sifted through the piles of garbage outside the saloons and whorehouses to find anything edible. Terry had not yet gotten that hungry, though he had often come close.

He sighed. Maybe if he asked Brian, just for a loan…but, no, he knew how his brother felt about his ambition to be a dancer.

"What kind of a damn fool thing is that for a man to do?" Brian demanded whenever the subject came up between them. "Sometimes I wonder if you're even a man at all."

There were times when Terry wondered that himself. He still remembered how natural it had seemed to him, that time at the

Mission School when he'd put on the blouse and jumper. He watched the girls here in the dressing room, admired their frocks, and sometimes wished he could try them on. Men didn't think of things like that, did they? Real men didn't, surely.

Brian was a man, certainly. He had run away from the school when he was only eleven. "There's more to the damned world than the Five Points," he'd said when Terry had tried to dissuade him. "I'm going to take it by the balls, I tell you, you just see if I don't."

He had, too. He'd started shining shoes and selling newspapers, and had graduated to picking pockets and selling dead rats to boys who liked to fling them at their nemeses. He'd soon found that he could do better with his fists. Strong and fearless, he quickly made a name for himself as a fighter upon whom people began to place bets. Most Saturdays, he could be found on a street corner, surrounded by a crowd of onlookers, many of them wagering. It wasn't long before the odds were considerably in Brian's favor.

When he beat one opponent nearly to death, he lost most of his challengers, but by that time, he was the undisputed ruler of the streets in their little neighborhood. There were men with businesses who were happy to pay a young man who was so fearless and so effective in silencing any criticism. The political bosses in their ward paid him, too. Many an anti-Tammany voter had been waylaid on his way to the polls, and left senseless in the gutter.

By this time, Brian had his own gang, The Boyos, and had wrested a small patch of turf from the Plug Uglies, the gang that had owned it previously. Brian's little band of followers did whatever he ordered them to do without question or hesitation, and he rewarded them with dregs of beer from the saloons, and stolen cigars, and sometimes with the whores who vied for his attention.

Most coveted of all, he showered on them his beaming approval. He swaggered and bullied and enjoyed the fear and toadying he inspired in others, and it was only in looking after his younger brother that he could be seen to have any tender side to his nature.

Terry knew he embarrassed his brother, and only a never explained, never even closely examined familial loyalty overruled his disapproval. That was private and rarely demonstrated between them, however, and almost never for the benefit of others. Sometimes, Terry found it mysterious, more than blood alone could explain. Whatever it was, though, it did not extend to Brian's approval, even in private.

"Goddam it, you act more like a girl than a man almost eighteen years old," Brian said more than once, but no one else would have dared to say it or mistreat Terry; at least not in Brian's presence, though one or two of his hoodlums snickered like the toughs at the loading dock and gave Terry scornful looks when Brian was not there to see or hear. Terry ignored them. They wouldn't have dared do more than snicker when Brian's back was turned. Their laughter couldn't hurt him.

Brian's largesse, however, went no further than providing Terry with the jobs he had arranged for him at various saloons about the neighborhood, doing the cleaning, emptying slop jars and other tasks of the most menial sort.

"I had to make my own way, didn't I?" Brian asked, "I wouldn't do you any favors by coddling you, either. And don't ask me to finance this foolishness you've got in your head," was his customary response whenever Terry had even hinted that he needed money for his dance lessons. "You ask me, you'd be better learning some sensible way of making a living—if you can even make a living dancing around on tippy toe. Seems a lot of crap to me, when you could be learning a real job."

"I can sew," Terry said. "I've sewn up things for some of the girls. If I had to, I could earn a living making dresses."

"There, see, that's what I mean," Brian was quick with his disapproval. "Sewing. Making dresses. What kind of work is that for a man?"

"Other men sew," Terry said. "Tailors and such."

Brian sighed. "You do what you like," he said. "I won't stop you, it's your life, but I'm not paying you to embarrass us both."

They'd left it like that for two years now. Sometimes, although he would never have voiced this to anyone else, Brian least of all, and despite his insistence to the Professor that he would make it one day as a dancer, Terry privately wondered if there was any possible chance that he would ever achieve that goal. Even more privately, so deep inside that he rarely faced it himself, he wasn't altogether sure that it was what he truly did want, so much as it was an avenue of escape from the city's slums.

He had a conviction, that came from he knew not where, that he was meant to escape, that some path had been laid out for him, and though he couldn't see that path, he often thought he saw signs and portents, invisible to others, that pointed him the way.

Was ballet the way, though? For all that he saw himself living a different kind of life, he never could quite picture himself dancing on the ballet stage. Really, the truth was, he'd have been just as happy to sing in the opera. Sometimes, at night, he had made his way to the Castle Garden down in Battery Park, while the operas were being performed. He couldn't afford a ticket to go in, of course, but he could hang around outside and hear some of the tunes. He even sang them himself, when he was alone, though, he mostly substituted la-la-la for the words he didn't know.

The opera, too, was a dream of escape, but that one was even further out of his reach than the ballet. He could learn to dance, at least. Common sense told him opera required a kind of schooling he couldn't hope to get. You had to go to Italy for that, didn't you? He almost never even got out of the Bowery. For the present, he could only watch for the omens, and follow where they led him. There was a part of him that believed, despite all evidence to the contrary, that one day they would lead him out of the Bowery.

There was a noise at the dressing room door. Startled, Terry turned to discover he was not alone. A gentleman in tails and top hat, a silk cape thrown carelessly about his shoulders, stood in the open doorway staring at him. He held a jeweled walking stick in one hand, and stroked a small, neatly trimmed goatee with the other.

Terry blushed, realizing he was stark naked before the stranger. Other men, he knew, thought nothing of that. Brian walked around his little rooms all the time with nothing on, sometimes unembarrassed even at being half stiff when he bragged about the women he'd had. Trying, Terry suspected, to inspire Terry to emulate his success. And, sometimes, too, it had seemed to him as if Brian were trying to get Terry to look at him, to notice that half stiff member—though why that should be true, Terry had no idea.

Stiff or not, Terry made it a point not to look at him, no more than a quick sideways glance now and then, just out of curiosity and, he didn't deny it, a certain admiration. His brother was far from handsome but there was something splendid about his naked body. Except that Brian's body was thick with hair, he looked like one of those statues Terry had admired one day when he had ventured north to the park, some Greek god or other, naked, the muscled flesh so perfectly captured that Terry had felt he could reach out and run a caressing hand over it.

Of course, he hadn't. He couldn't reach out and run his hand over his brother's furry body either, but sometimes he wanted to, just to see if it felt as hard and powerful as it looked.

Brian naked, however, was one thing. He himself naked was quite another. He had always felt funny about anyone else seeing him in the altogether. Even Brian. Certainly, he did not care for a perfect stranger seeing him with nothing on.

"I'm sorry," Terry told the stranger. He shoved his glasses on and snatched up his trousers, turning red all over. "The girls have all left already."

It was not unusual to see one of the city's playboys backstage. "Stage door Johnnies," the girls called them, and tittered among themselves as they talked about them and sometimes compared one to the other.

They came often, the moneyed roués, to fetch the girls, many of whom boasted of their "Johns," and admitted frankly that the gifts from their grateful admirers made the difference between living in comfort or struggling to survive, as Terry did.

One or two of the girls actually lived in apartments provided for them by their gentlemen friends. Sometimes the friend changed, but the apartment remained, a newcomer stepping casually, almost unremarked, into the slippers—and the bed—of his predecessor.

Terry did not blame the girls for their arrangements. There had even been times when he had envied them, and wished he had so simple a solution available to him. They, at least, never seemed to go hungry and they lived in quarters far more comfortable than his mean room in the lower east side, where the streets stank and the rotting tenements leaned drunkenly against one another.

"You're blushing," the man said, grinning. "How charming. Is that a trick of your trade? Can you do it at will?"

"I don't have a trade, sir," Terry said, and because the gentleman seemed not to have heard him the first time, he said, again, more distinctly, "The girls have gone."

"I didn't come to see the girls. I specifically waited until I was sure they were gone. As if you didn't know. I should think that would be obvious."

"But why?" Terry started to ask, struggling to get a leg into his trousers.

"Stop that. There's no need to cover yourself," he said sharply, and added, incongruously, Terry thought, "Do you know who I am?"

Used to being ordered, Terry stopped trying to clothe himself and looked full at the stranger. He knew at least *what* he was, if not who: one of the town's profligate rich; and, just now, he was very drunk. He swayed a bit unsteadily as he looked Terry up and down with a frank appraisal that made Terry nervous. He'd never had anyone look at him like that. It occurred to him, in an insight that provided no comfort, that there was something in it similar to the way the hooligans on the street looked at him.

But they, of course, had not been staring at him naked. No one had, up 'til this moment.

"No, sir, I don't," Terry said.

The stranger considered that for a moment. "That's probably just as well, come to think of it. You can call me Philip. That will do. You can't make trouble for me if you don't know who I am."

"Trouble? What kind of trouble could I make for you? And why should I, since I don't know you?"

"Well, as you are certainly aware, there's some things...secret things that some men favor, that can cause a man trouble enough, get him sent to prison even, if he's careless." He gave Terry a narrow-eyed look. "Or do you know what I'm talking about?"

Terry gave his head a shake, puzzled enough that for the moment, he had forgotten his nudity. "No, sir, I don't think I do."

Philip looked disbelievingly at him for a moment, and then gave a coarse laugh. "By God, I don't think you do. I never imagined. I just took it for granted, a tender little boy like you, doing this sort of nonsense," he made a sweep of his hand that took in not only the dressing room, but the entire theater. "Don't tell me I've got myself a virgin?"

Terry blushed. "I don't know what you mean," he said. "I've not been 'got,' if you'll pardon my saying so, and I don't think I want to be, whatever you mean by it." His glasses had slipped down his nose. He pushed them up again and began to struggle in earnest with the trousers, increasingly uncomfortable with the situation and with the way the stranger—Philip, was it?—continued to look him up and down so brazenly.

To his further embarrassment, Philip stepped across the narrow space that separated them and grabbed the trousers out of Terry's hand, so suddenly that Terry would have fallen if Philip hadn't grabbed hold of his shoulder.

"Stop that, I told you," he said in an imperious tone. "What do you think I mean, you little fool? I *want* you naked. I waited outside till you had your clothes off. I watched you in the mirror. Haven't you understood anything I've been saying?"

"No, I don't think…" Terry started to say.

"Why in the name of heaven do you think I've come here, when I knew you'd be alone, waited for you to get naked? What could a man like me want from a sweet little piece like you? A pleasant bit of chit-chat?" He laughed again, drunkenly, and pulled Terry violently to him. "I can see for myself, plain enough, what you're good for, and it isn't talk."

"No, please," Terry tried to protest, realizing at last what it was the man was driving at, but he was enveloped in a pair of strong arms, and lips smelling of whisky sought his. He twisted his own mouth away from them and felt a massive hand pawing at his naked backside. Philip dropped to his knees, dragging Terry to the dirty floor with him. Despite his struggles, Terry was turned forcibly onto his side.

"No, I tell you, I'm not what you think," he said, his voice breaking. "You've got it all wrong. I'm not a nancy."

"You are now," was the answer.

Terry felt a sudden pain, as if he had been impaled.

"By God, I think you really were a virgin," Philip said afterward. "I half didn't believe you. All the fancy boys tell you that, to whet a man's appetite. It's been a long time, though, since I got myself the real thing…Stop that sniveling."

When Terry continued to sob softly into the crook of his arm, Philip added, "I'm sorry if I hurt you," though there wasn't a trace of contrition in his voice. If anything, he sounded altogether too pleased with himself. "I've been watching you, following you, for weeks now, and when I saw you naked like that…well, I couldn't help myself is all. You've no one but yourself to blame, flaunting yourself the way you do. You can't set a fire and then cry when you get burned. What's that?" He started suddenly at a noise in the darkened theater outside. The gaslights fluttered in a sudden draft.

"The watchman, I expect," Terry said through his sniffles. "It's about his time."

"Damn." Philip jumped up and began quickly to rearrange his clothes. "Cover yourself, before he comes by." He grabbed a towel off a chair and threw it at Terry. "This won't do, then. I can't afford to be found out. We'll have to find somewhere else. What about your place?"

"My place? For what?" Terry was appalled by the question and what it implied.

"For the next time, you little fool, what do you think I'm talking about? If you're going to be my fancy boy, we'll need a place to be together. Obviously it isn't safe doing it here."

"I'm not your fancy boy," Terry said hotly. His glasses had fallen off in their struggle. He found them now and put them on. "And there isn't going to be a next time, either. What would give you that idea?"

Philip seemed not even to hear him "Where do you live?" he demanded. "Do you live alone?"

"I live in a boarding house," Terry said. "In the Five Points, but…"

Philip wrinkled up his nose. "A man like myself, it wouldn't be safe to be seen in that hellhole. And a nosy landlady, to boot, I suppose. They all are down there and I can't afford to be recognized." He thought for a moment, and sighed. "I have an apartment, of course, I keep it for…well, never mind who. It's not that simple, though, I can't just parade you in there. I'll have to make arrangements." He reached some sort of decision. "I'll send you the address as soon as things are in order."

"You must be crazy," Terry said, his manners fleeing before his misery. He wiped a hand across his nose and scrambled into his trousers. His backside felt damp—blood, he thought, but he was too eager to have himself covered up to worry about that. "To think that I would come to see you, after what you've just done. By God, if I told him, my brother would kill you. I swear to you, if you so much as dare to show your face here again…"

"Oh, you'll come. I know your type. You're all alike." The man laughed disdainfully. He took a wallet from his pocket and tugged a handful of bills from it, and tossed them disdainfully onto the floor. "I'll let you know where," he said.

With that, he left.

Terry glanced down at the money. He would like to have ignored it, stepped right over the scattered bills and walked from the room, holding his chin up the way he did with the hooligans outside the stage door.

It was too late for that, though. The stranger had already gone. And he couldn't afford to ignore the money. He was behind in his rent, he was behind in his dance fees, and he was hungry. And this was more money than he had ever seen at one time.

He was ashamed of himself for doing it, but he dropped to his knees nevertheless and began to snatch up the scattered bills.

Chapter Two

At first, afterward, Terry had been literally afraid that he would die. He had indeed bled from the assault, and he had a superstitious dread that he must surely have been impregnated with some horrible disease. People went blind just from abusing themselves, didn't they? And grew hair on their palms, although so far none had shown up on his. Neither of which had stopped him from doing it regularly any more than the guilt had. Surely the consequences of what had been done to him must be considerably worse. There was certainly no one he could ask, though.

For two days he huddled in his room, aching and ashamed, sure that if anyone saw him, they would know in a glance what had happened to him, as if it must be written on his forehead for all to see.

In time, though, he got angry. How dare Philip Whoever-He-Was think that he had any right to do what he had done? Terry had half a mind to tell Brian about it, as he'd threatened. Brian, he knew, would see that the assailant was punished.

Brian could find him, too. The city wasn't that big, and the people that Brian worked for were the masters of the city's vices. It would not be difficult to find out who among the city's wealthy young men had that peculiar taste. There were only so many means to satisfy it, after all, and they were all of them on the Lower East Side.

Much as he wanted to, though, he knew he could not tell Brian. In his heart, he knew that Brian would blame him as much as anyone. "What could you expect," he would say. "You've no one but yourself to blame."

Philip had said that, hadn't he: "You've no one but yourself to blame." But it was no stretch to imagine Brian saying it as well. And, really, Terry half believed it himself. He was almost eighteen, and most boys in this neighborhood were grown up long before that age, but he knew perfectly well that people didn't see him as a man, not the way they saw Brian or even the hooligans at the loading dock.

Brian said things like that often, mocking men dressed in tights, prancing about on a stage. "Sometimes I think you're more a woman than a man," Brian had said more than once. It was hardly surprising to Terry, remembering all his jibes, that someone should treat him like a woman, when his own brother thought he was less than a man.

And, "For Christ's sake, can't you walk straight? What do you expect people to think?"

The same as those hooligans thought, Terry realized now. The next time he went past them, he felt a peculiar beating of his heart and his breath seemed to catch in his throat. He had a fleeting thought of what Philip had done to him, and it was only a small step to imagine one of these young toughs doing the same—that tall one, perhaps, with the copper colored hair, who always looked at him differently from the others. Who had actually defended him one time, in a manner of speaking.

"Hey, girlie," one of the others had called as Terry went by, and made a grabbing motion at his crotch, "why don't you have a look at what I've got for you?"

The others had snickered and jeered, but the tall freckled redhead said, "Oh, leave him alone, why don't you, he's not doing you any harm, is he?"

"Oh, Finnegan's got himself a boyfriend, then," the first had said, and the others whooped with laughter.

"You want a boyfriend," Finnegan said hotly, and gave the other a couple of good punches with his fist, "here's your boyfriend, then, you ignorant mick."

Terry had taken that for a talisman of some sort, that he and the redhead were both Irish, as if it somehow formed a bond between them, though in truth probably they all were.

After that, however, when he glanced in their direction, it was always Finnegan to whom his eyes were invariably and inevitably drawn. The others looked at him with mocking scorn, but Finnegan looked at him the way a hungry man looked at a buttered roll. And, inevitably, whenever he looked at Finnegan, Terry could feel the blood suffuse his face. He hoped the tall redhead did not notice.

Now Terry found himself wondering; was that what Finnegan had on his mind all this time, that funny hunger Terry had discerned in his eyes—what Philip had done? Not what Terry had always imagined, not beating him up with his fists, but a different kind of assault altogether.

Oddly, considering that he lived in one of the city's most notorious neighborhoods where every kind of vice and perversion ruled, he had never actually thought about the act Philip had performed, had only been dimly aware that this was something men sometimes did to one another. Some men, at least, although he had never for a moment consciously imagined anyone doing it to him.

Now that it had been done, however, it seemed as if the image never left him. He could still feel the iron clutch of Philip's arms about him, the ragged breathing in his ear, the grunting as he gave up his seed deep inside Terry's ravaged bottom. It had been horrible, painful, humiliating…but it was there, the memory. It persisted.

It did not immediately reoccur, however, and he was determined that it would not. He avoided being alone in the theater. Each night, he hurried to be ready to go when the girls went, and left with them in a group, chatting quickly to cover his nervousness, and was relieved to see no one waiting for him.

He began to think it was something that had happened just once and would not happen again. That man—he disliked even honoring him by attaching his name to him and preferred to think of him as "that man"—he had been drunk, reeking of whiskey. Probably he had all but forgotten it by the time he sobered up in the morning. Maybe he was even ashamed of his actions, and suffered guilt for them.

Terry had a vision of his attacker kneeling in church, maybe Saint Boniface's down the street, begging forgiveness—although, no, surely a man wouldn't confess that, even to his priest. Men went to prison for what he'd done. Probably he was too frightened by that prospect to want to do it again. No doubt the enormity of his sin was Terry's greatest protection.

It was nearly two weeks before he heard from Philip again. Terry had not forgotten the assault. He could not close his eyes at night without reliving it in its entirely, but as the days passed and the physical pain lessened and, more quickly than he would have expected, vanished, he had begun to breathe easier.

As ugly as the incident had been though, he could not help but be grateful for the money Philip had flung at him with such scorn. Terry had been able to pay his back room and board, and his dance fees to the Professor, and there had been enough left over that for most of those two weeks—for perhaps the first time since he had left the Mission house in Brian's wake—he had kept his belly full. He'd even eaten his fill of those apples from the vendor's cart and found them every bit as delicious as he had imagined.

So, when a street urchin dressed in rags and smelling like a wet dog showed up at the dressing room one evening with a note for him, Terry was surprised, and hadn't an inkling who might be writing to him, until he unfolded the scrap of paper to read it. There was nothing on it but an address, and a time, two in the afternoon the following day. No message, no signature. And, really, none was needed. Who else could have sent it? Realizing, he felt his skin turn cold, and then quickly hot. His face burned red.

"An admirer?" one of the girls asked, and they all tittered. They had long since stopped flirting with the single male in their midst. Although few of them were any older than he was in actual years, they were all of them by this time well enough attuned to the interest of males to have seen that he had none for them.

Which was just as well, really, as they saw it philosophically. Even if he had shown any interest in one or the other of them, what would it have counted for? He was as poor as a church mouse, the same as them. Their lives had no provision in them for romance that did not come with money or some advantage attached to it. Terry was just a dance partner, almost like one of the girls himself. They talked the kind of girl talk usually not heard by members of the opposite sex, and they no longer troubled themselves about dressing and undressing in front of him, or took the slightest notice when he did so as well.

They had learned that he had an instinctive talent for makeup or arranging hair, and they often asked him to help with theirs.

"Oh, do something with these curls, won't you, pet," one of them would say, or, "Damn, I can't get my lips right, you paint them, Terry, you're so much better at it," and he did, expertly.

Terry crumpled the note up and started to throw it into the trash, but some instinct stopped him. He shoved it into the pocket of his trousers instead. He might have need of that address some day, though he could not imagine what that need might be.

"Just something from my brother," he answered.

"If he's asking about me," Rosaria, the oldest of the girls, said, "the answer is yes."

They all laughed. Brian was regarded as something of a prize, although not for his money and certainly not for his looks. All those fights had left him with a permanently swollen ear that looked like a cauliflower, a nose that bent to the left, and a big scar that ran from one eyebrow clear up until it disappeared into his hair.

There were women aplenty who seemed to notice these imperfections not at all, however. That aura of power that he wore, of manly ferocity, was a potent aphrodisiac to many. To young women such as themselves—poor, at the mercy of fate and the men who came around looking to pleasure themselves—power was something magical, more alluring by far than a handsome face, or a beautifully sculpted body.

Terry didn't keep the appointment that had been made for him the next day, but he waited with some apprehension to see what Philip would do about it.

He didn't have long to wait. They were leaving the theater

the next evening when one of the girls said, "Looks like we've got ourselves a Johnnie."

"Which one of us do you think he fancies?" Rosaria asked.

Terry looked in the direction they indicated and his heart sank. A splendid black calash was parked across the street, harnessed to a matching pair of black geldings, their manes and tails elaborately braided. Although the autumn weather had turned cool, the carriage's cover was folded back, to reveal the elegant deep red leather of its upholstery—and the carriage's lone occupant: Philip sat watching the stage door as they came out.

He gave Terry one fierce look, so quick that if he hadn't been watching for it, Terry would have missed it altogether, and rapped with his stick for the driver. The carriage drove away, the geldings' hooves beating a brisk, steady tattoo on the cobblestones. Philip pointedly did not look at them again.

"Looks like none of us caught his eye," one of the girls said, and they all forgot him in the next moment. Johnnies were nothing unusual.

He was there again the next day, in the same splendid carriage with its cover once more down, and again, they had no sooner emerged from the stage door than he drove off.

"Must be looking for someone in particular," one of the girls said, and another, "Maybe it's our little Terry he fancies."

Terry blushed and said, quickly, "Don't be silly. Whoever heard of such a thing?"

"Oh, I've heard of it," Rosaria said. "There's some as likes a lad better than a lassie, you know. Luckily for us, not so many, or who'd buy us our suppers and our pretty frocks?"

Everyone laughed. Terry forced himself to laugh with them.

The third time they found Philip waiting, Terry began to be genuinely frightened. What's more, the girls had stopped joking about it, and he saw one or two of them give him funny sideways glances that turned his face scarlet.

He decided he would have to talk to Brian about it after all.

Brian would be angry, but he would know what to do in any event. The following day, after his lesson, Terry rushed into his street clothes and left before the others, hurrying through the theater and slipping out the front door instead of the usual stage door.

He took a hack to Harry Green's bar on Houston Street. Harry's was the most popular saloon in the Bowery, and the finest. Everyone went there: judges and politicians and pickpockets and sailors and pimps, millionaires and every kind of scoundrel.

Almost every other building on Houston Street housed a bar where rotgut liquor laced with camphor and worse was served in filthy glasses, a nickel a glass. At Harry's, the liquor was the real thing, and cost far more than a nickel, and the whores were the prettiest in town.

Neither the pickpockets nor the pimps nor the whores plied their trade at Harry's, however, though it was not unheard of for the prostitutes to make dates for later with gentlemen admirers, or a pickpocket to follow a likely prospect out of the bar. Unlike at other bars, there were no rooms upstairs to let for a quick assignation, profanity was banned, and the women were cautioned to keep their voices down and mind their language.

"I'm not running a whorehouse," Harry said whenever the question was raised. "I've got important clientele. I take proper care of them, and they take proper care of me." It was well known that Harry had valuable connections in the city's government offices, and the police who sometimes gave other owners a hard time treated Harry with unvarying respect and, in return, drank for free, but carefully, never to excess.

Harry himself was presiding over the bar when Terry came in. He frowned disapprovingly; he thought Brian's little brother was a queer duck, and not the sort he wanted hanging around his establishment, in case anyone got the wrong idea about the kind of establishment it was. There were plenty of places in the neighborhood where boys like Terry, and younger, some of them as young as ten or eleven, hung about, and older men of a certain stripe came to drink and look them over and take their pick of the fruit on offer.

Harry's wasn't one of those places and he meant to keep it like that; but Brian was a valued employee—here, he worked as a bouncer, to see that Harry's respectability was maintained at all times—and Harry tolerated Terry's visits, so long as they were brief and infrequent, and Terry minded his Ps and Qs while he was there, which so far he always had.

Harry ushered Terry quickly to a table, not the best table, but not the worst, either, and sent a waiter to tell Brian his brother was here. By the time Brian arrived, a tray with two beers and two glasses had already been placed on the table.

"I heard you pulled up in a hack," Brian greeted him, sliding into the chair opposite Terry and pouring one of the beers into a glass. He slid the glass across the table to Terry, and drank directly from the other bottle. "Come into some unexpected money, did you?"

"One of the girls paid me something she owed me," he said. "I was too tired to walk, so I splurged."

Brian half drained his beer, regarding Terry across the bottle's rim. "Well, if you say so," he said. "What brings you here?"

Terry was on the verge of explaining, but he hesitated. Now that he was here, seated across the table from his stern-faced brother, he was less certain than he had been before that Brian would automatically want to defend his honor, not once he heard what the nature of the problem was.

"Can't I want to see my big brother occasionally?" Terry asked instead, taking a decorous sip from his glass and pushing his slipping glasses up. He saw that the glass was dirty and put it back on the tabletop.

"Nice to hear it. It just seems sudden, like," Brian said, scratching his hairy chest where his shirt lay open. "And the hack, and all."

Terry looked around and said, to change the subject, "How's business?"

"Here?" Brian looked around too, as if surprised by the question, and gave a shrug. "Same as always. Not much trouble. There never is here. Everybody knows, once you're tossed out of Harry's, you don't get back in."

"Like your work, don't you?"

Again, Brian shrugged. "It's okay. Lately, I've been thinking, though…oh, never mind, it's just something I've been chewing on."

"What?" Terry asked. "Tell me, I like hearing what you're up to."

"It's just this idea I been playing with, is all. They're talking a lot about the gold rush. Out west, you know. There's men making their fortunes overnight. They say you can just wade out into a crick and pick up nuggets of gold the size of a man's fist, and you're an instant millionaire. Makes you kind of think."

"But, you've got a job here," Terry said.

"Not much future in it, the way I see it. It gets kind of boring, if you want to know, the same old thing, day in and day out. Might be exciting, is what I was thinking, heading for the wild west. A man could be his own man out there and not be kissing somebody else's ass all the time, like you got to do here to get ahead."

"Seems like Harry treats you well enough," Terry said.

"Better than some. But he still wants his ass kissed, same as they all do. Makes me sore, sometimes. It ain't like he's any better than I am, don't seem to me." He took a big swig of his beer and said, in a wistful voice, "Think about it. A millionaire. Just walking out into a crick."

"You aren't actually thinking of going, are you?" Terry asked, wide-eyed. The thought of Brian's leaving…he'd be here alone, on his own…not that he saw that much of Brian, they weren't close that way, but they were brothers, and just having Brian for a brother was a kind of protection.

"I don't know. It's just something people are talking about a lot." He looked around the crowded bar again. "Oh, I expect I'll stay right here, where I am. I know a good thing when I've got it. Say, you don't happen to know Martin Van Arndst, do you?"

"Martin, who? What makes you ask that?"

"Because he's standing over by the bar, and he's been staring a hole in the back of your head. Like he knew you."

Terry knew before he looked over his shoulder who it would be. He took only the quickest glance and looked away. "No one I know," he said. "What'd you say his name is? Who is he, anyway?"

"Martin Van Arndst, I told you. The Van Arndsts are big money, blue bloods. The bluest. They own Fifth Avenue, folks say."

"What on earth would make you think I'd know someone like that?" Terry asked, trying to calm his jangled nerves. He took a bigger drink of his beer this time.

"Just as well," Brian said. "There's stories about him, people say he's got some peculiar appetites. I wouldn't want to think my brother was mixed up with anyone like that. People go to prison for what they say he does. Not people like him, most likely. People with money and important names, they're above the law. But someone like you, say, why, you'd be sitting in Sing Sing faster than I could say Jack Sprat." Brian's gaze was penetrating, judging. His eyes regarded Terry steadily. "That's if you was mixed up in anything like that."

"Oh, you needn't worry about me," Terry said. He really was afraid now to tell Brian why he had come, and about the man he knew as Philip.

Anyway, it was too late, wasn't it? He'd already said he didn't know him. If he tried to explain now, Brian would never believe that he had been innocent. Once you'd told a lie, nothing was quite honest after that, was it?

"Well, I guess you're right," Brian said. "He's leaving. Maybe he thought you were somebody else."

"Probably," Terry said, relieved.

When he left a short while later, without ever explaining to Brian what had brought him. Terry half expected to see Van Arndst waiting outside in his elegant calash, but there was no sign of him. To his great surprise, though, he saw that young tough from the loading docks, the tall redhead, Finnegan, standing in the entrance to an alleyway across the street.

For a moment, he half thought that Finnegan was following him, but the next moment Finnegan had disappeared into the alley, and Terry wrote off his appearance there as nothing more than coincidence.

He kept watching the entrance to the alley as he walked down the street, almost hoping Finnegan would reappear. The oddest picture popped into his head, of him and Finnegan strolling along together, like they were friends or something. But he didn't appear again.

And why should he? Terry asked himself. What a crazy idea, to think of him and that hooligan lollygagging together. If they ever really did come into contact with one another, he'd be far more apt to get a taste of Finnegan's fists than a saunter down the street.

As for Van Arndst, most likely he'd seen the looks Brian gave him, and had gotten scared off.

Terry devoutly hoped so.

Chapter Three

Terry wasn't surprised, though, when he got another note the next afternoon, delivered by another filthy urchin.

"How do you think your roughneck brother would like hearing about our little fling?" it asked, and again, there was no signature, only a time, three P.M., the following day.

Terry thought he knew well enough how Brian would feel, though it angered him to have what had happened described as a "fling." As if he'd had any say in it!

What should he do? What *could* he do? Ignoring Philip—no, he reminded himself, it wasn't Philip, Brian had called him Martin, Martin Van Arndst—anyway, whoever he was, ignoring him had accomplished nothing. If anything, it seemed to have intensified his determination.

Maybe, he thought, and the idea surprised him, it was the same as what he'd always sensed about running from those street toughs, knowing by some instinct that it would only encourage them. He had been running from Martin Van Arndst, in a sense, and that was exactly what it had done, made him all the more determined to repeat his obscene actions.

Very well, then maybe the answer was to stop running, to stand up to him. Not to submit to another brutal assault, but, surely the man must have some decency in him. He had been drunk that other time. Maybe sober he was a different sort. If he understood the enormity of the mistake he had made, if he could be made to realize that he had misjudged Terry altogether, perhaps he would see things differently, and agree to leave Terry alone.

And if he didn't agree voluntarily, there was always the threat of Brian's displeasure. However angry Brian might be with Terry, he was certainly not likely to excuse Van Arndst's actions—and Van Arndst obviously knew who Brian was, and his reputation. It would be worth bringing Brian's anger down on his own head if it convinced Van Arndst to leave him alone. He certainly hoped it wouldn't come to that, but just the mention of Brian might be enough to discourage Van Arndst's attentions, if nothing else did.

Yes, Terry decided. He still had Van Arndst's first note, with the address in it. He would go there—not tomorrow as invited, but this very day, catch him off guard, maybe sober. Surprise would almost certainly be to his advantage.

Convinced that he was doing the best thing, Terry again hurried to be out of the theater before the girls. He would like to have taken a hack again, determined to get this confrontation over with as soon as possible, but by this time the money Van Arndst had flung at him so disdainfully was nearly gone, and he walked briskly instead. The weather was turning quickly colder. Already there was frozen horse droppings and urine on the street. Terry's thin shirt provided little comfort against the chill wind that blew at him as he walked.

The theater was on Broadway, not exactly a prestigious address but certainly upscale compared to the teeming slums at the lower end of Manhattan. Van Arndst's apartment was on Fifth Avenue, not the further end where the mansions were, but nonetheless the distance from the Bowery was far more than the mile or two Terry trudged.

People were arriving early for services at Grace Church. Intent on their own salvation, they noticed not at all the solemn little figure plodding past them. Another time he might have paused to gaze wistfully into the windows of McCreery's, at the luxurious goods on display, the sort of things he could only dream of one day owning, but today he hardly gave them a glance. He crossed Union Square, so lost in his thoughts he barely missed being run down by a streetcar.

He arrived at Van Arndst's address, sweaty despite the cool air and in a state of apprehension, which only increased as he mounted two flights of steep stairs.

It was not Van Arndst, however, who answered his knock, but a woman. Tall, slim, imperious, she looked Terry up and down and said in a frosty voice, "Yes?"

Terry was so confounded by her unexpected presence—a woman? Nothing could have surprised him more—that it was all he could do to stammer, "Is Mister Van Arndst here?"

"Martin?" Her eyebrows shot up. "What could you possibly want with Martin?"

"I...it's a personal matter," Terry said, sorry now that he had come, wishing he could just vanish through the floorboards. "But, maybe this isn't a good time, I'll try him..."

"Alicia?" a familiar voice called from inside the apartment. "What is it? Who's at the door?"

"Some little street brat," she said, her voice rising in anger. "One of *those* boys."

Martin Van Arndst suddenly appeared behind the woman, looking totally shocked to see Terry. "You," he said, "what are you doing here. I told you..."

"So you do know him," the woman said in an accusing tone.

"Alicia, you see..."

"Indeed, I can see very plainly," she said. "I can see at a glance what kind of a young man he is, and I can certainly see why he would be coming here to look for you." Her voice took on a grating whine and she flung her hands wide in a gesture of despair and frustration. "Oh, Martin, you told me you'd given all that up, you promised me."

"I have, I swear it. It's not what you think," he said, and he turned on Terry with an angry scowl. "What are you doing here, you little guttersnipe? I told you never to trouble me again. Get out of here and leave me alone."

He reached behind the door, grabbing his walking stick, and

swung at Terry with it. Terry managed to duck his head but the cane hit his shoulder instead, sending a lightning bolt of pain down his arm.

"Ow," Terry cried, dodging another blow that almost caught his head. "Please…" He tore the note from his pocket and waved it. "Here, you said…"

"He's trying to blackmail me," Van Arndst said, swinging wildly with his stick, his expression livid. "That's why he's here. He wants money from me, to stop him spreading a pack of filthy lies."

"No," Terry cried, "that's not true, just read this," but Alicia might not even have heard him.

"Blackmail? You little wretch, how dare you," she said, eyes flashing demonically. "I'll see you in prison. You can't trouble decent people with your filth. Grab him, Martin. I want him arrested."

Terry backed away, open-mouthed, but when Van Arndst actually moved past her and tried to seize him, Terry's fright overwhelmed him. He tore himself from Van Arndst's clawing hand, his shirt ripping in the process, and began to stumble pell-mell down the stairs.

"Stop him," the woman cried, "there's a policeman on the corner. We'll let him deal with this." Loud footsteps followed Terry down the stairs.

He ran from the front door and right into a pair of arms. At first, in a panic, he thought it was that policeman. He didn't know what the policemen up in this neighborhood might be like, but he knew enough about the ones down in the Lower East Side. The best he could hope for from the roundheads there was a serious beating.

When he lifted frightened eyes, though, he found himself, astonishingly, looking into the face of that Irish tough from the loading docks. He was so startled, it took him a moment even to remember the young man's name—Finnegan.

"In here, quick," Finnegan said and all but dragged him into the alley next door. There was an enormous pile of garbage just a few feet down the alley and Finnegan shoved Terry to the ground behind it, and half fell across him. Terry's instinct was to jump up and try to run, but Finnegan held him so firmly he could hardly move.

"Lay still, damn it," he hissed in Terry's ear.

They heard footsteps pass the opening of their alley, and Alicia's voice said, "I can't believe he's just disappeared. We must find him."

"Oh, let him go," Van Arndst said. "I know where to find the little bugger, never fear. I'll see he gets his comeuppance."

Their voices faded and were gone. For a moment longer, the two young men stayed where they were. Terry was suddenly aware of the big, hard-muscled body lying atop his, warm in contrast to the icy pavement beneath him. He fancied he could feel Finnegan's heart beat, and hear his excited breathing. It gave him a funny feeling. A strange heat coursed through his body.

Finnegan got off of him then, all quick like, as if something had bitten him. Terry sat up, brushing some garbage from the torn sleeve of his shirt. His glasses had fallen off. Finnegan picked them up from the pavement and handed them to him, and Terry put them on.

"Sorry if I was rough," Finnegan said. "Wasn't no time to be polite, I didn't think."

Terry took a deep breath and pushed his glasses up and looked through the lenses into his benefactor's face, still only inches from his own, and almost felt as if he were drowning in emerald green eyes.

"I'm grateful to you," he said. "It's Finnegan, isn't it?"

"Tom," the redhead said, grinning broadly. "Tom Finnegan. You know me, then?" he asked, surprised.

"I've seen you," Terry said. "I'm Terry."

"I know. I've heard the girls call you by name." Tom Finnegan gave him an embarrassed smile. "When you come out of the theater, sometimes, is what I mean."

"But, what on earth are you doing here?"

"Following you," Finnegan said. "Same as—oh, I was just keeping an eye on you, like."

"Me? But what on earth for?" Terry couldn't have been more amazed.

"I have been ever since—well, especially since I saw that vermin, Van Arndst, had his eye on you. I knew he was up to no good."

"You know him?"

"I know of him, that's for sure. I've lived on the streets since I was six. You learn early on about his kind. Ain't a kid in this neighborhood don't know about him. Everybody knows to stay out of his way. But, I didn't figure you to know what he was like."

"I know enough," Terry said. He scrambled to his feet. Tom gave him a hand to help him up. "Well, I'm very grateful to you. I'd better get home, I think."

"I think better not," Tom said. He still held Terry's hand in his. Terry was altogether conscious of the touch of their fingers. "You heard them, they'll be looking for you. Probably the coppers, too. Does he know where you live?"

"No," Terry said, and then changed his mind. "I don't know. He might have followed me." He screwed up his face. "I don't know what to do."

"You could go to your brother," Tom said. He let go of Terry's hand. Terry's fingers clasped and unclasped, as if they had lost something valuable.

"You know my brother?"

Tom snorted. "Everybody knows Brian Murphy."

Terry gave his head a shake. "No, I couldn't. He'd kill me."

"He'd be sore, that's for sure. But…" Tom studied Terry's worried expression for a moment, and seemed to come to some sudden decision. "Look, come with me, okay. We need time to think, and this ain't the place for it, case they come back." He started down the alley, and paused to look back over his shoulder. "You coming then, or what?"

After a second's pause, Terry went with him. He didn't know what else to do.

Where Tom took him was the cellar of an abandoned tenement building. The surface of the nearby river was red with the descending sun. They climbed through a window that had been boarded up, but Tom pulled the boards easily aside and slipped through. He motioned Terry to follow him, and pulled

Victor J. Banis

the boards back into place when they were inside.

Although it was still daylight outside, the basement was in near darkness. Terry stood for a bit, allowing his eyes to adjust to the gloom. What he saw, finally, were makeshift living quarters: a moldy mattress on the floor, a box for a table with a candle atop it, and some scattered tins of food and a couple of apples. The place smelled of mildew and rotted garbage and excrement.

"Is this...?" Terry started to ask, and hesitated.

"I live here," Tom said. He followed Terry's gaze about the room, seeming to see it through Terry's eyes. "It ain't much, is it? But I've lived in worse, I can tell you. Anyway, nobody'll find you here. You're safe with old Tom Finnegan, as safe as in your mother's arms. As long as you want to stay."

"But...I can't stay here," Terry said.

Tom's smile faded and he looked crestfallen, but Terry, still looking around the cellar, missed that.

"No, course not," Tom said. "I expect you're used to lots better. This ain't exactly Fifth Avenue, is it?"

"Oh, I'm not used to that either, that's not what I meant," Terry said quickly, apologetically. "It's just, well, what about my things? And I've got my lessons. Besides, my brother wouldn't like it if he knew."

"Yes. Well." Tom kind of shrugged. "Are you hungry. I've got them apples, and there's a can of beans I haven't finished, if you'd like the rest of them. Go on, sit down, why don't you?"

He motioned to the tattered mattress. A large brown rat had crept onto it and Tom gave him a swift kick. Squealing, the rat vanished into the shadows.

Terry sat a bit gingerly and raised up the next moment to look at the cards he'd sat on, several decks, maybe four or five of them.

"I'm learning to play cards. To make money," Tom said, scooping them out of the way. "I plan to be a professional."

"A card shark, you mean?" Terry said.

"They ain't a lot of jobs open for a fellow like me," Tom said a bit defensively.

"Oh, I didn't mean to sound like a prig."

"Here," Tom said, and thrust one of the apples at him.

Terry took it and looked at it, but it looked perfectly fine, and he was hungry, now that he thought of it. He rubbed it quickly on his shirtsleeve and bit into it. "It's delicious," he said.

"I steal them," Finnegan said, looking altogether too proud of himself, Terry thought. "I'm good at it. That's how come I think I can get good enough with the cards, if I keep practicing. It's all in the hands. That's how they do it, the good ones. Look."

He took one of the decks and riffled through it, the cards flying so fast in his fingers they were no more than a blur. "Here, take a card," he said. "Any card, and look at it and remember it."

Terry did as he was instructed. It was the Ace of Hearts. "Now, stick it back in the deck, anywhere you like. And," Tom shuffled the cards again, screwed up his face in concentration, cut the deck, and turned one half over, to reveal the Ace of Hearts.

"That's…that's amazing," Terry said. "How did you do that?"

"I told you, it's all in the hands," Tom said, pouting his muscled chest like a pigeon. He looked at the card he'd revealed. "The old Ace of Hearts. Hah. That says something, me boy-o."

"What's that mean?" Terry asked.

"Love," Tom said. "Major heart stuff, real close, close enough you could just about…" he caught himself and gave his head a shake. "Oh, shoot, that's just some old gypsy blarney, reading the cards, it don't amount to a hill of beans, really."

For a moment, their eyes met, and it seemed as if something, some invisible current, passed between them. Terry had an urge, it swept through him, to lean forward, across the short distance that separated them, to come closer—but, for what? He remembered the feel of Tom's body atop his earlier in the alley, the warmth that had radiated from him, and now he saw in Tom's eyes that strange hunger he thought he had detected before.

"You're going to be a dancer, ain't that so?" Tom asked, breaking the spell. "That's what you're doing at that theater, ain't it?"

"Yes. I was going to be, anyway, before all this. Oh, I don't know, it was just a dream. I suppose they don't matter."

"We all have 'em. Least I do. Mine's gettin' rich from playing cards. I'll make it, too. And so will you, I bet."

Terry sighed. "Sometimes, at night, when I'm asleep, I have this other dream, a different kind of dream. The same one, over and over. I'm walking down this road, toward a city, a secret place, it seems like, hidden behind these great walls, and there are all these other people walking toward it too, and everyone keeps going faster and faster, and me too, until I am practically running, only, I don't know what it is I'm running to, I just know there is something waiting there for me, and I can't wait to get to it."

He had been speaking as if to himself, but now he blinked and looked at Tom. "I guess that sounds like a bunch of non-sense, doesn't it?"

"It sounds beautiful to me," Tom said, looking impressed. He gave a deprecating laugh. "All's I ever dream about when I'm sleeping is something to eat."

Terry moved his arm, and winced.

"What's wrong?" Tom asked quickly, all concern.

"Van Arndst hit me a good one back there, with his walking stick." Terry felt cautiously at his shoulder and winced again.

"Here, you better let me have a look at it, then," Tom said. "Take that shirt off, why don't you, and let's see what's what."

Terry hesitated for a moment. "Come on, then, off with it," Tom said, and he looked so serious and so concerned, Terry swallowed his shyness and did as he was told, slipping his torn shirt off.

Tom moved closer to him, put his hands on Terry's shoulder and felt it gingerly. To Terry's surprise, his big, callused hands were astonishingly gentle.

"There, is it?" Tom asked and Terry nodded mutely.

Tom felt around some more, lifted Terry's arm up and brought it back down. "Well, it's good and bruised, that's for sure," he said. "It'll hurt for a bit. Don't look like nothing's broke, though."

They sat for a moment longer. Tom had not taken his hand away. It rested lightly on Terry's shoulder, and Terry realized that Tom was looking at him that way again, only more intently than ever, as if there was something he was dying to say, and was afraid to voice it. In a way, it was how Martin Van Arndst had looked at him, but it was different, too. What had been in Van Arndst's eyes had been hard and cruel, and the light in Tom's was much softer, gentler, and Terry fancied he could see something else in it, too, like a silent, eager plea. Terry's face turned pink.

"I like it when you blush like that," Tom said. That only made the pink deepen to scarlet, which seemed to amuse Tom all the more. He grinned from ear to ear, as if Terry had just performed some clever trick for his amusement.

It was cold in the basement and, without his shirt on, even colder. A gust of wind blew through a broken window. Terry gave a shiver. When he exhaled, his breath made a little cloud.

"Say, I'm forgetting my manners," Tom said, business like all of a sudden. "It's cold in this place. I ain't got nothing to start a fire, either. Here. Let me warm you up."

He pulled Terry close, against his own body, and put his arms about him. It felt to Terry as if the other boy's body had the heat of a blast furnace, it all but burned his skin, and penetrated clear through him. He couldn't remember anyone's ever holding him like this—Van Arndst, the swine, had held him when he attacked him, but not like this, tight but gentle too at the same time. Tom's hands moved caressingly up and down Terry's naked back, like he was petting him.

"You could stay for the night, anyway," Tom said, and his man's voice was suddenly a little boy's, very shy and tremulous. "Just to be safe. Ain't got no blankets and no heat, but it'll be warm enough, if we...well...we can keep one another warm, can't we? Sleep close, like? I'll bet you wouldn't be cold at all if I was to keep my arms around you, all night, even, I'd be glad to. Warm and safe, is what old Tom promises you. If you was wanting to stay."

Only, Terry didn't feel at all sure he would be safe with Tom Finnegan, the way Tom promised. He wasn't sure he understood exactly what the danger was, but the quickening of his heart told him that Tom Finnegan's arms might not be the best place for him to spend a night.

"No, I think I'd better go," he said. He struggled to get to his feet. Tom's arms fell away.

"Suit yourself, then. Only, not home, I don't advise," Tom said, in his more manly voice, standing too, brushing some dirt off the front of his still dirty pants. "I doubt that would be smart. I think you'll have to go to your brother, regardless. He'll know what to do, at least. Van Arndst is vermin, but he's a rich man, and powerful. Them kind can be dangerous, to them like us especially."

Terry sighed. Tom was right. There was nowhere else for him to turn, and even if there weren't that other thing between them that he didn't understand, he couldn't very well stay here, could he? It looked like Tom was barely taking care of himself. How could he expect Tom to take care of him?

"I couldn't ask you to take care of me," he voiced his thoughts aloud.

Tom smiled, shy again. "I'd be proud to," he said, in something of a mumble that Terry could only just hear. "I'd like it, if you was to know the truth. You look to me like someone as needs a man to take care of him."

Terry remembered of a sudden the few coins he had in his pocket, the last of Van Arndst's money.

"Oh, say, I've got some money," he said. "Let me pay you for that apple, at least."

He took the coins out of his pocket and held them in his hand, palm up, toward Tom. "If you want," he started to say, but Tom looked so offended and glowered at him so intensely that Terry dropped the coins back into his pocket and offered his empty hand instead. "I can't tell you how grateful I am, for all you did."

Tom took hold of Terry's hand, but he didn't immediately let go of it. He swallowed noisily and took a step closer, so close that Terry fancied he could again feel the heat radiating from his body. He looked suddenly determined, as if he had made up his mind to something.

"Listen, before you go, if you was of a mind…well, we could…" he stammered, "I never said nothing like this before, never to nobody, but, since I been seeing you…well, I kind of been wanting to…I mean, not just anybody, is what I mean to say…"

He lost his courage at that point, though. It was his turn to blush, something Terry would never have imagined the tough boy doing. He left unsaid what it was he wanted and let go of Terry's hand abruptly, and backed away again. "I'll take you to your brother's," he said instead, in a gruff voice.

"I can find my way," Terry said, his own feelings awhirl as well, and put his torn shirt back on, but Tom gave him a derisive look.

"You need a man to look after you," he said again, firmly, "is my opinion. I think it's lots better if I was to take you. Come on."

When he put his hand on Terry's backside, to boost him out the window, Terry felt as if he had been touched with a white-hot branding iron.

The hand did not linger. The memory of it did, though. Terry could still feel it all the way to Brian's, as real as if Tom still had his hand there.

The river had turned black. They said almost nothing on their way. The clatter of an elevated train on Third Street seemed unnaturally loud in their silence. Tom actually seemed to be angry about something. A couple of times, he brushed his hand surreptitiously down across the front of his trousers, but Terry was afraid to look to see what he was pushing at, and kept his eyes stubbornly away.

When he had delivered him to Brian's door, Tom said, gruffly, his eyes down on his scuffed shoes, "You know where I live, then. Just in case you should ever, you know. It ain't much, but…" He shrugged and left the rest of it unsaid, and walked quickly away.

Terry pushed his glasses up and watched him until he had disappeared around a corner, without looking back.

"Terry, Terry, Jesus, what have you done to us?" Brian dropped his head into his hands with a groan of misery.

"I couldn't help it," Terry said, his voice breaking. "He forced himself on me, Brian. I tried to fight him off, really, I did." He sat for a moment, waiting for something more from Brian. When it wasn't forthcoming, he asked, in a small voice, "Will they really arrest me?"

Brian did look up at him then. "The woman, what did you say her name was?"

"He called her Alicia."

Brian groaned again and shook his head. "Alicia Langley. Damnation. It couldn't be worse."

"Who is she?"

"She's his fiancée, for starters," Brian said. "The one's going to marry him."

Terry considered that for a moment in confusion. "But, a man like that, the way he is—why would a woman want to marry him?"

Brian's smile was sardonic. "Female vanity. Women always think they can cure a man of that sickness. Anyway, bugger or not, Martin Van Arndst is regarded as a catch. The Van Arnsdts are at the top of the heap. People like that don't generally marry for love. It's all about social standing, and money, and influence. He's got the social standing and she's got the money and the influence. Her family isn't as old as his, but they've got a lot more money, and important connections in a lot of places. Her cousin is the mayor, for one thing. And what that means is, all it'll take is one word from her to him, and the police will be after you for sure. I'd guess they already are."

"What'll I do?" Terry asked. "Maybe I should run away. If you've got enough cash to get me a ticket I'll leave on the next train. To anywhere, it doesn't matter where. You won't have to worry about me."

"You think they'd let you get away with that? I guarantee you, they're already looking for you at the train station, and at your boarding house, too, and it won't take them long, I wager, before they come here. It ain't any big secret I'm your brother."

He gave Terry a ferocious glower. "I ought to kick the shit out of you," he said. "Getting me into this kind of mess."

"Go ahead, if it will make you feel better," Terry said in misery. "I deserve it, I know, and God knows, I couldn't feel any worse."

Brian gave a sigh and stood up, pushing his chair back so violently it toppled over with a crash. "Fuck," he said loudly. "Look, you stay here, let me have the boys do some sniffing around, see what's going on. Maybe she'll decide not to create a scandal. No matter how it's handled, it won't look good for him, will it? He's got a reputation to think of. Her too, as far as that goes."

He grabbed his hat off a peg on the wall and went to the door. "Keep the door locked, and don't open it to nobody. I'll have a couple of the boys outside, to keep an eye on things. If things start getting ugly, do whatever they tell you."

He gave Terry one last, accusing look, and went out.

It was mid-morning by the time Brian returned, carrying a large bag and followed by a couple of his thugs, who dumped Terry's meager possessions unceremoniously in a heap on the floor and went back out.

"It's worse than I feared," Brian said. "Van Arndst sailed this morning on the Lorelei, for Europe. By the time he comes back, all the stink will have died down. Those folks have short memories. And the roundheads have already been nosing around your boarding house."

"Then, how did you get all that?" Terry indicated his things.

"There's ways, and there's ways. Don't worry, my boys know what they're doing. Nobody even knew they were there. It won't be long, though, before the coppers connect you to me, and this place won't be hard to find. We've got to get out, while the getting's good. Get that stuff bundled up, whatever you'll want to take with you. Best travel light, though."

"But, if they're watching the train station, how will we get away?"

"There's a carriage waiting downstairs, with a driver and a good team of horses. A lady friend owed me a favor, I got her husband out of a jam—course, I got a little reward at the time for my services, but this is like insurance to guarantee her husband don't ever find out about that. We'll drive to

Philadelphia and catch a train there. They won't be looking for you that far off."

"But, catch a train to where?" Terry asked, already tying his things into a bundle. "Where'll we go?"

For the first time since Terry had arrived at the flat to share his story, Brian gave him a genuine smile.

"West," he said. "I've been thinking about those gold nuggets just waiting in the cricks out west for me to come along and pick 'em up. This convinced me to do what I was wanting to do anyway, I just couldn't make up my mind to it before, but now..." He shrugged.

"But, it takes money to travel all that distance, doesn't it?"

Brian brandished the bag he was carrying. "We've got it. I emptied Harry's safe while I was at it. This'll get us there, if we make tracks before Harry finds I cleaned him out. Once we're there, it won't matter. Nobody can reach that far and we'll have plenty of money of our own in no time. We're going to become prospectors. Now, get your ass moving and start getting ready, before we have the coppers at the door. And try to look grateful for me saving your skin, why don't you?"

"I am, Brian, you don't know..."

"And no more of that goddamn tomfoolery of yours, sashaying around on tippy toe and getting your butt fucked all over town like you was some two bit whore. Where we're going, the men'll be the meanest and the toughest, I'll wager they'll make the toughs here look like babies. It's time you started acting like a man, too, little brother, and forgot all that girly stuff."

For some reason, the remark about toughs made Terry think of Tom Finnegan. He found himself wishing that he and Tom could become friends. He'd never actually had a friend; Brian was the closest he'd ever come. And it really seemed as if Tom wanted to be his friend. He had even suggested Terry stay for a time with him, hadn't he? You wouldn't offer that to someone if you didn't want to be friends.

And, there was the way Tom looked at him, and the electric current that had passed through Terry when their hands had touched. Just remembering made Terry's face turn pink, as if Tom were right there, looking at him that way.

He found himself wondering what might have happened, if he had lingered a bit longer at Tom's quarters, what it was that Tom had come close to asking him, before he had lost his nerve. It had almost seemed as if he were hinting at some kind of physical intimacy—but, surely that couldn't be, not from someone as manly as Tom. Real men, men like Tom, didn't do those things.

And what if Tom *had* been leading up to something like that? Terry wasn't at all sure how he felt about it. He had hated what Martin Van Arndst had done to him…but, what if it had been Tom Finnegan, with that smile that was rare but sweet when it came, and not forcing himself on him, but, well, what if it had been different. Say, tender…something between friends.

Terry had never thought of that. How could he? He'd never really had a friend before. No one who had looked at him the way Tom had. And, as ugly as that business with Van Arndst had been, Terry had actually found himself tempted by the idea of something like that happening with Tom, had kind of hoped for a fleeting moment or two that was what Tom was trying to lead up to. Not exactly like it happened with Van Arndst. It really wasn't even the sexual part of it that he imagined, it was just, well, having Tom's arms about him, just being close together like that. Tom was kind of homely, with his little pug nose and all those freckles, but there was something about him that appealed mightily to Terry.

It couldn't have been that, though, that Tom had had on his mind, could it? Surely he had misread that look in Tom's eyes.

That was why he'd been afraid to stay, afraid that he had misinterpreted, and that he would make a fool of himself. Worse, that he would make Tom angry at him, when Tom realized what he was thinking.

Terry pushed those thoughts determinedly away. *Oh, what does any of that matter*, he asked himself despondently. *I'm never going to see him again anyway.*

He wished he could, though, just one more time. He wished, in fact, that he had stayed just a little longer at Tom's quarters, had been just a little more responsive to his friendly overtures.

Just to see.

PART II

ALDER GULCH

Chapter Four

Terry felt like he had been lifted up into the air, as if in a tornado, and set down in another world altogether.

It had taken them most of a year to get here—by train and by riverboat, and traveling for a time with a wagon train of Mormons. They'd gone first to California, but the mine fields there were already overrun with thousands of others who'd heard the same stories Brian had heard, of gold for the picking up of it—stories they had quickly learned had been greatly exaggerated. There was gold, to be sure, but coaxing it out of the ground and the creeks took work, hard work, and lots of it.

In any case, all of the likely spots there had already been claimed, and the claims closely guarded by suspicious, quick to shoot miners who kept an especially close eye on any newcomers. Gunfire was not an uncommon sound, and new graves were not an unusual sight.

They had no sooner arrived there, though, than news had come of a rich strike here, at Alder Gulch, and Brian had spent most of the money he had left to buy them a bullock cart and a horse, and they had lit out the same night they got the news.

Terry had turned eighteen on the long journey, somewhere close to Salt Lake City, but he felt as if he had aged decades. Already his life in the Bowery seemed as if it had happened to someone else, or in another lifetime.

Almost everything here was new and unfamiliar to him. The only things that remained from his old life were his few clothes, his brother, and the crucifix that now hung from the lintel above the door—the sole souvenir that he had of the parents he couldn't remember.

In truth, there wasn't much that he missed of that other life. He found himself daydreaming often of Tom Finnegan. Sometimes he dreamed of him at night, as well. He would find himself falling into Tom's emerald green eyes, saw Tom's full lips, almost like a woman's, descending slowly toward his own.

Always, though, he woke up before their lips touched. Sometimes, he would find himself in an aroused state. But, those dreams faded quickly. Tom was gone, thousands of miles behind him. That's all he was now, a memory, a dream that would never be fulfilled. A dream the nature of which Terry could never fully discern, even.

Far harder for him to give up had been his dreams of becoming a dancer. Some part of him clung to them still, but the possibility was so remote now as to seem little more than a fantasy. There was no dancing in a mining camp, if you discounted Lizette, who entertained at the local saloon, and sometimes there the miners danced jigs or clumsy two steps, often men dancing with men, as there were too few women to go around. But Terry had no desire for any of them as partners, and no interest in dancing a jig.

He had tried, when they had first gotten here, at least to keep up his practice, but even that had proven next to impossible. Brian had quickly built them a rough log cabin, with a hard-packed dirt floor, a whisky barrel for its chimney and flour sacks for windows. The roof of woven willow saplings leaked endlessly, so that in a heavy rain, the dirt floor turned to mud.

It was as good as most of the miners had, better than the lean-tos and wickiups many of them lived in, but the cabin was tiny—a single room, most of that taken up with stove and table, and one bed along the other wall, a straw-stuffed pallet that they slept in together. There was hardly enough room in the rest of the cabin for the two of them to move around in it when they were both there, let alone space to do a jeté.

Terry had tried a time or two doing some stretches and some leaps outside, but Brian had quickly put a stop to that.

"I ain't having you make a fool of yourself, worse yet, me too, showing off like that where everybody and his brother can see you," he'd said in a tone of voice that brooked no argument. "God damn, I tell you, we're having none of what happened back there, in the States. If you can't act like a man, then keep yourself inside where people can't see you."

"I can't live like a prisoner, Brian," Terry argued, but Brian was adamant.

"You either act like a man when you're outside, or you stay in, one or the other," was his final word. "No jumping around in the grass like a goddamn fairy."

Terry practiced when and where he could after that, at least enough to limber up, clinging to some faint hope that he might yet dance one day, but he was careful not to do it where Brian would see him.

Living with his brother, for the first time since they had been children, Terry had quickly learned there were two bodies of thought on any subject: Brian's opinion, and Brian's further thoughts on the matter.

Terry made it a policy mostly to keep his mouth shut. What else could he do? At least back in the Bowery he had been able to live alone and more or less pay his way, if just barely—but here he was entirely at Brian's mercy. Even if he could have found a job of any sort in the rough and tumble camp that was rather grandly seen by its inhabitants as the "city" of Alder Gulch, Brian wouldn't have heard of it.

"I'm making enough to feed us, ain't I?" he said when Terry tentatively suggested he might find something to do. "Best thing for you is to keep things cleaned and the food cooked, and you could wash my clothes while you're at it. My pants could stand up by themselves, just about, they ain't been washed in weeks. If you're going to act like a woman anyway, you might as well take care of the woman's work, and I'll be the man of the family, which is what I am anyway, ain't it?

Seems like to me you ought to be grateful, the way I see it, having a man to look after you."

Tom Finnegan had said something like that, too, hadn't he, Terry found himself thinking. Only, it seemed to him as if Tom had meant it in an entirely different way. It had sounded kind of sweet when Tom said it, at least in memory, but coming from Brian, it just sounded bossy. That thought, too, he kept to himself, however.

By the time they had arrived at Alder Gulch, the best claims here had been taken as well, but Brian had quickly found a job working for the Simmons brothers, who had better than a half a dozen claims of their own staked and were generally regarded as the richest men in the camp. They paid Brian a hundred dollars a week. Back in the Bowery, that would have been a fortune, but here a man could spend that much to rent a cabin if he hadn't the mind or the time to build his own.

Brian got a tenth of whatever dust he found for them as well, and he got to stand right there and watch as they weighed it, so there was no cheating in the payment of it. Already, he had a nice little pouch of dust buried in the dirt under their bed.

"When I've got enough, we'll set out on our own," he said. "I didn't come all this way to work for someone else, even if the Simmons brothers are good men to work for. They're fair, at least, which is more than could be said for some in this town. But it's still just kissing ass, ain't it?"

To Terry's undying shame and regret, though, Brian seemed to have accepted in his own mind that what had happened back in New York had been Terry's fault and not something odious that had been done to him by a drunken profligate. Once or twice, Terry had tried to talk to him about it, to make Brian understand his innocence, but Brian had made it clear he wasn't interested in hearing Terry's version of things.

"It's not gonna change anything anyway," was his final word on the subject. "Van Arndst is lower than a snake's belly, that's true enough, but you were his woman, weren't you? That's how anybody would see it, if they knew. How you went about getting his pecker up your ass don't make much difference. It was there, is all that matters. You're as much to blame as he was, the way I look at it."

Which was how it was left between them. The best Terry could do was to try to make himself at home in Alder Gulch—but, he had doubts that he would ever really be able to feel that way about this foreign setting in which he now found himself. He wondered, was this where his omens and portents had been leading him all this time?

At first, when they had set out, he had felt a genuine sense of excitement. Maybe this journey was the one for which he had waited and watched, the one that would carry him safely and cleanly to the future he had imagined. Maybe at last he would arrive at that walled city of his dream.

But, surely, this Alder Gulch was not that future. He could see, when he strolled about the town, that the setting must have once been beautiful. Surely, not long before, there had been a carpet of pine needles beneath the towering fir trees and the abundant alders.

The creek that came down from the mountains was tawny and sparkled in the sunlight, like jewels where it cascaded over the rocks, and the mountains themselves, still snow-capped in the middle of summer, loomed majestically against a sky almost obscenely blue after the soot-filled air of the Bowery.

All of it had been ravaged though, by the coming of these eager, greedy men. The creek was an ugly patchwork of sluices and chutes, entire fields of trees reduced to stumps and the carpet of pine needles was now a sea of mud that ran between rows of cobbled-together buildings. Only the sky remained pure, and the mountains that seemed to look down upon it all with a lofty and infinite scorn.

As he strolled, Terry looked around him with a combination of puzzlement and dismay. It was all so squalid, so dismal. Had he misread the signs, or only fooled himself all this time? What kind of future could Alder Gulch possibly hold for him? Even if Brian did get rich, and that began to seem more and more like a fantasy, no more real than Terry's dream of being a dancer, what could that mean for him? They'd still be here, in this horrible place. And Brian would still look at him with barely disguised disgust. At least, in the past, back in the Bowery, he had sensed an abiding if rough affection on the part of his brother, but Van Arndst seemed to have killed that as surely as he had destroyed Terry's innocence.

The men who passed by as he walked—there were few women, and those were obviously prostitutes—were all of a kind, lean, tough looking individuals with hard eyes, unwashed hair and shaggy beards. They wore black trousers and black hats and red or blue flannel shirts, and they looked curiously at the slim, willowy stranger in their midst, with his white cotton shirt and the cleanly washed gray trousers that clung tightly to his round little dancer's bottom.

A lone woman clattered by in a shiny black buggy, snapping her whip at a dappled roan. She was a big woman, ample rather than fat. Her dyed yellow hair was piled atop her head in careless ringlets, and her gown was as red as the buggy's wheels and too dressy for daytime. Terry stared as she drove by.

"Do not lust after the whore of Babylon," a voice said from behind him.

He knew who she was, then. Even he had heard of Belle Blessings, madam of the local whorehouse. She gave him a quick glance as she drove by—a new male in town was certainly of interest to her—and looked quickly, dismissively away, her practiced eye telling her in a glance that this was an unlikely customer.

"I wasn't lusting, Reverend," Terry said, turning to the speaker. "Just curious, is all."

"Let your mind seek in the Lord's way," the Reverend Davidson said. "For that is the path of salvation."

The Reverend was almost the first person Brian and Terry had met on their arrival here. Brian had scarcely claimed a space for their cabin and begun to build it with the wood from the bullock cart—the lone ox had been sold off for supplies—before the Reverend had shown up to welcome them to Alder Gulch.

He was a tall man, six foot six or more, gaunt and sere, as if the juices had been dried out of him, with long skinny legs like a grasshopper's, you wondered that they could support him, and neither his hair nor his beard gave any hint of ever having known soap and water, let alone a comb or a brush. He gave an odd impression of being too large for his skin, and you couldn't help thinking he might be a bit less peckish if it fitted him more loosely, but he radiated a kind of energy that made him seem anything but frail despite his leanness. His wide dark eyes flashed with an almost alarming intensity when he spoke, and the voice that emanated from that sunken chest was astonishingly deep and booming, even in everyday conversation.

He wore the same flannel shirt and dark, dirty trousers as the others in town and apart from his shagginess, and most of the men who had been here any time at all were similarly shaggy, there was little to distinguish him from them save for the little gold crucifix that he wore on a chain at his throat and fingered ceaselessly when he talked.

He had invited Brian and Terry to attend services at his "church"—really, nothing more than a lean-to attached to his own cabin. Terry had visited him there once. It was as primitive as the rudest shacks of the miners, its only decoration a roughly hewn wooden cross before which wildflowers were sometimes scattered incongruously on the dirt floor.

Occasionally on a Sunday morning one or two of the miners could be seen there, kneeling while the Reverend exhorted them to piety and led them in a hymn or two in a voice that made up in loudness what it lacked in tune.

"He catches them staggering home from the saloon," Brian said of the Reverend's parishioners, and Terry was inclined to think he was probably right. Curious, he had hidden among the trees his first Sunday in Alder Gulch, watching the Reverend's "service," and it had been evident that at least one of the miners was on his knees because he had difficulty standing.

Terry wondered what had brought Davidson to Alder Gulch. It did not seem that, like the others, he had come to seek his fortune, and if he had come expecting to "gather the lost sheep back to the fold," as Davidson himself put it, Terry could not but think his journey a wasted one. The sheep showed little inclination for being gathered.

"I'll keep that in mind, Reverend," Terry said now, "though it doesn't seem to me that there is much choice of direction here in the Gulch."

"Every breath is a choice," the Reverend said, "you walk toward the Lord or away from him," but Terry had already nodded and gone in his own direction, away from the Reverend.

The preacher made him uncomfortable. Those hard, dark eyes looked at him as if they wanted to penetrate his inmost thoughts, and Davidson's scowl seemed to him altogether disapproving. He was grateful that the Reverend did not follow him, at least, though he had the feeling that his eyes did.

Terry paused to look in the open doorway of the town saloon, The Lucky Dollar. The air inside was filled with stale cigar smoke and the scent of unwashed bodies. Men clustered at the bar or around the gaming tables, scuffing their feet in the sawdust on the floor and talking in overloud voices. Someone beat out a discordant tune on an upright piano and as Terry watched, a tall wiry man grabbed a woman from a chair, slapped her and shoved her reeling onto the dance floor. A disheveled miner grabbed her with a loud whoop and began to spin her around spiritedly, taking not the slightest heed of her sobs.

Fascinated and frightened at the same time by the aura of vice rampant, Terry turned away and continued his meandering. Two men standing outside the saloon glanced after him as he passed and one of them gave the other a knowing smirk and pursed his lips, but Terry did not notice them.

It was at this point that Brian found him and caught up to him, looking angry. "What are you doing?" he asked in a harsh whisper.

"Nothing. Just having a stroll, Brian," Terry said, surprised and puzzled as to why his brother should sound so angry.

"Looking for someone, was you?"

"No one in particular," Terry said. "Why?"

"I guess it don't matter who, in particular, does it?" Brian said.

Terry stopped short and turned to face his brother directly. "What's that supposed to mean, then?" he asked.

"I saw the way you looked at those two outside the saloon," Brian said.

"Who?" Terry asked, puzzled. "I didn't see anybody."

"I saw the way they looked at you, too," Brian said, as if he hadn't heard him. "I told you, Terry, I won't tolerate any of that whoring around of yours, like back in the States. You try that here, even once, and I swear it, I'll beat it out of you if I have to."

Terry flushed. It had become quickly clear to him that even if Brian did not want to talk about what had happened back in the States, it was never far from his thoughts. "Don't talk nonsense," he said. "I never even thought of such a thing. It isn't anything I'd do anyway. I've got no interest in having that happen to me again. Once was bad enough."

"Well, it hadn't better," Brian said. "You go on home now, and stay there. If they don't see you sashaying around like that and twitching your little tail, they won't be getting any ideas."

Terry started to object, but Brian wasn't hearing it. "Go on, now, do as I say, get yourself home. Clean the house."

"It's already clean," Terry said. "I cleaned it this morning."

"Clean it again, then."

Terry had quickly learned that there wasn't much privacy in a little one-room cabin. Most nights, he heard Brian abusing himself on his side of the bed. Terry recognized the sounds well enough. It was a vice that he had struggled with himself since boyhood, not always with success.

He was too modest to practice it where Brian could hear him, or even in the privy, where Brian might catch him unexpectedly. He had found a place a little ways off in the woods, surrounded by bushes, and where he could see and hear anybody who came close, and whenever the urge became irresistible, the way it sometimes did despite his determination to avoid it, he went there and, freeing himself from his trousers, had at it frenziedly, desperately almost, getting it over with as quickly as possible and afterwards feeling guilty and ashamed.

Brian obviously had no such qualms however, and seemed not to care if Terry heard him or not. Sometimes, it had almost seemed as if he wanted Terry to notice what he was doing. Occasionally he would cough, or shift from one side to the other halfway through the act, and when he finished, he often moaned aloud, and sometimes swore, "Oh, Jesus," or "Shit, damn."

The night after Brian had sent him back to the cabin, Terry heard Brian once again indulging in his solitary pastime. For some reason, listening to him, Terry felt himself responding in kind. He got stiff, and had to restrain himself to keep from emulating his brother. He had to prevent himself as well from turning so that he could watch.

He had never before been tempted to look while his brother indulged himself, and didn't understand where the sudden urge to do so now had come from, but the thought of Brian, his member exposed and swollen with his pounding, suddenly made Terry's own erection grow harder.

It was strange—until Martin Van Arndst had forced himself on him, Terry had hardly thought at all of what a man had down there, except the occasional, almost unavoidable glance at Brian when he had paraded around his apartment naked in the old days, or those worrisome times when the urge overwhelmed him and he resorted to abusing himself. Even then, he hardly even looked at himself, at what it was he was handling.

Now, out of the blue, he had this peculiar and worrisomely frequent urge to want to see Brian's member. Sometimes, even during the day when Brian was fully clothed, Terry caught himself staring at Brian's crotch, imagining what was hidden within his trousers.

Embarrassed when he realized what he was doing, he would blush and quickly look away, and hope that Brian hadn't noticed; but sometimes, it almost seemed as if Brian were teasing him with it. Terry would stare and, for no reason, Brian would scratch at his crotch, or actually take hold of himself through his trousers and tug things about to get them more comfortable, which usu-ally resulted in his making them more prominent, it seemed to Terry, though he tried not to notice that.

Despite all the times Brian had been naked around him, Terry had never taken more than the briefest of glances at him, and had only a vague idea of what was actually there. Now, he found himself wishing he had paid more attention to it when he'd had the opportunities; and, at moments like this, when he knew it was there to be seen, he was troubled by the curiosity it inspired in him, and the temptation that seemed to grow stron-ger the more he resisted it, to take a real look.

But why it should fascinate him so, he had no idea. It was just a male member, wasn't it? It could hardly be all that different from his own, and he saw nothing particularly attractive about that.

He rolled onto his side, his back to Brian and tried to force those sinful thoughts from his mind, determined to go to sleep. He hadn't heard Brian finish with his usual violent shaking and gasping, but he must have, because the slap of his fist against his belly had ceased and the bed no longer shook. Terry was glad. He would never have been able to sleep while Brian was still at it. His own erection began to shrink.

He had no more than begun to drift off, though, when he felt Brian scoot up next to him, behind him and Brian put a hand on his hip, taking a firm hold of him as if to keep him from floating away.

Terry had all but despaired of ever seeing any open dem-onstration of the affection that he had always longed for from his brother, that Brian had sometimes, if only rarely and only in private, demonstrated in the past. Now, half asleep, he happily snuggled back against him, savoring the warmth of his big broth-er's body, unsuspecting of anything untoward—until he felt a hard probing at his hole.

He sort of froze, not knowing what to do or say, not wanting this to happen but afraid to object, afraid of Brian's quick temper, and by the time he might have protested, it was too late, Brian made a spitting sound and slicked himself up, and a moment later he pushed his way in and was working it quickly deeper, as if in a hurry to have the deed accomplished.

Terry nearly cried out, and bit his lip instead, knowing that any objection on his part would be sure to make Brian furious. Brian did not like to have his authority challenged, and somehow Terry felt sure that would be all the more the case with what he was up to now.

It was less painful than it had been that other time, with Van Arndst, maybe because it had been done before and probably—but he didn't think about this until much later—because Brian's member was considerably smaller, skinny and nowhere near as long as the other man's had been. It was more uncomfortable than anything else, having that hard thing shoved up inside him like that.

At the same time, though, there was something else, something he couldn't quite shape into words. Brian no longer held on to his hip but had put his arms about him, hugging him close, and their tight embrace, their bodies pressed so firmly together that he could feel the wiry thatch of Brian's chest hair against his bare back, Brian's hoarse breath against his cheek, all gave him a feeling he'd never had before, of fulfillment, almost, or completion. It was as if in joining them, Brian had somehow made him whole in a way he had not been before, as if Brian were, both literally and figuratively, sharing his own manhood with him.

Their mouths were so close, no more than an inch or two away from one another. Terry turned his face a little and it seemed to him that Brian brought his lips closer too, as if he meant to kiss him, the way Tom did in Terry's dreams, and Terry parted his lips eagerly, to welcome the kiss…but like those dream kisses, this one failed to materialize. In the instant before their lips actually touched, Brian turned his head quickly away, and fucked at him more furiously than before, almost like he was angry, until his whole body stiffened, and Terry felt his brother's spunk spewing inside him.

Brian held him for a moment longer, and giving a sigh, as

if he'd just run a long distance, slipped out and rolled onto his back. They lay in silence for a long time, neither of them moving. It was Brian who finally spoke.

"We don't need to be telling anybody else about this," he said.

"I wouldn't, Brian, you know that," Terry said.

"And I don't want to hear no sniffling about it, either. It ain't like I was the first in."

It was a moment before Terry said, his voice carefully devoid of any emotion, "No, it isn't."

Another silence. "Don't you be fooling around none with any of the boys in the camp, either," Brian finally said. "Now that I've taken care of it for you."

"I wouldn't," Terry said.

"They're a bunch of tough hombres, those boys. If they started thinking you meant a piece of ass when they wanted it—the way you walk, and all—it could lead to all sorts of trouble for us. For me, especially. Bad enough, you being so sissyish. I don't want anybody getting any ideas. I'd have to start passing out some knuckle sandwiches."

"I won't make any trouble," Terry said.

"That's how's come I did it, in case you're wondering. It's not something I care about. I could see you was getting all twitchy like, the way you was sniffing around all those men in town and swinging your butt, I knew you was hankering to get it plugged good. This way, you won't need anybody else. I can't change the way you are, but if it'll keep you out of mischief, I'll see you're taken care of steady, you needing it so bad and all. I reckon I can keep you satisfied good enough. That's the best thing, you ask me."

"You're right," Terry said. "This is best."

"Course I'm right. It's good you can see that, too. Shows you got some sense, anyway, even if you do have that damn foolishness in you." He paused for a moment. "Don't go getting any ideas about how I am, either," he added. "I told you, I mean to keep you out of any more trouble, is all. If that's what I have to do, well, then, that's just what I have to do."

"I understand."

"I just hope you're grateful, is all."

"I am, Brian. Honest."

"Well, then." After a moment, Brian turned on his side, his back to Terry, and in a little while, he had begun to snore, but it took longer for Terry to fall asleep.

Brian awakened him during the night, scooting up to him again, as hard as before, shoving it in without preamble, holding Terry in such a crushing embrace that Terry thought his ribs would surely break, and this time pumping it in and out at a furious pace so that in little more than a minute he had emptied himself again into Terry's sore backside.

He pulled it out at once, almost before he'd finished shooting, and again turned his back, and went to sleep.

Terry wondered how he was supposed to act the next morning. He was up first, as he usually was, and when Brian stirred and opened his eyes, Terry found himself blushing, and quickly looked away from the sight of a naked Brian clambering out of bed, his erection poking out in front.

It was quickly apparent, though, that the subject wasn't meant to be broached, at least not by Terry. Brian said nothing of what had happened and for most of the day, he avoided meeting Terry's gaze—but, once or twice, turning from what he was doing, Terry found Brian's eyes on him, his expression one Terry could not read—speculative, almost, weighing. And, oddly petulant.

It made Terry self-conscious. He blushed again and again, and was awkward, spilling things and bumping into the table and the stove it seemed every time he turned around.

Usually, Brian would say something about that sort of thing, but this day he was silent—and watchful. Stealing glances at him, at his scowling face when Brian wasn't looking at him, Terry had a sudden insight that his brother blamed him for what had been done. But, Terry couldn't understand it. How could he, Terry wondered? It was he who had done it.

After that, however, it was done pretty much every night and, surprisingly often, twice a night, and almost never anything said. Once, while Brian was plugging him and without even thinking about it, Terry had taken hold of his own stiffness and started working it the way he did out in the bushes.

"What are you up to?" Brian asked him, pausing in his strokes. It was the first he had ever spoken while he was doing it.

Terry, who thought it should have been obvious what he was up to, considering all the times Brian had done it to himself, said, embarrassed, "I'm abusing myself."

"Well, stop it. You can do that when you're on your own if you need to, a man can't help it sometimes, but I don't want to see it."

"I've heard you doing it plenty of times."

"Well, see, there's the difference, that's cause you're queer and I ain't. A real man wouldn't be interested in listening to another man having at himself, would he, if he didn't have dick on his mind?"

"It's not like that, it's just, well, it's hard not to hear."

"Listen, you get this straight, you hear? A hole's a hole as far as a man's concerned, there's nothing queer about what I'm doing. If I didn't know different, this could be a pussy I'm fucking instead of a butthole, but I don't need to be reminded of what you got up front, either. That makes it queer, see, if you got to listen to a guy whack his pecker while you're giving him what for. You just enjoy getting poked good, I'm doing this for you, ain't I? You save that other business for some time when I'm not around, I don't give a shit about that, just not when I am taking care of your little pussy, you hear what I'm saying?"

"It's not a pussy, Brian," Terry said, embarrassed even to use the word, even in the dark.

Brian, who had begun to pump him again, once more paused. "You want this, or not? 'Cause I can find other places to stick it into if you don't want me to. Better places. I ain't doing this for my own sake, you know."

Terry sighed. "No, go on," he said. "I want you to."

It wasn't true, but it was close enough to the truth—and instinct told him it was what Brian wanted, needed, to hear. For some reason, he didn't resent that. What had happened between them made him feel oddly protective of Brian, as if it were Brian who was being used against his will, and must be comforted for it. As if it were Brian who suffered.

Terry pushed back against him, welcoming him. "Please. Don't stop. Really, you're right, I want it. I'm grateful to you for taking care of me, like you said."

"Just remember, then," Brian said, and fucked him harder than ever.

What Terry had said wasn't altogether a pack of lies, either, if it wasn't quite the truth; but he knew Brian would never understand the truth of it. Terry wasn't altogether sure he understood it himself.

In a way, Terry did want him to continue what he was doing. It still gave him no particular pleasure, no bodily pleasure at least, having Brian pounding in and out of him, sometimes so violently that their bodies came together with loud slapping sounds. When he was doing it, Brian went at it with a single minded intensity, like an invading army determined to overpower its enemy, as quickly and as decisively as possible.

At least, though, it wasn't painful anymore, not the way it had been at the beginning, except when Brian was particularly rough. And there was a kind of pleasure in it for Terry, if it could be called a pleasure. It was more a sort of satisfaction, actually, that he took in the feeling that it gave him, a strange sense that it meant he belonged to Brian, in a way he had never before belonged to anyone.

It came to him gradually that it was almost as if they were married instead of two brothers, and it gave him something that he thought must be akin to happiness, a sense of relief—of homecoming. It felt as if he'd been lost and now he'd come to some place he'd been looking for—to be the means of Brian's satisfying himself, even to be used as Brian's convenience and at his will.

Having no say in it, Terry need feel no guilt over it, the way he did when he abused himself, with increasing frequency now. This wasn't anything that he was doing; it was being done. There was nothing he could do about it. He wasn't to blame. If Brian wanted to use him that way, well, that was his privilege, wasn't it? He was the boss, the bigger, the older brother. Terry couldn't stop him even if he had wanted to.

And the more he thought about it, the more it seemed to him that Brian was right, anyway, in the things he said. Terry knew he would never be a man, not a man like Brian, or the miners here in the camp. Sometimes he wished he had been born a woman. Sometimes he felt like he was anyway, just the way Brian put it, only he had this male body and not the female one he should have been born with. There was nothing he could do about that, either, except be Brian's woman when he wanted him. And, once he'd gotten used to it, once it no longer hurt, he didn't mind.

What was more, despite Brian's protestations that he got no pleasure from it, Terry thought that Brian's body said otherwise. Certainly he seemed always hungry for it, ever ready to go.

That, Brian's pleasure, or at least his physical satisfaction, was the pleasure as well that Terry took in their doing it, and he was content enough with that—more content in a way, truth to be told, than he had ever been in his life. How could he have known, that the way to the love he'd always longed for was to let himself be used as a woman? It was probably unmanly, too, to want to be loved, cared for. Real men didn't, it seemed. But he did, he always had. And this was as close as he'd gotten yet to what he thought love was.

Once, while Brian was pounding at him, hugging him close in a fervent embrace, his wiry beard rasping against Terry's smooth cheek, his other beard grinding against Terry's tender buttocks, Terry found himself suddenly thinking of Tom Finnegan back in the Bowery, with his red hair and his homely grin, and the way Tom had looked at him, especially that afternoon in his living quarters.

This must have been what he was thinking of, Terry thought in a flash of insight, what he had recognized and been afraid to acknowledge in the glint of Tom's green eyes, what Tom had been about to suggest that day, just as Terry had instinctively suspected, and Terry had a fleeting regret that something like this hadn't happened between them.

When he was having his way, Brian's thrusts were accompanied with loud, short grunts and his breath grated on Terry's ear like the beard that left Terry's cheek raw afterward, and occasionally when he reached his finish, he would break wind in a noisy and noxious cloud.

Sometimes, when he had rolled Terry over onto his belly and climbed atop him, Terry imagined that it was some wild animal that rode him, a wild pig or a forest demon, perhaps a satyr, and not a man at all. He found himself dreaming of how it would be with Tom, and in his fancy those feral grunts that mounted steadily in volume and tempo as Brian's climax neared were instead tender sighs and soft words of affection sweetly whispered in his ear.

He tried to imagine what Tom's member must look like, how it would feel buried in him. He wondered if Tom would kiss him, not fading away as it did in his dreams, but their lips finally coming together. Would Tom love him while he did it? Sadly, he would never know now. Tom was thousands of miles and an entire lifetime away.

But if not with Tom, maybe one day with someone else, maybe even someone with copper hair and flashing green eyes. If he ever had the chance again, if someone ever looked at him that way in the future, well, he would know now, wouldn't he, what it was that they wanted, what they could do for him that apparently couldn't be done elsewise?

For the present, though, there was Brian, pummeling him night after night, side by side or hunched atop him with his hairy legs forcing Terry's wide, pumping him full of those man juices that afterward seeped out of him to stain their pallet. And, when Terry had thought about it, it came to him finally that this was what the miners did with those whores in town, wasn't it, or what a husband did to his wife at night?

The way he began to look at it, it was a lot like that for him and Brian, like a husband and wife, the whole business: living together, him cooking and cleaning and looking after the house and Brian going off each morning to work the claims and coming back to him at the end of the day. And at night, those urgent couplings and Brian's tribute offered up to him over and over, the same treasure a man gave his wife. And night after night, Brian gave him the gift of it, just as if he were Brian's wife and Brian were his husband.

He knew better than to say anything like that out loud. He liked the feeling, though, of knowing that, if only in this way, he was Brian's and Brian was his, the same as if they were married. If this was what it took, what it meant, to belong to someone, to belong to Brian, then he was content enough to do it.

It wasn't real love, of course. He knew that. Or real happiness, either. It wasn't complete. He knew they weren't really man and wife, that when Brian did it to him, Brian was pretending that he was with a woman, and wanted nothing to remind him that it was a man, let alone his own brother, that he was rutting with.

But it was the best relationship Terry had ever known, the only truly intimate relationship he'd ever had, and the closest he had ever come to love. Maybe Brian didn't love him, the way a man loved his wife, but he truly believed that Brian loved having his way with him. And Terry had discovered that being loved, being wanted and needed, was what he loved more than anything else, was the most like happiness of anything he had yet experienced in his young life.

Still, no matter how often his brother had at him and no matter how hard, there was something else in him, something that ached, like a boil that needed lancing, and it seemed that no matter how far inside him Brian reached, it was never far enough to pierce that and drain the poison from it.

Maybe, he sometimes thought in the heat of the moment, and shocked himself thinking it, maybe if Brian were only a little longer, went just a little deeper; and when Brian was in him, when Brian was getting close enough to his climax that he ceased to pay any attention at all to the body in front of him, to anything that Terry did, and was aware of nothing but his own pleasure, his need, then Terry would stop being just a passive recipient and actively push himself back, hard, against Brian's abdomen, opening himself to take Brian as deeply as he could, all of it with each lunge, would have welcomed the balls too—and not until Brian had gotten him so enflamed, his butthole aching, his own cock burning hard and begging for attention he dared not give it, not until then did he call them even in his mind "butthole" and "balls" and "cock," when normally he thought "opening" and "eggs" and "member"—he would have welcomed Brian's balls, too, then, if they had gone in, would have swallowed up Brian's body in its entirety, taken all of him too into his "pussy," if he could have, to fill himself completely, to finally possess altogether the man possessing him so violently.

But it never was deep enough. The poison was still there.

Chapter Five

It soon began to seem, however, that no matter how fully nor how enthusiastically he submitted to Brian's desire, it did not make his brother any happier. Indeed, Brian grew steadily more unhappy as their time passed in Alder Gulch, like something was aboil deep within him and had, increasingly often, to be spewed forth, like a volcano erupting. Most of all, his taste for Alder Gulch had paled dramatically.

"I'll never get rich here, working for Simmons," he complained. "I didn't come all this way to be nobody's goddamn servant."

And, "I hear there's people getting rich up around Butte, maybe that's where we should have gone."

Terry grew alarmed at the prospect of picking up stakes and moving again. As bad as Alder Gulch was, he knew that there were worse places. He had seen some of them on their travels.

Brian was right, however, when he said he wasn't going to get rich here. For one thing, everything was so expensive. The pay he got from the Simmonses went as quickly as he made it and the stash of gold dust that they gave him for a bonus had ceased to grow.

If he only didn't spend it all at The Lucky Dollar saloon, Terry found himself thinking, but he dared not say. Brian had taken to drink. He spent most evenings now at the saloon, and when he came home, he wasn't always drunk but he was never quite sober, either—and he was usually angry about everything in general and nothing in particular.

"What a hell hole this is," he would rant, shedding his clothes and leaving them in a heap on the floor for Terry to pick up. "I had things better than this, back in the States. Should have stayed where I was." He would pause in his mutterings and then add, in a still angrier voice, "Only, I couldn't very well, could I, thanks to my pansy little brother. I should have let them throw your sorry ass in prison, is what I should have done," and he would glower at Terry as he staggered naked about the cramped room, scratching at his furry backside and looking for something upon which to vent his anger and frustration.

What he generally found was Terry. Most of the time, his abuse was only verbal, and Terry had long ago learned to block that out. Sometimes, though, and increasingly, it was physical.

"It's your fucking fault," he would say, grabbing Terry's arm and twisting it viciously. "You're the one's to blame," and then, too often of late, he would hit him, slap him openhanded or even punch him with his fists. Terry could do nothing but try to duck the blows or put up his hands to protect himself.

Luckily, like the mountain storms that sometimes swept through the camp, uprooting tents and sending paper and empty tin cans sailing down the muddy street, Brian's fits of temper were as brief as they were violent, and they soon ended with him flinging Terry to the bed, and assaulting him with renewed fury. In that regard, at least, his penchants remained undiminished. If anything, they grew stronger, though satisfying them seemed to bring him no relief from whatever demons ate at him.

Terry tried, when it was happening, to make it as good as he could for Brian, to find every possible way to enhance his brother's pleasure in their sexual couplings, but no matter what he did, no matter how compliant he was, it only seemed to make Brian angrier with him. Even when he ceased to be just a passive partner, and tried actively to participate in their sex, for Brian's sake, that too infuriated Brian.

"Christ, you don't have to love it so much, do you?" Brian demanded one night when Terry had been churning and twisting beneath him, hoping to distract Brian from his unhappiness and trying, too, to get it over with more quickly. "It makes me sick, the way a stiff dick gets you all worked up, like you can't get enough of it. I swear…" and he paused long enough to box Terry's ears soundly before he resumed his poking.

Brian's physical abuse, at least, accomplished what his tirades hadn't altogether; they kept Terry more and more at home. Too often, now, he sported ugly bruises, and for a while, a badly split lip, and another time his eyebrow was cut open. He was ashamed to have anyone see him like this, afraid they would know at a glance how he had gotten these marks and, worse, why.

He became frightened that people would know that he and his brother were lovers, and certainly it was him they would blame, not Brian. It seemed to him, the next time he encountered Reverend Davidson, that the preacher looked at him differently, as if he knew what they had been up to, which of course he couldn't.

"It will heal the soul to confess your sins," the Reverend said, accosting Terry on his way one morning back from the creek with a bucket of water. "Kneel, son, I am here to unburden you of them."

"You'd be more of a help if you unburdened me of this water," Terry said curtly, and hurried by. He was already late and Brian would be waiting angrily for his breakfast. He couldn't help thinking, though, as he went, that there had been something knowing, even sly, in the way the Reverend had eyed him when he spoke.

Always shy, he became something akin to a recluse. And what did it matter, he consoled himself? There was nothing in the town of Alder Gulch for him, after all.

Really, apart from Brian, there was nothing anywhere for him, was there? As bad as things were, they would surely be worse without Brian.

Brian was all he had.

He thought that, at least, until the stranger came to town.

At first, when Terry caught that glimpse of red hair through the trees that separated their cabin from the much grander one that belonged to the Simmons brothers, he had a wild thought that Tom Finnegan had followed him here, had come to rescue him and carry him off. They would be together, the way he and Brian were together, but more completely, more fully, and when they did it, Tom would hold him, not in those angry embraces of Brian's, but gently, tenderly, and kiss him, and whisper to him those sweet nothings he could almost but not quite hear in his dreams.

He was on his way to the creek to fetch water, as he did each morning. Dawn was just breaking through the treetops. He went early, often while it was still dark, because Brian scolded him incessantly that he must as much as possible avoid being seen, and Terry had long since begun to collude with Brian in keeping himself out of sight.

The path took him close to the Simmons' cabin. Usually he hurried by, trying to be as inconspicuous as possible, but this particular morning, he heard someone cough and instinctively he glanced in that direction, and his heart skipped a beat at that single glimpse of hair glinting in the early morning sunlight, hair the color of copper.

His heart in his throat, Terry left the path and crept through the pine woods, moving from tree to tree, until he was close enough to see the man with the red hair.

It wasn't Tom, of course, how could it be? It was a stranger, tall, lean, his muscles rippling as he washed himself, shirtless, at the pump outside the Simmons' cabin. He finished, dried himself with his shirt, and laughed at something Walt Simmons said as he came out the doorway.

Terry stared at the young stranger as if seeing a ghost, and a dizziness came over him all of a sudden. His legs could barely support him and if he hadn't been leaning against an alder tree, he was sure he would have fallen, fainted dead away. Even alone, unnoticed, Terry blushed furiously while he stared.

The redhead took a step or two in Terry's direction and for a second Terry thought he had been detected and almost ran away, but the stranger paid him no attention, showed no sign at all of seeing him there. He stopped a few feet away from where Walt

Simmons was busy now washing himself at the pump, fumbled with the buttons at the front of his trousers, took himself out of them, and began to take a loud, splashing pee.

Terry could not take his eyes from that lightly held member spilling its water so noisily. He watched in a trance, seemingly unable even to get enough air into his chest to breathe properly, until the stranger had finished, had shaken it vigorously, maybe a shade longer than might have been necessary, like he was teasing Terry with it, and put it back in his pants. He turned, still unaware of the watcher in the trees, and strode in the direction of the cabin, past Walt Simmons with a quick, laughing exchange of words, and disappeared inside.

Terry would have stayed, waited for him to emerge again, would have followed him wherever he went, not for any purpose except to be able to see him, to look at him, to feast his eyes. Yes, feast, because it was like that in a way, there was a hunger in him that the redheaded stranger had both aroused and fed, and that only the sight of him could feed afterward.

Terry couldn't stay there, though, watching the Simmons' cabin. He was already putting himself at risk of Brian's anger, quicker than ever to erupt these days, as if he were all the time angry about something, at someone—too often, it seemed, at Terry, although Terry could think of nothing he had done to earn Brian's anger.

Brian would be stirring by now, expecting his breakfast to be ready for him, maybe even wanting to relieve himself before he got out of bed, the way he occasionally did in the mornings, despite however many times he'd done it during the night.

For once, Terry found himself hoping that he would, wanting it in a way he had never actually wanted it before. He remembered the sight of the redhead as he peed, and with his fly hanging open, Terry had caught a glimpse of the bush at its base, like spun gold, gleaming in the dawn's yellow light.

The muscles in his backside seemed to twitch at the memory, to pucker involuntarily. The thought of having the stranger buried inside him suddenly excited him in a way that prospect had never excited him until now

He hurried back to the cabin, trying as he went to push his own surprise erection into a position in his pants where it would not be obvious to Brian, knowing full well that if Brian saw him stiff, that would kill any possibility of his wanting the other.

To his disappointment, however, Brian was already out of bed, washing up at the water bucket warming on the stove.

"Where the hell you been?" Brian demanded when Terry came in. "Where's my breakfast?"

"I just stopped to watch the sunrise and listen to the birds," Terry said. "It's such a beautiful morning, I forgot the time."

"Well, the birds don't have to work, like some of us do," Brian said peevishly. "And them of us as has got to go to work would like to have our breakfast ready for us before we do, if it ain't asking too much of you. Jesus, it's like I can't ever do enough for you, Terry, can I? I work all day making a few pitiful dollars and spend my nights keeping you satisfied, and you can't even cook my breakfast on time for me. I ought to be kicking your pansy ass instead of poking it."

"I'm sorry," Terry said, and hurried to get eggs into a skillet, and forgot all about his erection, which had already shrunk up.

He didn't forget the redhead next door, though. Even flipping the eggs, careful to get them exactly the way Brian liked them, he could still see the handsome stranger holding his member in his hand, the stream of pee splashing on the ground, and that gleaming bush just visible at his fly.

He had a sudden urge: he wanted to run his fingers through that golden fleece. He almost fancied he knew how it would feel, too. Silky. Not like his own wiry black bush, he was sure, or the coarse hair that so often rasped at his buttocks while Brian ground against him.

The mere thought of that made Terry's face turn red, so red that Brian noticed.

"What's wrong with you?" Brian asked shortly. "You look like a beet."

"It's the stove," Terry said. "It's hot."

Brian looked at him, and the stove, and back to Terry. "Don't seem like it's any hotter than usual," he said, but Terry set his breakfast before him then, and Brian lost interest in the subject.

The memory of the redhead continued to haunt him as the days passed. He knew who he was now, at least. Brian came home that first day to tell him. He was Walt Simmons nephew, Joshua Simmons, come out from Philadelphia, where the family had business enterprises, to try his luck with his uncles in the gold fields. And he had his own claim, too, a small one that his uncles had ceded to him, that he worked when he wasn't panning in theirs.

"Seems okay," Brian said about him. "A bit hoity-toity, seems like, but he'll get over that soon enough, a place like this. Don't do for a man to think himself too grand."

Terry thought Joshua Simmons plenty grand, but he kept that to himself, and though it took some doing, Terry contrived to see him from time to time—frustratingly, never again with his member on display as it had been that first morning. He was always clothed now when Terry saw him, mostly at the claims. He often worked alongside Brian, and Terry had the inspiration of bringing Brian's lunch to him, so he could manage to steal careful glimpses of the man who had stolen his heart so completely—always careful glimpses, quick and furtive, lest Brian catch him at it and guess at once what had caused this sudden concern on Terry's part for his noonday well-being.

Of course, now that Terry saw him properly, Joshua Simmons did not look much like Tom Finnegan. They both had red hair, it was true, and green eyes, but where Tom had been homely, just missing ugly in fact, Joshua was as handsome as a god.

Once, Joshua had spoken to Terry, had said, "Howdy, I'm Joshua Simmons," and held out his hand for Terry to shake, but Terry had been struck dumb, could not even look into that smiling face, had barely touched his fingers to the offered ones, and the next moment had fled, pushing his glasses up on his nose and blushing in confusion.

At first, the first few nights after he had seen Joshua, Terry was more excited than he had ever been with what Brian did to him. He could not keep the thoughts of Joshua Simmons out of his mind, could not stop remembering how he had looked exposed the way he had been.

Remembering, he responded deliriously to Brian, so that once Brian had said, not sounding pleased, "Shit, it's like trying to ride a bucking bronco, the way you fling it around," but despite his derision he apparently liked it well enough. He had fucked him then with a gusto beyond anything he had ever demonstrated before.

Only, afterward, he had gotten angry about something—Terry had ceased to pay any attention to what it was now that set Brian off, it seemed like it could be anything at all, or even nothing.

Terry had been almost asleep afterward that night, and out of the blue, Brian had smacked him across the back of his head, and without a word of explanation, had rolled over and gone to sleep.

Terry's new-found enthusiasm for Brian's assaults quickly vanished, though. It wasn't the way he imagined it would be with Joshua. From remembering how Joshua had looked soft, he had come to imagine him hard, and from that, it was only a small distance to imagine that it was Joshua who was in him, panting violently as he buried himself again and again.

Somehow, though, he knew it would be different with Joshua. Everything about Joshua was different, even the way he talked, the kind of well-modulated voice and proper grammar that spoke clearly of his upper class background, so different from Terry's or anything here in The Gulch. Even here, in this crude location, it was obvious that Joshua was a gentleman. Certainly there was nothing of Brian's vulgarity or rough-shod manners about him.

As quickly as this new passion for being ravaged by his brother had come over Terry, it faded, faded altogether, so that what had been in the beginning agreeable, if not particularly enjoyable, now was almost intolerable.

For the first time ever in his life, he actually wanted to be fucked, wanted the feel of a man, hard and excited, driving into him, but it wasn't Brian that he wanted up there, it was Joshua.

That would never happen, he was as sure of that as anything, but that didn't stop him wanting it, and imagining it; and, compared to those fantasies, Brian grew ever more disappointing.

Even odder, Terry's fantasies grew until he not only wanted Joshua Simmons with him, in him, he wanted him as well for his husband. He imagined himself being true to him, faithful to Joshua alone. The thought of Joshua's fidelity hardly occurred to him at all. It was different with men. Despite his nightly ministrations, Brian somehow had the energy still to pay occasional visits to Belle Blessing's whorehouse, and Terry just assumed that Joshua would have passions as well that he would need to satisfy in other ways, with other partners.

For himself, though, in his fantasies Terry remained true to Joshua. The thought of having relations with anyone else, Brian included, became odious to him, and it was all he could do not to protest when Brian, as was their custom now, had his way with him nightly.

He knew better, of course, than to voice those feelings, and he did his best to conceal them, even continuing to pretend the enthusiasm that he no longer felt. With each night, though, his unhappiness with it increased.

How this might have gone was unimaginable, but something miraculous happened. One night when Brian had finished with him and gone soundly to sleep, sawing logs with a vengeance, Terry crawled out of bed, restless, unable to fall asleep. He put on his trousers and slipped from the cabin.

He had no particular goal in mind, and if he had consciously considered going toward the Simmons' cabin, he'd have told himself right up front that it was a pointless journey—who could he expect to see there, in the middle of the night? Nevertheless, of their own accord, his feet took him in that direction.

He stopped among the trees, imagining Joshua Simmons, remembering how he had looked that other time—and just as if his thoughts had conjured the real man up, Joshua suddenly appeared, stepping from the cabin door into the moonlight, wearing nothing but his trousers, the same as Terry. He came in

Terry's direction and, like before, opened his fly, took himself in hand and began to pee noisily.

Terry stared spellbound, breathing open-mouthed and wishing it were his hand holding that magical root, shaking it now that the stream had ended.

Only, Joshua did not tuck it back into his trousers as he had that other time. Instead, he continued to shake it, and then, as it quickly lengthened and swelled, he began to stroke it, until it was standing at full attention, and Joshua's hand was sliding up and down its long shaft.

Joshua paused, looked around as if he somehow sensed the presence of his audience, though he could not have seen that far in the pale light. There was a big rock near where he was standing, screened from the cabin by a thick stand of bushes, and he stepped to the rock now as if he'd been there before and, tugging his trousers down about his ankles, sat and spit into his hand and began to work himself in earnest while Terry stood and stared as if in a dream.

He had never witnessed anything so thrilling, had never felt so breathlessly excited. He put his hand down and began to rub his own growing erection, spreading his legs to give him a better grip of it—and, as he did so, a twig snapped under his foot.

Joshua's hand froze and he looked in Terry's direction. "Who's there," he demanded in a low voice.

Terry told himself he should run, remain unseen and unidentified, but like a sleepwalker, so mesmerized that he did not even blush, he found himself stepping around his tree, walking quickly in Joshua's direction. Joshua watched him approach, recognition finally relaxing his wary expression.

"Oh," he said, "it's the little Murphy boy, isn't it?"

"Yes," Terry said, his voice little more than a croak.

Joshua looked past him, as if there might be someone else in his wake, and back at Terry. "What are you doing, creeping around here in the middle of the night, checking on people? Why aren't you home in bed? It's the middle of the night."

"I…I'm sorry," Terry managed to whisper, "I couldn't sleep. I didn't mean to spy on you, I was just out for a stroll and…and I couldn't help seeing you."

To his surprise, Joshua grinned at him, not at all embarrassed, it seemed, at being discovered at what he was doing.

"And found me pounding the old pud, huh?" he said, and to Terry's amazement, began to stroke it again, as brazenly as if Terry weren't standing right before him. "Well, you've caught me tending to the beast, so to speak, not much point now in pretending I wasn't. I guess you won't object if I finish what I was doing." He glanced down at the front of Terry's trousers. "Looks to me like maybe you've got the same problem there. You just going to stand and look, or you going join me? It won't bother me any if you want to do the same," he said.

"I…oh, no, I…I couldn't, Terry stammered.

Joshua laughed softly and shrugged. "Do what you want," he said.

In the next moment, Terry did exactly that. He suddenly dropped to his knees in front of his idol, knowing that what he was doing was insane, that it could get him beaten, maybe even lynched, but he couldn't help himself, he was consumed by a desire he had never experienced before, that swept through him and over him, like a mountain brush fire.

"Hey—what're you doing?" Joshua said, startled.

Terry fully expected to be punched any second now, beaten into a pulp, but he no longer cared. He had to do this. He put his hand over the hand in which Joshua held himself and, reaching past it with his fingertips, touched Joshua's golden bush, the way he dreamed of doing. He had been right, too: it did feel like silk. It was worth dying, wasn't it, just to run his fingers through that godly fleece?

Joshua didn't punch him, though. He took in a sharp breath and leaned back, resting his elbows on the rock to brace himself and spreading his legs wider to make more room for Terry to kneel between them. After a fleeting pause, he took his hand from his cock, relinquishing it to Terry.

Terry took hold of it gladly, with a boldness that surprised even himself. For all the months now in which Brian had been riding him nightly, as much experience as he had of it, he had never had more than a glimpse of Brian's member, of anybody's except that earlier, all too brief glimpse of Joshua's, had never held Brian's in his hand—never held anybody's member but his own.

And how different it was now to clasp Joshua's, to fill his sight with it. It appeared to him the most beautiful thing he had ever seen. Up close like this, it was enormous, far bigger than Bryan's, and without the fleshy curtain that hung down over the head of Bryan's. What a splendid thing it was, and how wonderful it felt in his hand, hard and yet soft too, like velvet. It filled his hand. His fingers could barely close around it. It smelled sweet and sour all at the same time and, still slick with Joshua's spit, it seemed to gleam like marble, the column pale, almost white, and the bare knob at its end, its heart shape looking altogether appropriate to its love drunken admirer, was darker, almost black in the moonlight that splashed through the trees and over them.

Without thinking, Terry leaned down and kissed the tip of that knob, with no thought of anything more, and just like that, it slipped between his lips and he had it in his mouth.

He had never done this before, had never even imagined it, hadn't known, even, that this was something else men could do to one another; but now, doing it for the first time, it seemed so utterly right to him, like he had been waiting all his life for this magical moment, to hold a cock in his mouth. Even the word, which had always somewhat embarrassed him when Brian had used it, suddenly seemed utterly right to him. It was cock-like, wasn't it, upright and proud; and it was surely altogether right to have this one special cock in his mouth, to begin sucking on it as if he had always known this was how it was done, what it was for, what he wanted.

He might have been in some kind of delirium. He ran a hand up Joshua's hard-muscled thigh, found the big, ponderous globes suspended there, covered with more of that silky down, and cupped them in his hand, as if weighing them. Above him, Joshua barely stifled a moan of pleasure, and raised his butt off the rock he was sitting on, arching his back, fucking himself at Terry.

It was quick, far too quick. He put a hand on Terry's head, shoved it down mercilessly and pushed in, the whole length of it, and erupted, shooting a flood into Terry's mouth, making him gag and cough. Terry swallowed all of it that he could, but there was too much and it came too fast and he was too unskilled at the art, couldn't get the hang of how to manage so much, so fast. Trails of it dribbled out the corners of his mouth.

It finished shooting at last, the torrent dwindled to couple of little spurts. Terry continued to suck on it, savoring the aftermath more than he had the actual event, until Joshua suddenly shoved his head away, so violently that Terry fell back clumsily on his rump in the grass. Joshua stood up abruptly, tugging his trousers up.

"I'm...I'm sorry," Terry stammered, turning red. "I couldn't help..."

"You want to be careful who you try that with," Joshua said, buttoning his fly. "There's some wouldn't take kindly to it."

Terry had not even bothered to take off his glasses when he had fallen to his knees, and they were filmed up from the encounter so that when he looked up at Joshua he saw him as if through a mist.

He took them off and wiped the lenses on the leg of his trousers, and put them on again. Joshua had pushed against them with his belly while he was coming and the one arm was bent, so that they hung lopsided on his nose, but Terry did not try to fix them.

"You're not mad at me?" he asked.

Joshua didn't answer that. He turned to go back to the cabin, and paused, like he was listening for something.

Terry couldn't help himself. "Was it...?" he started to ask. "Did you...?" He wanted to ask, "Did you like it? Was it as magical for you as it was for me?" But the words caught in his throat.

Joshua ignored the stammered, unfinished question. "You don't tell anybody about this, and I won't either, you hear? There's men get real upset about your kind. They like to beat the shit out of them, and worse."

"You can…if it'll make you feel better. What I did was bad, I know. If you wanted to…well, you know." He couldn't help thinking he ought to be punished for what he had done.

"Just keep your mouth shut, is all."

"I won't tell anyone," Terry said quickly, fervently. "I swear to you, I won't, cross my heart."'

"Not even your brother," Joshua said, and added, emphatically, "especially not your brother. He's one of those who hates queers worst of all. Said he'd kill one if he ever found one here in camp."

With that, he was gone, never pausing nor looking back. He disappeared into his cabin. The door closed.

Terry sat for a long moment in the damp grass, looking after him, wishing him back. He could not help being aware of the irony of the warning Joshua had given him. He thought of Brian, fucking him nightly, so obviously pleasuring himself. And Joshua, too, he had certainly seemed to enjoy what Terry had done, at least while he was doing it.

Two different men, two different ways of having their pleasure from him, and what was paramount on both their minds was that nobody else must know. Clearly, both of them thought what they had done was wrong.

It must be wrong, too, Terry could see that, if everybody said it was—but that hadn't stopped his brother or Joshua either one from doing it, or enjoying it mightily, at least until after it was done, until after they had spewed out their juices for Terry to take from them.

But, how could it be so wrong, if they all wanted it, if both those men loved it as much as they obviously had, as long as he was willing to do it for them—more than willing, in Joshua's case? And somehow he felt sure that if Joshua were to do to him what Brian did, he would love that, too. Not so much for the act, but for who it was done with. But what did they have to complain about, to regret?

After a bit, Terry got on his knees, and knelt at the rock as if it were an altar, and kissed the spot where Joshua had been sitting, and imagined that it still held the warmth of his naked buttocks.

There was a noise in the woods nearby, like something moving. For a moment, Terry thought that Joshua might have returned, and he looked about hopefully, but there was no one there. Just some animal, prowling, he thought.

He scrambled to his feet and hurried away then, savoring in his mouth as he went the lingering taste that Joshua had left there, trying to recall exactly how it had felt when he was coming, how it had tasted. At the time, it had been an ordeal, trying to take it all, it came so fast and so plentifully, but now, in a romantic haze, he thought of it as a kind of nectar, as sweet as honey, like honey mixed with cream, almost. He wished he could taste it again, in full torrent, to have his mouth filled and overflowing with it, instead of this ghost that teased his taste buds but would not quite coalesce into memory.

He had never for a second thought about what spunk might taste like. He'd never actually even seen Brian's. His jism, as Brian called it. That all went up his backside, and he hardly troubled to look at his own when he'd coaxed it out of himself and shot it onto the ground in his little patch of bushes, always, once the deed was done, in too much of a hurry to stuff himself back into his pants and get away before anyone discovered him.

He got back to the cabin, but he couldn't go in now, would never be able to sleep, as enflamed as he was. He took his spectacles off and straightened the bent arm, and put them on again, but it was no use, he could not distract himself from his arousal. He went around the corner of the cabin, in case Brian might come out for any reason, and took himself out of his trousers, and began to work himself furiously, reliving as he did so the experience with Joshua.

Over and over, it ran through his mind, and as he shot onto the ground, he would have sworn he could feel Joshua's load once again splashing into his mouth, like the flood of those cascades upstream, where the creek spilled down from the mountains into Alder Gulch.

Chapter Six

Joshua Simmons lay in bed for a long time afterward, thinking about the little Murphy boy, and what he'd done to him outside in the clearing. Remembering, his prick got hard all over again, and he wanted to relieve himself, but he was afraid his uncles would hear him.

Not that both of them didn't do the same thing often enough. Many a night he'd heard one or the other of them, and sometimes both at the same time on opposite sides of the room. For whatever reason, he had always chosen to see to his needs privately, going outside as he had earlier, usually to that sheltered cove with the big rock in it. But, two trips outside in quick succession—if either of them was awake, they were sure to wonder. He rolled over on his belly instead, grinding his stiffness into the mattress.

His emotions were all awhirl. He was angry, though he wasn't sure whether it was himself or the young man who had sucked him off so enthusiastically that he was most angry with. Guilty, too, and afraid, because he knew damn well that a man could get into lots of trouble indulging in pleasures like that. Even back in the States, it was a dangerous thing to do, but here, with all these rugged miners, it was practically inviting disaster. He remembered all the times Brian Murphy had railed against queers.

"There's lots of them back in the Bowery," he would say. "That's one of the things brought me west, to get away from shit like that," and other miners would shake their heads in agreement and spit out the corners of their mouths, angry just to think of a man stooping to such disgustingness.

So, it took no great imagination to think how they would respond to the news of Joshua letting himself be pleasured the way he just had been. A beating was the least one could expect, and getting run out of camp to boot.

That it had been a pleasure, though, he couldn't deny. He couldn't tell himself a lie that big, not even to assuage his guilt or his anger. He'd never experienced anything before that had felt so unbelievably wonderful as that steady, eager sucking. He could only suppose that Terry must have done it a lot, to be so expert at it.

He found himself wondering who he had done it with. Someone here in Alder Gulch? It was hard to imagine, but some man, maybe lots of them, had had the pleasure of that boy's skillful ministrations. So, then, not everybody was so dead set against it, not in private, anyway. He even experienced a tinge of jealousy, thinking of someone else having that pleasure instead of him. He wondered briefly who it had been, and thought over the men in camp, but he could think of no likely candidates, though one or two of them were good looking enough that he could imagine they would attract little Murphy's attention.

He had never had a blow job before, but he had come close, that time back in Philadelphia, and he was sorry now that it hadn't happened then, regretted all the loads he'd wasted since in jacking off, when he knew now how much better use they could be put to.

At least, he supposed that was what Samuel Winslow had had in mind, that time he'd gotten him off alone in the carriage house during the lawn party. Looking back, he could see how carefully and skillfully Winslow had arranged it, lured the unsuspecting younger man away.

Unsuspecting, however, had not meant unwilling on Joshua's part, not once he began to get some inkling of what Winslow had on his mind, even if he hadn't been clear on the intended specifics. He'd been plenty willing enough, eager for something, for whatever Winslow had in mind, the moment Winslow had put his hand to the front of Joshua's trousers, had begun to fondle the cock that had almost instantly reared up, ready and eager. Well, a young man's generally was, wasn't it? There was nothing queer about that.

Winslow hadn't sucked him them, but, looking back on the scene, Joshua felt sure now that it was only because there hadn't been time. They'd gotten no further than trousers lowered around their knees, eagerly fondling one another. He couldn't clearly remember now, he thought Winslow had actually started to stoop down to do it, but that might be only his imagination gilding the interrupted lily.

Interrupted by Joshua's sister, Elizabeth, coming toward the stall where they were sheltering, saying, in a voice that startled them because they had been so engrossed in the pursuit of their pleasure that they hadn't even heard her enter the carriage house, "Joshua, where did you go, I want to…"

And there she had stopped, staring wide-eyed, her mouth forming an O of surprise, while both men scrambled to get their clothes restored, their throbbing erections concealed. Not in time, though, not before she had seen them, in quite enough detail to tell her mother about it soon afterward, who told their father, who summoned Joshua to a hasty and heated conference in his study, Samuel Winslow quickly having fled the premises and, as it subsequently turned out, the town of Philadelphia.

At least, Joshua had been able to assure his father quite honestly on one point: "No, sir, I never did anything like that before. I didn't even know, until it was happening, what he was leading up to. He caught me…" and checked himself. He'd been about to say, "with my pants down," and realized in time that his father might think he was being flippant. "Unawares," he'd finished instead.

The result had been the decision to send Joshua west, to work with his uncles in the gold fields. "In which virginal garden, I feel certain," his father had said, "you will not find any snakes like Samuel Winslow to tempt you to that vice again, just in case you have any inclination for that particular apple."

His father had been wrong, though, hadn't he? Right here, in Alder Gulch, which was surely as far from the civilized world as you could get, here had come the serpent, in the form of a boy as little and as tempting as any girl could be, blushing like a girl, too, and with enormous, doe-like eyes and lips like a woman's, and when he had sucked Joshua dry, lips that were bruised so red they looked as if they had been painted—here he had come to do what Winslow hadn't had time to do on that other occasion, but which Joshua was sure was what he had been planning.

And, by God, Joshua thought, and after all had to turn on his side and deal with that aching cock, how he had loved having it done. Inclination? Yes, damnation, once he'd had it done, he could not pretend he didn't want it again.

Wanted it too much. It scared him, scared him a lot. And once his cock had been relieved, he made a vow that he must resist that inclination with all his might. He would not make the mistake of repeating that sin. He wasn't a queer, and he had no intention of becoming one, and that little devil Terry Murphy, with those frightened-looking eyes, was not going to make one of him.

Of that much, he was determined.

Terry went to the claim with Brian's lunch the following day. Joshua was, standing shirtless in the creek, his skin sleek in contrast to the thick fur that matted Bryan's chest.

Joshua ignored Terry's presence altogether, turned his back determinedly on him and refused even to look in his direction, although scratching at his crotch the way he did only made Terry more aware of it. Terry lingered longer than he usually did too, in hopes of some sign, of approval or even disapproval, anything but this being stonily ignored.

He hung around too long, however. After a bit, Brian paused in eating the hunk of roast venison Terry had brought him, and gave him a curious look. "Something on your mind?" he asked.

"I was just wondering how you liked the venison," Terry said, straightening his glasses.

Brian looked at the meat in his hand, and back to Terry. It was the same haunch of venison they had been eating for a week or more. "Nothing wrong with it, that I can see," he said. "Why?"

After which Terry could do nothing but shrug and say, "I just wondered, is all," and take his leave.

He heard Brian say, when he was some distance away, "I swear, it's like having an old woman nagging at you."

Terry would like to have looked back, to see what Joshua's reaction was to that remark. But he was too afraid that Brian might see him. If Brian ever suspected how he felt about Joshua Simmons...He got enough blows and slaps and curses as it was. He couldn't even imagine what would come of that.

"We're out of flour," Terry said. "I need some money to buy some."

"There isn't any money," Brian said. He saw Terry glance toward where the gold dust was usually buried in the dirt. "No gold dust either."

"What," Terry started to say, but Brian cut him off.

"It's the way you spend, throwing my hard-earned money around. For all I know, you're paying some miner to plow your back pasture. Like I didn't work hard enough to take care of that for you. Wears me plumb out just trying to keep you satisfied, but probably it still ain't enough for you, is it?"

"There's never been anyone else doing that," Terry said. "You're the only one." Which, as he saw it, was the truth. What he had done with Joshua didn't count, did it? That was a different sport altogether, one that apparently had never even occurred to Brian, and Terry hoped that it didn't. That was something he'd done only for Joshua, and wanted to do with no one else. It was the only gift that he had to give his idol.

"Well, the money sure goes somewhere," Brian said. "That was supposed to be our stake, that gold dust, that was going to get us to Butte, and it disappears faster than I can make it. I don't know what you do with it."

And off he went to The Lucky Dollar.

Later, though, Terry had an idea. He broached it cautiously with Brian. "I could get a job, you know," he said. "I could help with expenses."

"What kind of job could you get?" Brian asked. "Peddling your ass? You thinking of going to work for Belle Blessings?"

"I used to work at the bars back in the Bowery," Terry said. "I thought there might be something I could do at The Lucky Dollar. Or, now that you mention it, maybe at Belle Blessings'. Not that, but, maybe she needs somebody to clean, or empty the slop jars, or the like."

"You ain't working at no whorehouse," Brian said, "and that's final. You know as well as I do what everybody would think, seeing you sashaying in and out of there. Next thing people would be remarking on I had a nancy for a brother. There's enough of them already wonder about that, I expect, without making it any clearer for them."

He had not said, however, that Terry could not get a job at The Lucky Dollar, and Terry took that for at least a tacit okay. The next afternoon, he washed up, glad for a change that he didn't have any bruises to hide, and strolled into town, to The Lucky Dollar.

The man behind the bar gave him a scowl when Terry came through the swinging doors of the saloon, and looked about to order him out. Terry said, quickly, "I was looking for Mister Willis."

The bartender jerked his head toward the rear. "He's back there, in Lizette's dressing room."

Lizette was the saloon's entertainer. She sang and danced, and in between times mingled with the miners, drifting from poker table to poker table and sometimes disappearing for a spell with one or the other of them, to the room she had upstairs.

Terry made his way past the stage to the curtained doorway that led to the rear, ignoring the curious looks he got from some of the poker players always crowded around the tables. There were voices in the distance and he followed them along the narrow corridor, and found himself at the open door to Lizette's dressing room.

It was immediately obvious that Lizette and Lem Willis, the saloon's owner, were having a quarrel. Terry paused in the doorway, not wanting to listen, but not wanting to interrupt either.

"I'm leaving," Lizette said just as Terri arrived at the door. "I'm going to Frisco, tonight, with old Jake."

"You can't leave just this minute," Willis said, obviously angry. "I've got a room full of miners out there, waiting for you to come on stage."

"Let them wait, what do I care," she said. "Old Jake is in a hurry, and I don't mean for him to go without me."

"And you're just leaving me in the lurch, is that how it is?"

"Listen, I'm sick of you. I'm sick of this saloon and this whole damn town. Old Jake's been saving up his dust, he's got a fortune, practically, and I mean to spend some of it for him. No more dirty mine camp for me, I'm going to live in the city and be a lady."

"Well, what about all this stuff?" Lem gestured at the racks of dresses and the dressing table littered with jars and bottles. "What am I supposed to do with it?"

Lizette laughed. "You can eat it, for all I care. All those cheap dresses? You think I could wear them in Frisco? This is what I'm taking." She picked up a small carpetbag from the chair. "Travels fastest who travels lightest, is what they say. Anything else I need, Jake can buy it for me when we get to Frisco."

"Listen, you," Willis said, but she didn't wait to hear him out.

"No, you listen. It's goodbye and good riddance." And with that, she threw open the back door and went out, slamming it after herself. From outside, they heard a man's voice say, "About time, I was fixin' to go without you."

"You ain't going nowhere without me, you old sugar," she said, and her laugh quickly faded.

"Good riddance is right," Willis said, staring at the door through which she had disappeared. "Damnation! I ought to have thrown the ungrateful bitch out on the street a long time ago." He turned, and saw Terry standing in the doorway. "What the hell are you looking at?" he demanded, "Who are you?"

"I'm Terry Murphy. Brian's brother."

"The mean son-of-a-bitch? I didn't even know he had a brother, unlest it was Old Nick. Well, what do you want?"

"I came by," Terry stammered, "I'm looking for work. I thought, well, maybe I could get a job here, at The Dollar. Maybe you needed somebody."

Willis laughed mirthlessly. "You want a job? Why don't you put on one of those dresses and go out there and dance for those damn fool miners. That's what I need, sonny." He stormed out, muttering angrily to himself.

Alone in the dressing room, Terry glanced about. The room was untidy, the air heavy with cheap perfume. His eyes fell on the dressing table. It was littered with toiletries, shabby little pots of rouge and black for the eyebrows and lashes. He picked up a Spanish fan that lay there and snapped it open.

Back in the Bowery, in the dressing room at the theater, Rosaria had entertained her fellow dancers often with her fan. "In Spain, a señorita doesn't need words to tell a man what she wants to say, she can say it all with her fan," she told them.

Clicking the fan open and shut, Terry strolled to the rack of dresses that stood along one wall, the costumes Lizette had left behind.

*Why don't you put on one of those dresses...*Willis' words seemed to echo inside his head. He thought of that time as a child when he'd dressed as a girl, how different he'd felt. He took one of the dresses from the rack and held it up before himself and looked speculatively into the standing mirror. The dress was black, vaguely Spanish in style, and lavishly trimmed in ruffles.

Even at a glance, he could see it would fit perfectly.

Chapter Seven

Willis was back a bit later. "You still here?" he said, coming in, "I thought I told you…"

He stopped inside the dressing room door and gaped in astonishment at the beautiful woman seated at the dressing table, scarcely able to believe what he saw. "Jesus H. Christ," he swore aloud. "It can't be, but…but it is, isn't it? It's…is it really you, Murphy?"

"Not anymore," Terry said. "Not tonight. Tonight, I'm Lola Valdez. And I'm going to dance on your stage."

"You must be plumb loco. Do you have any idea what kind of men those are out there?"

"A pretty good idea."

"They'd kill you for fooling 'em like this."

"They won't know, if you don't tell them," Terry said. "Look at me, Mister Willis. If you didn't know, would you ever suspect?"

"Someone will."

"You go out there and tell them there's a new entertainer just arrived in town tonight. Lola Valdez, you tell them, just back from a triumphant tour of the continent, where she danced for the crowned heads of Europe. And tonight, Lola dances for The Lucky Dollar Saloon."

"They'll string me up with you," Willis said, but after another long, hard look at the face in the mirror, he gulped and shook his head, and hurriedly disappeared out the door.

Terry followed him more slowly. He paused at the edge of the moth-eaten curtain, peering past it at the crowded saloon. For just a moment, his legs felt like they would fail him.

"He's right," he told himself. "You must be crazy, Terry Murphy, to think you could get away with this."

There was a mirror tacked up just off stage. He looked at himself carefully in it. His hair hadn't been cut since he had come here, and by this time it naturally hung all the way down to his shoulders. He'd used Lizette's pins and a couple of Spanish combs to pin it up, and let the dark curls tumble down either side of his face.

He'd had to leave his glasses behind in the dressing room, so he saw things through a faint myopic haze that, he did not realize until later, gave his glances a peculiar intensity. He had outlined his eyes to make them look even bigger and darkened his lashes. His mouth was painted a little fuller than it really was, and he'd made his complexion a bit lighter with powder, carefully not too much, and painted roses of rouge on his cheeks.

Other than his face and neck, there wasn't much skin to be seen. He'd put on a trio of red petticoats under the black dress, and cinched it all at the waist with a gold chain. The skirt came down far enough to cover his stockinged legs but managed nevertheless to offer glimpses of scarlet ruffles when he walked. There were more ruffles that hid most of his bodice as well, and he had pinned a flowery lace shawl around his shoulders, that screened the rest of it while the glimpses of flesh showing through it created the illusion that they was more to be seen than there actually was.

If someone who knew him, and especially someone who had any reason to suspect, looked closely enough, they might recognize him. But, who knew him here? Hardly anyone. He had almost never come into town, and then only briefly. They wouldn't be seeing him up close, either, but from a distance, and as they had said more than once in their dance classes back in the States, distance lends enchantment. Besides, there was no reason for anyone to suspect, to think he was anyone but who Willis was announcing to them at this very moment—Lola Valdez.

Willis came offstage, looked at Terry and, with a nervous grin, shook his head in wonder. "Go on, get our fucking necks wrung for us, if you're going to do it," he said.

Still, Terry hesitated, until someone in the saloon yelled, "Well, where the hell is she?" and someone else echoed, "Let's get her out here, then, and see what those crowned heads were so het up about."

No, Terry told himself. *I'm not crazy. I can do this. And I'm not Terry Murphy, either. I'm Lola Valdez.*

And the moment he stepped out past the curtain, strolled to center stage, sashaying and making the ruffled skirt and the petticoats swish and sway with each step he took, that was who he became, and Terry Murphy was left behind in the wings.

Lola held the Spanish fan before her face and gazed out at the men over the top of it, smiling with her eyes as Rosaria had demonstrated for them, her gaze sweeping the room. It was a gesture that said, "I find you very attractive," and her huge, dark eyes, just slightly out of focus, conveyed that message to every man in the packed room.

Something happened that had never before happened at The Lucky Dollar. The room went silent, a thunderous silence. No one spoke. Even the slap, slap, slap of the cards at the poker tables went still. A hundred mouths hung open, a hundred pair of eyes were suddenly riveted on the little figure standing before them.

"Like a rose, suddenly appearing in the filth of that dirty room," one of them would put it later, a description that would be long remembered by many.

It lasted half a minute, that eerie silence—a full minute, longer yet. You could almost hear the seconds tick by until Lola took the satin skirt between her fingers and lifted it ever so slowly, ever so slightly, offering more flashes of scarlet petticoat and one slender ankle—even an inch or two, but no more than that, of net-clad calf.

She gave the fan a quick, sudden snap, revealing her face in full for the first time, and smiled, brightly—and there was not a man in the room who wouldn't have sworn afterward that the smile was aimed directly and personally at him.

Pandemonium erupted. Male voices bawled like cattle in lightning, boots stomped, fists pounded on tables—so much noise that the very rafters shook and you half feared the roof might collapse, the building fall in on itself from all the noise and commotion.

Lola took a single step, rolled her shoulders. The silence fell again, as completely as before, as quickly as the noise had exploded.

She hardly knew afterward what she did. She was aware of the pianist banging out something on the piano, trying to follow the rhythm of Lola's dancing feet, the notes nothing more than a discordant jangle.

No one cared. No one heard them. There was attention for nothing but that slim-waisted figure twirling about on the stage, tossing her fan, flashing her ankles, laughing and winking and weaving in hellish abandon. When she spun about, they saw more womanly leg than it was possible for a man to see anywhere outside of Belle Blessings' whorehouse, and these legs were shapelier by far than any to be seen there. The mining camps didn't generally get the prettiest women. Certainly, here, none as pretty as this.

At first, they watched in a stunned, almost disbelieving silence, but then men began to cheer and clap, and now they were throwing money onto the stage, vying with one another to see who could throw the most: coins, paper money, even and increasingly, little bags of gold dust.

Lola rewarded them by dancing still faster, with ever greater abandon, until the stage was littered with tributes to her spell and she could hardly step without bringing her slippered foot down on piles of money or bags of gold.

Finally, she leapt into the air, gave a final spin, and sank in a weary heap to the floor of the stage, panting from exertion.

"She's fainted," someone shouted from the audience and there was a shifting of many feet and a scraping of chairs being pushed back.

At once, Terry sat up and scrambled to his feet, knowing that he dared not let them rush to the stage to help him.

He smiled out at the audience and curtseyed, and again there was that roar of approval, and finally, for the first time in his life, Terry knew love, felt it sweep over him in great waves from those cheering, shouting, clapping men—all their loneliness, all the grubbiness of their lives in this dismal place, their affection and desire, their excitement, coalesced into a great bubble of happiness that enveloped Terry and that it almost seemed he could float away in.

There was movement about the room, and no doubt some of them would have charged right up onto the stage, but Willis had the good sense to quickly whisk the curtain closed, and the last glimpse the miners had of Lola Valdez was the kiss she blew to them.

Terry quickly scooped up the money strewn across the stage, making a pouch out of his skirt to hold it, and ran for the dressing room. He had barely gotten there when Willis followed him in. The saloon owner was grinning from ear to ear, showing his blackened teeth, his face flushed with excitement.

"By God, you did it," he cried, dancing a jig. "You did it. I can't believe it. The toughest, orneriest men this side of creation, and you had them eating out of your hand."

"Yes," Terry said, sinking into a chair and looking at himself in the mirror. But it was not himself he saw, not the sissy boy whom others taunted or used for their pleasure, not the unwanted orphan, the butt of a lifetime of jokes. He saw someone beautiful, someone very much wanted, someone who brought happiness and pleasure to all who beheld.

He saw Lola Valdez.

He was still out of breath. *I'll have to get back in practice*, he told himself, and realized in that instant what he had not even contemplated before. He had not thought beyond this single night, beyond the challenge of walking on to that stage and winning over these hardened miners; but now, he realized in a burst of insight that what he had done was not some one-time thing, a mere lark. He had found his role in life. From this night on, he was Lola Valdez. The beautiful Lola Valdez.

"Listen to them," Willis was saying, "they're screaming for you. You've got to go back out there."

"No," Terry said. "We want them screaming for more, eaten alive with wanting to see Lola. You go out there and tell them if they want to see more, they'll have to come back tomorrow night. And they will. I guarantee it. Every man in this camp will be here tomorrow night, Mister Willis, to see Lola dance."

Willis shook his head admiringly. "Jesus, you're right," he said. "They'll be fighting one another to get through the door tomorrow night, to see Lola dance. Christ Almighty! My fortune is made."

"And you'd better put a couple of the boys outside the door to this room. Those men are feeling pretty rambunctious right now. We wouldn't want anybody to get back here. They might get a big surprise."

Willis chortled. "They might at that. I'll see to it." He made to go.

"And, Willis, aren't you forgetting something?" Willis paused, one hand on the door, and gave him a puzzled look. "My pay," Terry said.

"Your pay? Why, there must be five, six hundred dollars there," Willis said, looking at the piles of coins and paper dollars and the bags of gold dust that Terry had dumped on the dressing table, "maybe a thousand. You expect me to pay you in addition to all that?"

"Gifts," Terry said, waving a dismissive hand at the money, "from my enthusiastic admirers. That's got nothing to do with my employment. You paid Lizette, didn't you? And she wasn't anywhere near as good as I was. I want to be fair, though. I'll settle for what you paid her."

"Not a penny."

"Or," Terry said, "you can go out there and announce to all those excited miners that Lola Valdez will not be dancing for them again." He shrugged.

Willis glowered angrily at him for a moment. Terry only smiled back sweetly. Finally, with a snort of anger, Willis took a handful of coins out of his trousers' pocket.

"Gold dust," Terry said.

"Gold dust?" Willis echoed. Terry nodded. "You are crazy."

"Gold dust," Terry said again.

They regarded one another unflinchingly for a moment more, but it was Willis who blinked and looked away. He took a small bag from the jacket of his pocket, and threw it on the dressing table, and stormed out, swearing a string of profanities under his breath.

Terry picked up the bag and weighed it consideringly in his hand. He looked at himself in the mirror, half amused and half astonished. It was the first time in his entire life he had ever really stood up to anybody, ever stood his ground.

Already, he was a different person.

An obviously angry Brian was waiting for him, pacing the floor when Terry rushed in breathlessly a little later.

"Where you been?" Brian demanded. "If you've been up to any of your foolishness…"

"It's not what you think," Terry told him. "I swear it, Brian." Well, then, what?"

"I got a job. I told you I was going to look for one. I'm working now, at The Lucky Dollar saloon. And, look what I've got."

He had not brought all the money home with him, not even the greater portion of it. He'd made up his mind about that, while he had hastily changed himself back into Terry Murphy. Brian couldn't be trusted with the money. That was obvious. And, if Terry were ever going to be free of his brother, he'd need money of his own.

That, too, was an idea that had never before occurred to him: free of his brother. Suddenly, though, from the moment the thought had entered his mind, that was what he wanted, what he knew he was now working toward.

Because, he had a dream, a dream that someday he and Joshua would live together the way he and Brian did now, as man and wife—only, he knew it would be different with

Joshua, that Joshua wouldn't beat him and taunt him the way Brian did. He even, for a fleeting moment, imagined Joshua kissing him, though that, surely, would never happen. Men like Joshua didn't kiss other men, certainly didn't kiss men like Terry Murphy.

That didn't mean the rest of the dream couldn't happen. It wouldn't, though, so long as he remained under Brian's unsparing fist. So, yes, the money had to be kept from Brian. Most of it, he'd hidden in his dressing room, hoping Willis wouldn't think to look for it. He'd have to make arrangements. The Simmons brothers had a bank of sorts. Or, maybe Belle Blessings could help him some way.

He'd brought home some of it, though, enough to assuage the anger that he knew he would face when he got here. Now, he tossed the little bag of gold dust and a handful of coins onto the table, for Brian to see.

"What the hell?" Brian picked them up, opened the bag and poured some of the dust into his hand. "Where'd you get this?"

"I told you, I've got a job now. At The Lucky Dollar."

Brian turned suspicious eyes on him. "Doing what? What would old skinflint Lem Willis pay you this kind of money to do?"

Terry had to steel himself to keep from shouting with glee. If Brian only knew how much more money he'd made tonight. More money than he had ever seen in his life, and for one night's dancing. And all those nights yet to come. He would be rich, he couldn't even imagine how rich, but richer than he would ever have dreamed possible.

But, that dream, he wasn't about to share with Brian.

"It's a secret, what I'm doing. I can't tell you just yet." Terry laughed with his excitement.

"You'll tell me, or so help me, I'll beat it out of you," Brian said. "If you're fooling around with some man, I want to know."

"I told you, it's nothing like that. I just can't tell you right now. It's a surprise. You'll love it, I promise."

"When are you going to tell me, then?"

"Tomorrow," Terry said. "Tomorrow night. You come to the Lucky Dollar tomorrow night, and you'll understand everything."

Brian glowered at him, but Terry refused to say more. "Come to the Lucky Dollar," was all Brian could get out of him. "Tomorrow night."

When they were in bed, though, when Brian slid up behind him for his usual nighttime exercise, Terry rolled over, away from him, onto his back.

"I'm awfully tired tonight, Brian," he said. He surprised even himself. He hadn't any idea that he intended to do this until he had done it, but the gesture brought its own conviction with it. Just like that, he knew that was over. He was done with it.

"What the hell? Since when do I need your permission to fuck you, I want you to tell me? I been doing it all along, haven't I, and I ain't heard any complaints out of you till now."

"No, not till now," Terry agreed, but Brian missed the irony in his voice.

"Well, then, seems to me like you liked it well enough. Seems to me like you couldn't get enough of it, the way you was always after it. So what's so goddamn different about tonight that all of sudden your little pussy is too tired for a good dicking?" He put a hand on Terry's hip and tried to shove him over on his side. To his further astonishment, Terry resisted.

For a moment, Terry thought Brian might get violent, might force his will on him. Terry almost relented, as he had always done in the past.

But, no, he wasn't just Terry now, just a vessel for his brother's sperm. He was Lola Valdez, too, maybe more Lola than Terry. And Lola was nobody's slave. Lola lived her life as she wanted. She was still new to him, but already he knew that much about his other self.

"I need some sleep," Terry said, somehow managing to make his voice firm. "Really. I'll make it up to you, I promise. Tomorrow night. You'll understand everything then. Just let me sleep tonight, please, I'm asking it as a favor."

Terry braced himself for the blows he half expected. After a minute though, Brian said, "I ain't in the habit of begging someone to take my pecker. Especially not someone of your kind. I'm only going to ask this once, plain and simple—do you want to get dicked tonight or not?"

Terry took a deep breath, and said, just as plainly, "No." He held his breath, waiting for what seemed an eternity.

"Well then, fuck it," Brian said finally, loudly. "Fuck you. I don't need that scrawny ass of yours. I don't even like fucking it, you know that, I only do it to make you happy, you ungrateful little pansy."

Shortly, Terry heard his brother's hand slapping against his belly, and after a while, his heightened breathing and a low moan as he reached his climax. Terry waited until Brian had finished, had gone to sleep and was snoring loudly before he let himself drift off to sleep, smiling into the darkness, remembering the roaring approval of the men at The Lucky Dollar.

Surely that—the feeling of mass desire that had swept over him as they cheered and stomped their feet—surely that was the love he'd dreamed of finding, what he had been moving toward all this time. Surely that was the emptiness that had always ached within him.

Chapter Eight

Terry had been entirely right in his prediction. The Lucky Dollar was crammed to the rafters the following night, and when Lola traipsed on stage, her skirts swishing, the previous night's roar of approval faded into insignificance compared to the bedlam that erupted this time.

This night, Lola danced with a new confidence, a new sense of her power over these enraptured men. She flirted and toyed with them, reveling in her beauty, her desirability, soaking up their delight in her and sending it back to them magnified a hundred times.

Once, pirouetting swiftly from one side of the stage to the other, she caught sight of Brian, standing just inside the door. Her heart skipped a beat. Joshua was standing alongside him. When next she looked, though, she couldn't see either of them. The crowd had shifted, men jockeying for better positions.

That glimpse of Joshua electrified her, like a charge of lightning in the blackness of night. From that moment, she was dancing for one man alone, for Joshua Simmons, and she danced as no woman since Salome had ever danced, danced not for a man's head, but for his heart—and if not his heart, then she would settle for that other part of him. Whatever she could have of him. That was all she asked.

Even at a glance, the money was surely double what had been thrown on the stage the first night. This time, Lola was better prepared. She had left a big gunnysack hanging just off stage, and no sooner had Willis whisked the curtain closed, his two goons dashing into position to prevent any of the excited miners from rushing the stage, then Lola snatched the bag from its peg and darted hastily about the stage gathering the coins, the paper bills, the bags of gold dust, and hurried to her dressing room with them.

Willis was already there. She had no more than rushed into the room than he grabbed her in an enormous bear hug and whirled her about the room.

"By God in Heaven, you were magnificent, better than the first time, even," he said. He paused, his eyes flashing with excitement, and looked Lola up and down, grinning his delight. "Damnation, I don't care what you've got hanging down there, I've never laid eyes on anyone I wanted to fuck more than I want to fuck you right now, you little witch. I swear, you plumb got me hexed."

Terry struggled free of his embrace. "That isn't part of our arrangement, I'm afraid," he said, and before Willis, looking angry at the turndown, could argue, Terry said, "My brother will be back here any minute. Tell the men at the door to let him in. Oh, and, Willis, don't forget my pay."

Willis scowled ferociously, but the mention of Brian worked like a charm. He took the bag of gold dust from his pocket and threw it on the dressing table, and made for the door.

"Make no mistake, we ain't finished with that subject, my pretty little fellow," he said with a sullen expression as he let himself out. "If you're making a fortune for me, I'm making one for you, too, and I'm taking as much of a chance as you are, maybe more. I expect to be rewarded for my efforts. You just get that into your head."

When he was gone, Terry let out the breath he had been holding. That was a complication he hadn't foreseen, and one he'd have to take cautions over. It was still too new to him, this effect he had on men—even where, like Willis, they knew the truth about Lola

Valdez. Even knowing, Willis was still as aroused as any of the men out there in the saloon. Maybe more so, Terry thought. Maybe the contradiction only added zest to his appeal. That was something he could never have imagined, but the idea had no sooner popped into his head than he was certain it was true. What funny creatures men were, he thought, smiling at the thought.

For the moment, though, Willis was not the most important thing he had to deal with. There was still Brian to face. How would he feel about what Terry had done? It wasn't easy, predicting what Brian might or might not do about anything. Now, more than ever, he couldn't afford Brian's violence. Lola could hardly dance with a black eye or a split lip.

Terry's eyes fell on the bag with his night's earnings. Surely, the money would make a difference. Terry could think of no more compelling argument than that, not with Brian, at least. Maybe, after all, he would have to buy Brian's tolerance with the lion's share of his earnings.

Even if he gave Brian most of it, though, and kept only a small portion of it for himself, his share of it would multiply quickly enough at this rate. Hastily, he took several bags of gold dust and a couple of handfuls of paper money and put them with his cache at the bottom of Lizette's battered wardrobe trunk and piled dresses and underthings atop them.

He sat down at the dressing table, but he made no effort to remove his makeup or Lola's gown. Better, he thought, to face Brian as Lola than as Terry. Some instinct told him already that Lola had the courage to stand up to men that Terry himself lacked.

It really was as if he had become two people, living in one body, and the two people were quite different from one another. Just how different, he didn't know yet. He'd only made Lola's acquaintance the night before—but he had a notion that there was a lot he would have to learn about her.

It wasn't Brian who came to the dressing room, though. When the knock came at the door, and Terry opened it cautiously, the merest crack, one of the guards posted outside said, "There's a man out here, says his name is Simmons."

Terry's heart skipped a beat. "Let him in," he said, and a minute later, there was Joshua, looking him up and down, neither smiling nor frowning.

"It is you, then," Joshua said finally, shaking his head in disbelief. "I thought it was, but I told myself it couldn't be, that it was too crazy."

Terry glanced in the direction of the door, closed behind him. "Is Brian...I thought I saw him with you."

"He was. He left. You hadn't much more than started dancing, and he swore a blue streak, and barged out the door."

Terry didn't know what to say. He looked hard at Joshua's face, trying to read his mind, what he was feeling, but his face was a mask. A moment before, Terry's thoughts had been filled with Brian, with his approval or disapproval. But the appearance of Joshua here, in his dressing room, had crowded everything else from his head. He'd have to deal with Brian—but later. For now, he was alone with Joshua.

"Was I all right?" Terry asked finally.

"The dancing?" Joshua looked around the dressing room as if the answer might be written on one of the walls. "I guess so. I don't know anything about that stuff. Everybody seemed to like it, that's for sure. I thought some of those men were going to whip their tallywhackers out and beat off right there in the saloon."

He looked, finally, directly at Terry, into his face. "By God, you're beautiful," he said in a hoarse voice. "I never..." Their eyes met, and held.

Terry would never have dared approach Joshua in this moment—but Lola had no such qualms. She took a hesitant step in Joshua direction, and then another, not timidly, but afraid she might spook him like a skittish horse. She was standing only inches in front of Joshua now, so close that, little as she was, she had to tilt her head back to keep their eyes locked. Brazenly, she smiled a challenge up at him.

Suddenly, violently, Joshua took hold of her, hugged her fiercely, and brought his mouth down to Lola's, kissing her, hard, brutally, bruising her lips. Lola surrendered to him utterly, sank into his arms, parted her lips for the tongue that invaded them.

It seemed to last an eternity, that kiss, and they were both of them breathless when it ended, and again, they stared into one another's eyes.

"Josh, I…I love you," Terry whispered hoarsely, and Lola repeated it, less shyly, "I love you."

"Don't say that," Joshua said, cutting the air with a dismissive hand. He looked over Terry's head, as if he could no longer bear to look directly at him. "Men can't…it isn't normal, Terry."

"Then don't love Terry, if you can't," Lola said. "Love Lola."

"What kind of crazy talk is that? Terry, Lola, they're one and the same."

"They're one," Terry agreed. "But they're not the same."

Joshua shook his head, bewildered. This was too foreign to his experience, like nothing he had imagined in his wildest dreams. He couldn't make any sense of it. He was standing in front of a beautiful woman, the most beautiful woman he had ever laid eyes upon—only, he knew she wasn't a woman. She was Terry Murphy. A queer.

Terry said, taking advantage of his confusion, "I've loved you since the first moment I laid eyes on you." Alone with Josh, Terry might have blushed to make such a confession, but Lola was there in the room as well, and Lola was not the blushing sort.

"I went for a walk in the woods one morning, and you were at the pump outside your cabin. You had your shirt off and you were washing up, and you didn't see me, but it was like I'd been struck dumb. And then, you took yourself out of your trousers and peed, and I saw you, well, like that, exposed, and I couldn't get you, I couldn't get that, out of my mind. That's why I was so bold, that night at the rock, I'm usually not, but I couldn't help myself. It was like I was possessed. I haven't thought of anybody but you since that first moment I saw you, not even when I'm in bed with Brian, when he's…" He caught himself, but not quite in time. Joshua narrowed his eyes, frowning, and looked into his face again.

"I didn't hear that," he said, but Terry didn't care now, the cat was out of the bag, wasn't it? And Josh would have to know eventually, wouldn't he, if they were ever to be anything to one another, the way he dreamed?

"I can't help it, Josh, it's not me, it's what happens. He does it. Look at me. How could I stop him? And you know what he's like. Nobody crosses Brian."

"But, I never knew about...the way he talks, and everything, about queers. I never dreamed that he...and you..."

"It doesn't matter, I tell you," Terry insisted. "It isn't me, when he's doing it. It's just..." He shrugged helplessly. How could he explain to Joshua what he couldn't understand himself? "It's something he has to do, is all I can see. Maybe he really does hate queers. Maybe it's himself he hates, for doing it, but something inside him makes him have to, with me, anyway. Maybe it's because we're brothers, makes it different. But whatever it is inside him, whatever he's doing, I'm not doing it with him, is what I'm trying to say. Since that first night, it's you, always you. He's in there, inside me, he's doing it to me, yes, but it isn't him I'm feeling poking at me that way, it's you."

Joshua shook his head. "Jesus, Terry, you shouldn't be telling me...I oughtn't to know about that shit. I don't *want* to know, any of it."

"You have to know, because it isn't just him anymore, and it isn't just me. Everything has changed, since that first moment I laid eyes on you. I meant what I said, Josh, I'll never deny it. I can't help it. I love you."

"And you think I'm going to love you back? Jesus, how could I? I don't. I couldn't, not in a million years."

"I don't care, then," Terry cried. "I don't care if you don't love me. Only, just let me love you. Let me..." He paused, consumed with desire for the handsome man before him, and in agony because he didn't know how to communicate his desire, his love—his need.

And Lola, too, needed him, loved him, desired him. And Lola was not to be denied. Terry had already learned that much.

"Do you want to…" she started to ask, but Joshua let go of Terry as suddenly as he had seized him, so quickly, so unexpectedly, that Terry swayed and had to brace himself against the back of a chair with one hand to keep from falling.

"Christ I don't know what I want," Joshua said. "I do—but I don't. I'm not that kind of man, I tell you, I'm not a sodomite, Terry, I swear to God I'm not, and yet…well, you look like a woman, all right, it's like kissing a woman, that's for sure—but I know you aren't. So, how can I feel this way? Cause you've sure got my dick roused, in case you didn't notice."

Terry hadn't noticed, until now, but once his attention was called to it, he saw it plain enough, and was glad for what he saw.

"Then, let me, please," Lola said, and reached for the erection she could see straining mightily against the front of Joshua's trousers, but it wasn't Lola's hand that Joshua felt take hold of him, it was Terry's, and Josh's prick knew the difference in an instant. No sooner had Terry's fingers touched the buttons there than Joshua jumped back, as if a snake had bitten him.

"I've had too much to drink," he said, stumbling toward the door to the alley. "I've got to go. I've got to get my head straightened out." He threw the door open.

"I'll come to the woods later," Terry said. "To our rock. If you want…"

"I don't know what I want," Joshua said once again, and ran out, leaving the door to swing in the breeze.

Terry went to it and stared at Joshua's back as he ran down the alleyway like something was after him and disappeared around a corner.

He still had to deal with Brian. Brian had not yet come by the time Terry had carefully removed every trace of makeup—no telling who might pass him on the street—and let his hair down again, and changed back into his shirt and trousers. He was Terry Murphy once more, and for the moment, Lola Valdez was nothing more than a beautiful ghost.

Victor J. Banis

But, there was one thing he had to do, had to know, before he faced Brian. He left the bag of money in the trunk with his stash, took the back door key down from the nail where it hung by the door, and slipped from the saloon. Out front the bar was still noisy, but that was only a distant and discordant murmur back here.

He hurried through the town, avoiding the main street, following instead the alley that paralleled it. Outside of town, he skirted the cabin he shared with his brother, where he could see light in the window, and went directly to the rock—their rock as he thought of it now, his and Joshua's.

There was no one there. Terry wanted to cry, he was so disappointed. He had been so sure Joshua would meet him here. He went to the rock and sat down upon it, gazing morosely into the distance. He had failed, then, he hadn't convinced Joshua even to consider a future for them.

He was so absorbed in his unhappiness that he didn't hear Joshua approach until Joshua was practically standing before him.

Joshua said nothing, he just walked up before Terry where he sat on the rock, tugged his fly open, and pulled out his dick—already fully hard. He stepped close for Terry to take it.

Terry did, taking hold of it and stroking it lovingly, breathing in the smell of it, feeling that silken bush with the tips of his fingers. Yes, it was even more beautiful than he had remembered, more magical. He gazed at it lovingly.

That wasn't what Joshua had come for, though, to be admired, however lovingly. He put an impatient hand on Terry's head and drew Terry toward him. Terry opened his mouth, and the thick, purple head slid between his lips, over his tongue, was shoved brutally against the back of his mouth, down his throat.

As violent as the entry was, Terry welcomed it, put his hands on Joshua's hard butt and pulled him in even tighter, deeper. What did he care if it choked him, if it hurt? It was what he wanted. All he desired, all he could think of: to have Josh in his mouth.

There was nothing tender or romantic about it, the way he had imagined since their first time. Joshua fucked his mouth roughly, angrily, holding Terry's head tightly in both his hands, so that Terry could not even pull back long enough to catch his breath or swallow the spit collecting in his mouth, until he thought he would surely be choked to death by it, and he almost retched on the come when Joshua finally let fly.

Terry didn't care about the discomfort. He was happy just to be the vessel for Joshua's outpouring. Nothing else mattered but that sublime moment when Josh surrendered the gift of his manly fluids to him.

Joshua's mysterious fury seemed to have rushed out of him with his semen. He left his cock in Terry's mouth for a long moment after he had finished shooting, letting Terry suckle on it gently, lovingly, kissing it and laving it with his tongue, which was how Terry had really wanted to have it. Like he was nursing at it—and it was like that, for him. He felt as if he had been fed by the offering that Joshua had poured into him, as if those spurting fluids were his sustenance.

Finally, Joshua tousled Terry's dark curls in a tender gesture that might have been meant for affection. He pulled out, stepped back, put his dick quickly back into his trousers and turned away.

He disappeared into the night, the darkness swallowing him up, without having spoken a single word.

It was enough for Terry, though. Joshua's actions had said everything that he needed to know. Joshua wanted him too. Maybe he didn't love him, yet, but wanting him was enough for a start. Maybe that was a kind of love, the best kind of love he could hope for, at least at the beginning: being wanted, giving a man pleasure, serving as the vessel for his relief. He would make Joshua happy that way, keep him sated, contented. The rest of it, the real love, would come in time, he was sure of it.

Happier than he could remember ever being, Terry went back to the Lucky Dollar for the money, and trudged home with it, weary now and, as he got closer to the cabin, increasingly apprehensive about the welcome that awaited him.

When he got there, he found Brian shoving things into his saddlebags.

"What are you doing?" Terry asked from the doorway, staring.

"Doing? What the fuck do you think I'm doing, I'm fixing to leave. We're headed for Butte, tonight. Get your things together. We'll take turns riding and walking. Though I ought to make you walk the whole damn way. It'd serve you right, after that shit you pulled."

"Butte? I'm not going to Butte. And why on earth should you? We've just made our fortune, Brian. I've made it for us. Look, here." He threw the bag at Brian's feet. "Count it. It's all yours. More money than you could make in a year working the Simmons' claim—or in Butte either, I'll wager. You don't have to work ever again if you don't want to."

"A fat lot of good that money'll do either of us, won't it, if we get strung up by our balls, when those men at The Lucky Dollar realize how you've been making fools of them. What in the name of hell were you thinking of, making a spectacle of yourself that way? Not to mention, making a fool out of me. I ought to wring your neck and instead, here I am trying to save your little pansy ass again. Now, do as I say, and start getting yourself ready. I aim for us to be out of here before dawn, just in case any lynch parties come looking for us."

"No one's going to come looking for us, Brian. Why should they? No one in that saloon has the slightest idea who I really am, and they're never going to find out."

"I knew. I recognized you in a heartbeat, the minute you stepped onto that stage."

"You, yes, but who else would? Nobody, I tell you. I've hardly been seen in town up till now, not for weeks, anyway, and I'm going to be seen even less in the future. And they're only going to see Lola Valdez up there on that stage. There's no reason for anybody ever to suspect Lola is Terry Murphy."

"If that ain't rich. Lola fucking Valdez." Brian snorted his derision. "Simmons did. He was standing next to me tonight, and I saw him look at you funny-like when you started twirling about."

Terry started to say something, started to say that Joshua Simmons wasn't going to tell anyone, for reasons of his own, because he wouldn't want anyone to know Lola Valdez—or Terry Murphy, depending on how you looked at it—was servicing him out in the woods.

But that would take some explaining that he didn't want to do. So far as Brian was aware, Terry Murphy and Joshua Simmons barely knew one another, and Terry meant for it to stay that way, for the time being anyway. Brian was too volatile. There was no guessing how he would react to that news.

"You're imagining things," he said instead.

"Well, I'm not imagining this. I'm telling you, we leave for Butte tonight. And I'm telling you for the last time, start getting your little ass ready."

Terry took a deep breath. "I'm not going," he said.

Brian straightened from his hasty packing and shot him an angry look. "Who the hell do you think you are, defying me when I give you an order? How'd you like me to remind you who's boss around here?" He balled up his fists.

Terry steeled himself. "Not any more, Brian. I'm done taking orders. From anyone."

"Goddamn you," Brian said, and came toward him, raising his hand to strike him, but to his amazement, Terry didn't cringe from him the way he expected him to. Brian stopped, his hand back to swing, and stared at this stranger before him.

"Who are you? I don't even know you," Brian said, looking altogether confused. "You're not yourself at all anymore. Is that what putting on a dress did to you?"

Yes, Terry wanted to say, but instead, he said, "Count the money, Brian, why don't you, before you do anything. It's a small fortune. And it's just the beginning. I can make that much every night, maybe more."

Brian glanced over his shoulder at the bag lying on the floor, He went to it and picked it up, and dumped the contents on the floor.

"And what am I supposed to do, while you're making us rich?

Maybe you think I should take over the cooking and the cleaning, like I was your woman? Am I supposed to let you fuck me now?"

Lola almost said, *maybe you should, Brian. Maybe that would make you happy, because the other way surely isn't doing it.* But Terry bit his tongue. At least for the moment Brian seemed more interested in the money than in Terry's little rebellion. Better to keep it that way.

"No," he said instead, "we'll go on just the way everything was, or mostly. I'll still do the cooking and the cleaning, all that stuff. I'll take care of everything. Only..." here he hesitated, but it had to be said, while he still had the nerve. "Only, I don't want to be fucked anymore. That part of it's over."

Brian stared at him as if he were unable to understand the words Terry had spoken. When he responded, it was to ask, instead, "Where's the rest of it?"

"The rest of it?"

"The money. There's more than this. Those peckerheads were throwing money at you like it was water. Where's the rest?'

Terry gave a sigh. "In my dressing room," he said.

"Let's us go get it, then," Brian said.

The saloon was still booming, despite the late hour. Terry let them in through the dressing room door, lit a lamp, and went to the wardrobe trunk where he had stashed his share of the money.

Brian snatched it from him, bent down and emptied the trunk, flinging dresses and petticoats and scarves about the room, until he was satisfied there was nothing more in it.

"This all of it?" he asked.

"Everything," Terry said. "I swear, I'll bring it all to you every night, every penny of it."

"Not to me you won't," Brian said. "I've already told you, I'm leaving, for Butte. You can stay here and get yourself killed, or fucked to death, if that suits you better. It's got nothing to do with me anymore. I wash my hands of the whole frigging business."

"You're going to leave me here, on my own?" Terry asked, astonished. He had thought surely the money would buy Brian's acquiescence. He had thought too of being on his own sometime in the future, but not like this, not here in Alder Gulch, with no one to protect him. "You brought me to this God forsaken place, Brian. How am I supposed to survive here, in this hell hole? I'm your brother, for God's sake."

"From now on, I ain't got no brother," Brian said. "And you'd better forget you ever had one, too."

With that, he was gone, taking the money with him.

Terry sank down upon the chaise lounge in one corner. He felt drained, spent. He thought about going after Brian, trying to dissuade him, but he didn't feel like he could face him again.

Maybe it was best this way, though, when he thought about it. Brian leaving. Still, the prospect of living alone and vulnerable worried at him. Brian was right about one thing, at least—men did sometimes look at him funny, Terry could see that, too, and now that he'd had some experience of it, he had a pretty good notion what it was that he saw in their eyes.

Sharing the cabin with Brian, he'd had no fears on that score. Even the toughest men in The Gulch would think twice before crossing Brian. But, alone...and the cabin, too, was vulnerable, new men arrived every day, and who was to say if one or more of them might decide to usurp it for their own quarters? There wasn't much he could do to stop them if someone got the idea.

Of course, he could move into one of the rooms here, over The Lucky Dollar. The one, say, that Lizette had occupied before she left, and that was still empty.

But that would attract too much attention, and practically advertise his connection with the saloon. It wouldn't take much imagination for one of the miners to put two and two together.

A thought entered his mind all of a sudden. Maybe, just maybe, he needn't be alone in the cabin. Maybe Joshua could be persuaded to share the cabin with him, now that Brian was gone. Of course, he'd had that in mind all along, eventually establishing himself as Joshua's woman, the way he'd been Brian's—but, he'd assumed he'd have plenty of time to get Joshua used to the idea—used to the sexual convenience, at the least, and he felt sure that was far from accomplished at this point in time.

Well, his hand had been forced, hadn't it? It needn't make anybody wonder, either, Joshua's moving in with him, now that he thought about it. The Simmons cabin must already be crowded, and it was slated to be more crowded before long. Brian had told him just a few days ago that Pete Simmons, the younger of the two brothers, had sent for his family back in Philadelphia. His wife, a son and a daughter were already on their way west. In no time at all, they would be there in the cabin as well, and Joshua would almost certainly have had to make some other arrangements for himself.

What could be more obvious, than for him to move into Brian's cabin, now that Brian had left town?

Thinking about the possibility, Terry stretched out on the chaise. He closed his eyes, remembering how it had been earlier with Joshua, those exciting memories crowding everything else from his mind.

He found himself imagining what it would be like it they shared a cabin together, he and Joshua. It could be every night, the way it had been with Brian—only it would not be like that, either, not at all. It would be like a dream come true.

With a smile on his face, with that thought drifting happily through his mind, Terry fell asleep.

Chapter Nine

He woke stiff from the unusual sleeping accommodation, the first light of dawn stealing timidly through the murky little window high up in the dressing room wall. For a moment, he wondered where he was—then he remembered everything: last night, the quarrel with Brian, Brian's leaving. And Joshua…

He jumped up, remembering the rest of it, his decision to approach Joshua about moving into the cabin. That was, if Brian had actually gone, and that hadn't been a lot of angry hot air. Impatient to know, Terry pulled himself together and hurried through the still sleeping camp.

It was no longer night but not yet day and as he went he saw the town through new eyes. The pale light cloaked its scars and gave the dirty street and the slapdash houses a patina that would fade when the sun rose. In the silence, he could hear the rush of the creek, not far off, and above him, just visible against the rosy sky, the mountains hinted at something eternal and mysterious. Terry's spirits lifted with the mists that wafted upward from the damp ground.

Yes, Brian was gone. He had taken everything of value, too. The stove was still there, with the barrel for a chimney. He couldn't very well have loaded them on his horse. The flour sacks still hung at the windows and Brian had left Terry's crucifix hanging over the door, but there wasn't much else left.

What did that matter? A day, two days of dancing at The Dollar, and Terry would have plenty of money to buy everything he needed—except what he needed and wanted, most, the man to share the space with him.

He'd buy Joshua, too, if that was the only way he could have him—not with money, he felt sure Joshua was too high-bred and too proud for that, but he could buy him with a place to live, and someone to take care of it for him. A wife, if only in the most menial sense; but, maybe, in time, in every other way as well.

He couldn't wait to broach Joshua with the idea of moving in. He'd have to convince him, of course, assure him that this was strictly a business arrangement, something practical for both of them.

As for the rest of it, well, there was certainly no secret now about how he felt, but there wasn't much danger of him forcing himself on the bigger man, was there? That would have to be strictly up to Joshua. He could have whatever he wanted, however and whenever he wanted it. And if he didn't...but, Terry knew beyond a doubt that he did, even if Joshua himself didn't yet know it. He enjoyed it too much to deny himself what was there and obviously available to him. That rest would come too, in time. Terry was convinced of it.

So sure was he, that his fantasy had become their reality, he halfway expected to see Joshua waiting for him at their rock, already primed to make the proposed move. He wasn't there, of course. How could he be? It wasn't until after they had been together the following night that Terry had even conceived of his plan.

He had never actually approached him at the Simmons' cabin, though, and as he came near to that, he slowed his pace. It was still early morning, barely after dawn, and he wasn't at all sure what he should do next. Would Joshua be angry at him for coming here to look for him? He certainly wouldn't want Joshua's uncles to get any ideas—and if Brian's endless badgering of him had left any lasting effect on Terry, it was his awareness now that men did look at him suspiciously, maybe not knowing, but instinctively sensing something about his nature.

Brian had known, hadn't he, and Martin Van Arndst? And, Joshua must have known, too, on some level of awareness, or why hadn't he stopped Terry at the beginning that first night, why had he left himself so blatantly on display, if not as an invitation to what he perhaps unknowingly wanted?

So, yes, men knew, some men, anyway, if not all and if only half consciously. But it wouldn't do for Joshua's uncles to know, to put things together, because then Joshua would most assuredly never move into the cabin.

He paused, debating whether to continue or to go home and wait until he saw Joshua under some other circumstances, when Walt Simmons solved the problem for him by coming out the cabin's door, and saw him standing twenty feet away, looking indecisive.

"Something I can do for you?" Walt asked, heading straight to the pump, but pausing there.

"I...I wanted to see Joshua," Terry said, making an effort to lower his voice from its usual near-soprano. Unconsciously, he spread his feet wide, pretending the kind of macho stance common to the men in the camp. "I wanted to ask his advice about something."

"You're Brian Murphy's little brother, aren't you?" Walt asked, looking him up and down in a way that made Terry think his lower voice and affected posture had made no impression on him at all.

"Yes," Terry said, forgetting and letting his voice go up again. "Is he here? Joshua, I mean."

Walt began to work the pump handle. "To tell you the truth, I'm surprised you're here," he said. Water gushed out the faucet and Walt bent down, splashing it on his face and his chest and, filling his hands, took a drink of it. "In the Gulch, I mean."

"Where else would I be?" Terry asked, puzzled.

Walt finished his bathing and used his shirt to dry himself off. "On your way to Butte. I just figured you'd gone with your brother," he said. "Same as Joshua."

"Joshua?" Terry stared at him stupidly. "He's not here?"

"He left with your brother. Brian came by, nearly the middle of the night, woke everybody up. Said he was getting ready to head out, to go to Butte. He'd heard there were better diggings there. And, did Joshua want to come with him? And just like that, Joshua threw his things into his saddlebags and the two of them lit out of here, not more than an hour or two ago, I reckon. Surprised me, actually. I didn't know the two of them were on such friendly terms. Brian's kind of a…" He caught himself and left the sentence unfinished. "Anyway, they went. I guess Joshua was looking for greener pastures same as your brother."

He paused to put on his shirt and run damp fingers through his hair. When Terry only continued to stare at him, saying nothing, Walt added, "I just figured you'd be going with them."

"No," Terry managed to stammer finally. "No, I…I decided to stay behind."

Walt looked at him curiously, as if he couldn't imagine any good explanation for that odd piece of information, but was too polite to ask.

Terry had none to give him, either. "Well, I wasn't really sure about that, about Brian's telling me Josh was going, too. I was half asleep when we talked about it last night. When I woke up just now, I couldn't remember for certain if that was what he'd told me or I had just dreamed that part of it. I thought I'd better check." He turned to go. "Thank you kindly. I'm sorry to intrude."

"Always welcome," Matt said, but he was already on his way back into the cabin.

Terry hurried away, but, out of sight of the Simmons' cabin, he slowed his steps and, when he got to the rock, their rock, he sank down on it, and dropped his head into his hands. His eyes brimmed with tears. The hot sun, risen now to a harsh glare, mocked his earlier optimism.

Josh had run away from him. That was what it came down to. He hadn't been able to deal with what had happened. Had been too afraid, maybe, of wanting it to happen again. Maybe he'd wanted it too much. And Brian, by some instinct, had stolen his rival from under Terry's nose, without even actually knowing he had a rival.

Terry fought back his tears. It was no good sitting here crying over it, he told himself after a bit. He got up, wiping his eyes with a sleeve, and made his way back to his cabin. *His* cabin now, not theirs. It had always looked so tiny before, but now it looked enormous. The man he had counted on to fill it for him wasn't here, wouldn't be coming here.

He was on his own, in a way he had never been before. In a place he hadn't wanted to come and where he knew he stuck out like a sore thumb. Where, there was no use pretending, he was in near constant peril.

Well, somehow, he'd just have to cope, wouldn't he? He didn't know what he was going to do next, but wringing his hands and weeping wasn't going to accomplish anything, that was for certain.

Lola would know what to do. He'd leave everything up to Lola.

It was less than a week later that Terry came home from The Dollar and, still some distance from the cabin, he saw a shadowy figure slip out the door and hurry off into the trees. It was too dark and the distance too great for him to identify who the visitor had been.

Terry stood for several long minutes, worried, waiting to see if anyone else came out, or that one came back. Finally, when nothing happened, he went on in.

There was no sign of anything disturbed. There wasn't much, really, to disturb. Since Brian had left, Terry had bought himself a new pallet for sleeping, and some essentials: and a big pot for cooking, a bucket for water. He couldn't buy too much at any one time without making someone suspicious as to where he was getting the money.

He was still keeping Lola's earnings in the wardrobe trunk in her dressing room. Not the safest of places but, all in all, probably safer than here, as long as it didn't occur to Willis to go looking for it, and so far it hadn't.

So there was really nothing of value here to interest anybody. Nothing except the cabin itself. Or him, if someone had that on his mind. But in that case, surely whoever had been here would have hung around and waited for Terry to come home.

Of course, it might have been someone just checking the lay of the land, snooping around to see what was here. Or, was it another man, like Brian or Joshua, who needed time to work up his courage to do what he wanted to do all along?

The problem nagged at him. There wasn't much law here, except the law of the strongest. If someone decided they wanted the cabin, they could put him out without much trouble. What could he do about it? But, if someone did, where would he go?

There was even less hope for him if one of the miners decided he wanted Terry's body. It would be like Brian, only worse. At least Brian was his brother. If he hadn't wanted Brian's sex, he had certainly wanted Brian's approval. But the thought of being at the mercy of anyone who wanted him, of any of the unsavory denizens of this wild place…

He tried to think, while he prepared for bed, of who he could go to for help, if only for advice. He took the big cast iron skillet and put in on the floor by his pallet, but probably that wouldn't be much use against a strong man armed with a gun. It occurred to him belatedly that he didn't even own a gun. Probably, he was the only person in Alder Gulch who didn't. Even the few women had guns, he imagined.

He was almost asleep when the answer came to him. He was vulnerable. He knew that. This was a man's world, and he knew very well that he wasn't man enough to hold his own in it.

But, women did. Women had their own strengths. Some women. One woman in particular did very well for herself here in The Gulch.

Tomorrow, he'd go to see Belle Blessings.

The black woman who answered the door when he rang the bell opened it only a crack. "We're not open yet, sir," she said. "Till after noon. You come back then," and would have closed the door, but Terry put a foot inside to prevent it.

"I didn't come for that," he said. "I want to see Miss Blessings. Please. It will take only a minute. I want to talk some business to her."

The woman looked undecided, but she could do nothing about the foot in the doorway. She swung the door open with evident reluctance. "I'll see," she said. "You wait in there," and motioned him into the parlor.

He hadn't long to wait. Belle Blessings appeared only a few minutes later, pausing just inside the room's door. She looked as if she had just been roused from bed, though it was already midmorning.

"Lydia said you were asking especially for me," Belle said. She was taller than he was, and well-upholstered, as Terry had heard her described. "If you were looking for a girl...well I don't as a rule entertain the gentlemen any more personally, except in special circumstances." She raised an eyebrow.

Terry blushed, but he met her gaze evenly. "No, that wasn't why I came. I wanted to talk to you, is all."

She regarded him a moment longer. "Very well," she said, smiling faintly. "I've a little time. Sit, why don't you?" She gestured toward one of the horsehair sofas. "Would you like a sherry?"

"No, nothing, thank you," Terry said. Since she remained standing, so did he. She waited for him to explain, but now that he was here, Terry found it difficult to talk.

"Business, I believe you said," Belle prompted him, with a meaningful glance at the big clock on the mantle.

"I have some money," Terry blurted out. "Quite a bit of it. I wanted to put it someplace safe."

"You'll want to talk to the Simmons brothers, then," she said with a smile, but in a business like voice. "They are the closest thing we have to a bank, but they're quite trustworthy."

"I can't...well, they'd want to know where I got the money," he said. "They'd wonder and..." She looked so suspicious that he added, hastily, "Oh, it's not illegal, or anything but—well, it's hard to explain, actually."

She gave him a shrewd look. "Do I know you?" she asked. "You look familiar."

"I'm Terry Murphy. Brian Murphy's brother."

Victor J. Banis

"I know your brother. Not terribly well, let me quickly add, but he did come by now and again. I suppose I must have seen you around town a time or two as well, though to be honest, I can't exactly recall where or when."

Terry had been looking down at his feet. His raised his eyes now and met hers frankly. "Maybe at The Lucky Dollar," he said.

"The Lucky Dollar? Why, I hardly ever go in the place."

"You were there two nights ago," Terry said.

She seemed surprised that he knew that. "Why, yes, I was," she said. "I went to see that new entertainer everybody is talking about, that Lola Valdez. My business has been dead while she's on stage, though I must say it picks up nicely after she's done. Were you there as well?"

"You might say that." He paused and took a deep breath. "I'm Lola Valdez," he informed her.

She stared at him wide-eyed, as if she thought he had taken leave of his senses. Terry slipped his glasses off and lifted his hair, so that the curls fell about his face as they did when Lola's hair was pinned up.

"Why, you are," she said, and then burst into a little tinkle of a laugh. "Sweet Jesus, you fooled me, all right." But she quickly grew sober. "Same as you fooled all those men. Let us hope, certainly. You know, every man in this town is head over heels in love with Lola Valdez. Not just in Alder Gulch, either. There's men have come from twenty, thirty miles away to see her perform. If word was ever to get out…" She narrowed her eyes. "Who else knows of this besides the two of us?"

"Willis, of course, but he has good reason to keep his mouth shut."

"I should say. He's making a fortune. No one else?"

"My brother," Terry said, an unmistakable note of bitterness creeping into his voice.

"And that's how's come he lit out of here all of a sudden, the way he did?" she said, nodding her head shrewdly. "And left you behind. I wondered about that, you looking, well, not exactly like someone could take care of himself in a place like this. He didn't approve, I take it."

Terry gave her a rueful smile. "That's putting it mildly. And Joshua Simmons knows, but he went with my brother. Neither of them is going to tell anybody. Even if they were still here, they wouldn't want anybody to know."

"There's nobody else? Men, maybe, that you've been, well, let's say, friendly with?"

"No, I've hardly even spoken to anyone else here in town. Oh, Reverend Davidson. But he isn't like to go to the Dollar, is he, to see Lola dance? Anyway, I don't think he's, well, he isn't exactly bright, is he?"

"Someone said once, I don't remember who," Belle said, "that very tall men are like very tall houses, the top story is likely to be the poorest furnished." She sat down heavily in a big stuffed chair, folded her hands in her lap, and looked him over with new interest. "Yes. I can see it, knowing. But I would never have suspected. And I doubt any of those miners will."

"I keep them at a distance, to be safe," he said.

"And the money…yes, that would be a problem wouldn't it? I see what you mean. The Simmonses are generally discreet, but still, they'd have to wonder. And then, wondering, they might put two and two together."

"Exactly," he said. "But, I live alone, now that Brian is gone. My money isn't exactly safe there. I've been keeping it at the saloon, but I don't trust Willis either."

"Wise of you," she said dryly. "That skunk, he'd steal the gold out of his mother's teeth if he caught her smiling." She sat for a moment, contemplating her lavishly ringed fingers. She seemed to hear something in the hallway outside the room, although Terry had heard nothing.

"It's all right, Wonkle," she said past Terry, "The gentleman is only here to discuss some business with me."

Terry looked to see whom she had addressed. An Indian man appeared in the doorway, looking not at all chagrined at having been discovered lurking close by.

"Wonkle keeps an eye out for my safety," Belle informed Terry. Terry must have looked disbelieving. Wonkle was small, hardly any taller than he was, and as lean as an alder sprig.

As if reading his thoughts, Belle smiled and said, "He doesn't look like much of a bodyguard, does he?"

"It's none of my affair what," Terry said, but she interrupted him.

"But it might well be, and it's best if you know what to expect. That shawl there, on the mantle, toss it into the air, why don't you?"

Terry thought it an odd bit of advice, but he did as she said, balling up the lacy shawl and giving it a toss.

Just like that, it was pinned to the wood of the mantle right in front of him by a bowie knife. Terry blinked and looked from the knife, still vibrating, to the Indian standing just inside the door. He hadn't even seen him pull a knife, let alone throw it.

"He's just about as quick with a gun, too," Belle said. She gave Wonkle a nod and he crossed the room so lightly that you could hardly have heard his footsteps, tugged the knife from the mantle and handed Belle the shawl, and left as quickly and as soundlessly as he had come.

Terry looked after him with a worried expression. "But, now he knows, too," he said. "All of it, maybe, if he was listening the whole time."

"You needn't trouble yourself over Wonkle," Belle said, "I'd trust him with my life. Have done, many times. He is entirely devoted to me." She looked after the vanished Indian, and then back to Terry. "Well, it's a very singular situation, isn't it? I've never considered playing banker for anyone else…but, yes, I expect your money would be as safe here as anywhere. Safer, really. I keep most of my own here, in cash. I suppose…I'll have to charge you something, for taking care of it for you."

"I'd be very grateful," Terry said. "And it wouldn't have to be forever. I thought, if I could find some way to get it transported to San Francisco in due time. They have real banks there, don't they?"

"I do that periodically with mine, if you want to know. Best that we keep that to ourselves, though. My arrangements are pretty quiet, and I've got people I can trust. And there is Wonkle. Those who do business with me are well aware of his loyalty. Yes. I think that will be the best thing. You bring your money by and…"

"I have it here," he said, and indicated the valise at his feet.

She smiled. "I see you are a young man who likes to be prepared. You must have been very confident that I'd agree."

"I was hoping, was all," he said. "And, as long as I'm here, I was hoping for another favor, too, if you could help me."

"I'll try." She could not help a smile. He was an engaging young man, for all that he looked so little and helpless.

"I need a gun."

She nodded, her expression quickly grown serious. "Yes. I can see why you might. But why come to me for that? There's plenty of men in this camp who could sell you one. Willis probably could, as far as that goes."

"No doubt. But I need, well, something special. Lola Valdez can't exactly strap a Colt on her hip, can she? I've heard there are guns better suited to a woman, though, something small. I thought you might know more about that."

She smiled. "Wait here for a minute," she said and went out of the room. She was back shortly, and handed Terry the smallest gun he'd ever seen.

"It's a two shot," she said. "They call it a Derringer."

"It looks like a toy."

"It wouldn't do much harm at any kind of distance, but up close, it'll kill them just as dead as a Winchester," she said.

"If I've got to shoot anyone," he said, "I expect he'll be plenty close enough by the time I do it."

"I figured," she said. "Just remember, even here, they string people up for murder. I imagine the Vigilance Committee would string you up quicker than others. Most of these men would probably think if a man wanted to have his way with someone like you that you'd have no business objecting."

"I think that's probably true."

Belle sighed. "Well, if it ever comes to that, you come here to me first thing, all right? I've got plenty of friends, and not just here in Alder Gulch, either. You promise?"

"I promise," Terry said. "How much do I owe you for the gun?"

"How about if you have a drink with me, and we'll call it even. I think after the surprise you've given me, I could use a shot of whisky, and I hate to drink alone."

"You've talked me into it," he said.

She went to the table by the window and poured whisky from a cut-glass decanter into a pair of glasses. Terry stood up to take his from her.

"Now, do me one favor," she said, "Turn around, slow, and let me have a good look at you." She eyed him critically as he did so. "It's your bottom," she said. "Most men have really little ones. Yours is more filled out. Not big and flabby, but well-formed. You already were a dancer before you came here, weren't you?"

He nodded. "I wanted to be, anyway. I studied a lot of ballet."

"It shows. It builds up those muscles in the backside. That's a big part of how you can fool everybody the way you do. In a dress, it looks like a woman's bottom. Your legs, too. What do you do about bosoms?"

Terry blushed, but he answered her frankly. "I tuck a couple of handkerchief down in my bodice."

She smiled and patted her own ample chest. "A woman's bosoms are her glory, in my opinion," she said. "Tell you what, why don't I come over this evening while you're getting dressed. I think we can give you a little more glory than that, if you don't mind my advice."

He smiled back, genuinely glad now that he had come here. He felt as if Belle Blessings was the first friend he had made here in Alder Gulch. The first real friend he'd ever had anywhere, when he thought about it.

"I'd be grateful for your help," he said.

She looked him over again. "You know, even without the Lola Valdez rigmarole, you're not a bad looking boy, especially without the glasses. And so young and all."

"I'm eighteen," Terry said. "Almost nineteen."

"You don't look more than fourteen, fifteen years old, to tell you the truth. And you've got a vulnerable air about you, some find that mighty appealing. There's women would kill for those eyelashes of yours. It might surprise you to know, there's more men than you'd suspect who like a little variety on their plate. There's places in 'Frisco, they call them peg houses. You could do very well for yourself in one of them. Or here, for that matter, if you'd want to move in with the girls and me. And nobody would bother you. There's only a select few customers who'd ever know, and I could see they kept their mouths shut. They wouldn't want to be strung up either."

"Thanks, but no thanks. Don't get me wrong," he added quickly, "I've got no quarrel with what you do. The way I see it, you are providing a civic service. But mostly up to this point, other people did with me what they wanted and I didn't have any voice in it. Only, well, lately, I've had this funny feeling, like someone was stalking me."

"Wouldn't surprise me," Belle said. "But you've seen nothing?"

"No, it's just, I don't know, maybe I'm imagining it, but I can't help being uneasy."

"And that's why you want the gun?"

"Yes," Terry smiled and nodded. "I've made up my mind that from now on, if anything like that happens, money or muscle won't have anything to do with it. It'll be strictly because I want it. And, to be honest," he added, "there is someone I want...well. I sort of got an affection for this particular individual, only..." he hesitated.

"Only, he didn't feel the same? About doing it with a fellow? Even a fellow in a dress?" Terry nodded with a wistful expression. "It wouldn't be that Joshua Simmons, would it?" she asked, lifting an eyebrow.

He laughed. "I've heard you can read men's minds," he said. "I never believed it before now."

"If a woman expects to survive in a place like this, she's pretty well got to know what a man's thinking." She clucked her tongue and gave him a shrewd look. "Well, you picked yourself a handsome devil, I'll say that. I'd have liked a crack at that young man myself, but he never came to see me. Sort of made me wonder. You have any better luck?"

Terry blushed but he laughed, too. "Just once," he said. "Well, twice, but the second time, he was awfully drunk."

"They like to say that. I suppose that's what scared him into skipping town with your brother?"

"I'm afraid so," Terry said with a sigh.

"Well, you want my best guess, he'll be back. Sometimes men have to wrestle with things a bit before they get them sorted out. Wrestle with themselves, really. If he'd only done it once, that might have been the end of it. Sometimes they try on a shirt and decide it's not for them. But once is an experiment, twice is a bugger. He'll do it again. Mark my words."

True to her word, Belle was there in Terry's dressing room that evening to help him transform himself into Lola. She made a better job of Lola's bosoms than he had done, and made some changes in her makeup. When she was done, they both surveyed Lola's image in the mirror.

The makeup was a bit more tart-like, without being too garish. "They're seeing you at a distance," Belle explained as she worked on the lips and the rouged cheeks. "What looks over done up close like this is just right from across a smoky room. I can tell, you've hardly got any beard at all, but even so, you want to keep that close shaved, there's nothing will give you away so quick as that showing through the makeup."

She added some big golden earrings she'd brought, great hoops that hung almost to Lola's shoulders and swung widely whenever she tossed her head. She rearranged the hair a bit, too, so that it better framed the perfect oval of Lola's face, and tugged one curl loose from the combs, so that it fell across Lola's forehead.

"Like a man had disarranged it, running his fingers through it," Belle said. "They won't think that out loud, but it will cross the mind of every man looking at you. Everyone of them will wish it was him had set it loose. You'll have to learn to dance in high heels, though," indicating Lola's dance slippers.

"I'm not sure…"

"It just takes practice," Belle said. "You've got strong legs and feet. It won't take you long to get used to them. They make your legs look shapelier than ever and there's something about a woman in heels that gets a man right worked up." She looked Lola's reflection over critically. "Well, there," she said, "I think that's about as much as I can do."

Lola smiled at her in the mirror. "It's perfect," she said. "I don't know how to repay you."

"Hmm. We haven't discussed my fee for handling your money," Belle said.

"Anything you like. I don't mind," Lola said. "You may be saving my life, you know."

"Saving it, maybe, for that Joshua Simmons?"

"Do you really think he'll come back?"

"He'll come back," Belle said. "If he saw you tonight, looking like this, he'd never have left in the first place. A man would have to be plumb loco."

Her eyes met Lola's in the mirror, and Belle grinned naughtily. "Well, are you going to tell?" she asked. Lola cocked a puzzled eyebrow. "I'm an inquisitive woman," Belle said, "least where men are concerned. When it happened with him. Was it a wasted claim or a lucky strike?"

Terry might have been too embarrassed to answer, but Lola's grin was as naughty as Belle's. "A bonanza, definitely," she said.

"A real mother lode."

Belle gave a happy whoop of laughter, and Lola quickly joined in.

Chapter Ten

Terry's success only continued to grow. Each night, after Lola's performance, Terry took the money he'd garnered and carried it to Belle's, knocking at the back door as arranged and, when Wonkle opened it, handing across the bag and quickly leaving before anyone saw him or what he was up to.

The money was accumulating rapidly. Even Belle was impressed. "You've got more of their money by now than most of these miners have themselves," she said. "What are you planning on doing with it, by the way?"

Terry really had as yet no clear-cut answer to that question. He knew that the money meant independence for himself, but how exactly he meant to spend that independence he hadn't yet decided, except that it would not be in Alder Gulch forever.

At first, he'd had a vague idea of returning to the States, but now he wasn't sure. What would he be returning to? His life there hadn't been so wonderful, had it? He thought of young Tom Finnegan, but things changed quickly in the Bowery, and there was little guarantee that Tom would still be there. It was nearly two years now since they'd stood together in Tom's little basement quarters, and Tom had had ambitions—which meant, by now, he was probably somewhere else, maybe plying his trade as a card sharp.

Anyway, there were other people there too. By now, Martin Van Arndst might well be returned from Europe, and Alicia

Langley was almost certainly there, which meant the threat of prison still hung over Terry's head. There was Harry Green, too, whose safe Brian had plundered, and there was no telling if Harry would hold him responsible for that.

So, no, New York was not the best answer—but what was? San Francisco? There were plenty of tales about the grand life in that city. They said the Barbary Coast made the Bowery look like a children's nursery, but there was more than that to Frisco.

Only people said it was expensive. So, he'd have to wait until there was money enough to ensure that he could take care of himself. He did not mean ever again to be dependent on any man, which to his mind meant subservient to his whims. He'd had no choice but to submit to Brian, but he had vowed that he would never again be so helpless. In the future, he meant to pay his own way. He'd be beholden to no one.

But Willis remained a worry for Terry. The Dollar's owner had not again tried to force his attentions on Terry, but Terry was not unaware of the glances Willis often cast in his direction, and it took no great wisdom to read what was in them. And Terry had experience enough of how determined a man could be when his privates had made up his mind for him.

It was after the show one night, and Terry was stripped naked when Willis unexpectedly came into the room.

"You should get into the habit of knocking, Mister Willis," Terry told him coldly, snatching his robe off the chair, but not before Willis had taken a good look at his naked backside.

"Don't see much reason for modesty between the two of us," Willis said, not looking away. "I'm paying for it, ain't I? Seems like I got a right to see it if I want."

"You're not paying for my backside, Willis," Lola said. "You're paying me to dance, and you're getting your money's worth. Ogling me while I dress is not part of our bargain. Now get out."

Willis went, but not before giving him an icy glower. "You'll pay for your hoity-toity manners one of these days, mark my words."

Terry breathed a sigh of relief, but he was not so naïve as to think Willis had ceased to be a threat. He went to the door and locked it from the inside.

In the meantime, Lola danced nightly—in heels now, as Belle had recommended, and whether it was the improvement in the shape of her legs or not she couldn't say, but the miners' infatuation for her seemed only to grow with each night's performance. Certainly they continued to shower her with their growing largesse.

For the time being, Terry all but forgot the danger that he was ever in, pretending to be a woman—pretending, in particular, to be Lola Valdez, whom every man in town loved—and desired.

Who was going to tell the truth, after all? Brian and Joshua had gone. On that score, he had nothing to fear from Willis. Willis knew who he was, but he had every reason to keep his mouth shut. Terry trusted Belle and, since she trusted him implicitly, he trusted Wonkle as well. There was no reason to think anyone else would ever suspect the truth.

Apparently, though, someone had.

He had taken to locking the dressing room door at night when he changed out of his costume. He had to wait for Willis to come, to pay him, but he waited as Lola, and not until Willis had gone out again and the door was locked after him did Terry begin to take off his makeup, his dress and petticoats.

He had not thought, however, to lock the door before his performance. Then, Willis was busy in the saloon, and no one had ever ventured backstage—it was afterward, after they had seen Lola dance, that men got rambunctious, and the locks and the guards outside were necessary.

So, it was a shock to Terry, seated at the dressing table early one evening, pinning up his hair, to look into the mirror and realize that someone was standing just inside the door, watching him.

"Reverend Davidson," he exclaimed, his heart thumping.

"What are you doing in here? This is a woman's dressing room. You aren't supposed to be in it."

"The Lord opens the doors for his servants," Reverend Davidson said, smiling in a knowing way at the image in the glass.

"Does the Lord say it's all right for a man of the cloth to watch a woman perform her toilette?" Terry's mind was racing. He had his petticoats on and over them, a chiffon robe, but he hadn't yet put on his makeup. How long had the Reverend been there? How much had he seen?

"The wages of sin are death," the Reverend intoned in his most sepulchral voice.

"Is it a sin, to dance?" Terry asked. "To bring a little gladness into the lives of these poor, lonely souls? They are certainly grateful for it. Perhaps God is as well."

The Reverend's eyes sparked with flames. "Do not take the Lord's name in vain," he said, and he looked so righteous, so angry, that Terry felt a little shiver of fear run down his spine.

"You must leave," he said. "I have to get ready for my show."

The Reverend did not move, but his grave demeanor melted somewhat and a slow smile spread across his face. Terry found that no less frightening. It was hardly a warm smile, and there was something worrisomely conspiratorial about it, as if they shared a secret. Alarmed, Terry could only hope that was not so.

"If you don't leave," Terry started to say, but the Reverend only grinned more broadly, more confidently.

"Oh, I'll go," he said. "I've got prayers to say."

Terry breathed a sigh of relief. Perhaps after all, the man hadn't seen enough to put things together. He'd long ago concluded the Reverend wasn't the brightest man around.

"Perhaps you'll say a few for me," he said. "One needs all the help one can get."

"I will indeed pray for you," The Reverend said. "And for myself."

With that somewhat mysterious pronouncement, he left.

Terry got up from the dressing table, meaning to lock the door, but halfway to it, he stopped and shrugged. Locking the barn after the horse is stolen, he thought. In the future, though, he would see that it was locked before he began his transformation. He'd never thought of anyone's wandering in while he was making up, but it wouldn't do to have it happen again.

But, how much of that transformation had Reverend Davidson seen? That remained the question, and it nagged at Lola while she danced. She was not at her best, and although the crowd in the saloon clapped and cheered and threw their money as usual, she sensed, with the growing rapport she shared with them, that they too knew something was amiss.

It was autumn, the summer fading quickly at this elevation. One of those violent storms that sometimes blew down from the mountains began to rage outside, the flashes of lightning visible through the Dollar's swinging doors, and once a peal of thunder, like the shot of a gun, brought her to a stop for a heartbeat or two, frozen in place and staring at the swinging doors as if there might actually be a gunman standing there. The miners murmured briefly, reminding her, and she began at once to spin and twirl again, but her nerves were jangled. It seemed to her like an omen of ill to come.

She was particularly glad when the performance was over, and she barely paused to blow that goodnight kiss and scoop up her earnings before she dashed to her dressing room.

Willis confirmed her disappointment with her evening's dance "What's wrong with you tonight?" he demanded when he came to pay her. "You looked like the dogs was barking at your backside,"

Despite the fact that she too had been unhappy with her performance, she snapped back at him. "The miners seemed to like it. And anytime you're not happy with what I do here, you let me know. I can find other places to dance."

"You try to leave me," he warned her, "and I'll see they string you up by them balls you ain't supposed to have."

His threat didn't impress her. Willis couldn't tell on her without putting his own neck at risk. No one would believe he hadn't known the truth all along, and the miners would not take kindly to his having led them on all this time.

It was the Reverend Davidson who continued to gnaw at her.

Normally, when he had paid her and left, Lola saw no more of Willis for the night, but this time the saloonkeeper came back when Terry was almost ready to leave.

"It's an ugly night out," he said. "I was thinking it might be best if I was to walk you home."

"I'm not afraid of a little thunderstorm," Terry said.

"Maybe not. But there's been someone hanging around your cabin lately, I've caught a glimpse of him a night or two."

"What are you doing there anyway, hanging around my cabin?" Terry demanded. "I don't remember asking for any protection."

"I've got an investment to protect, don't I?" Willis said. "And you're all alone out there in the woods. If someone was to get any funny ideas…"

"I can deal with them," Terry said. "And I can find my own way home. Alone."

Willis shrugged, but his little ferret-like eyes studied Terry coldly. "Suit yourself," was all he said.

Terry half suspected Willis' tale of someone hanging around was only a ruse to gain his own entry to the cabin. In any case, he did not care for the idea of Willis' hanging around, watching him. And he didn't think Willis' protection counted for very much, either—who was going to protect him from Willis?

He was careful, before he left though, to be sure Lola's little Derringer was in the pocket of his trousers, just in case.

It was raining hard, great torrents of water pouring down. Thunder rumbled and the occasional sheet of lightning flashed as Terry walked through town and out to the cabin, hurrying and dodging puddles where he could. Even so, he was quickly soaked and his shoes and the hems of his trousers were covered in mud before he got there.

He was almost to the cabin when someone stepped in front of him, directly in his path. Terry gasped with fright and stopped dead, thinking in the first startled second or so that it was Willis.

"Kind of late, ain't you?" Reverend Davidson asked.

Terry put a hand over his heart. "Reverend," he said. "You scared me half out of my wits."

"You've got more serious things to fear than an earnest servant of the Lord," Davidson said.

"Right now, I think I'm most afraid of catching pneumonia from this weather," Terry said. "If you don't mind, I'd like to get out of it."

"I don't mind," the Reverend said, and moved from the path, but when Terry began to walk again, the Reverend fell into step alongside him.

Terry stopped outside his door. "I'm sorry, Reverend, but it's late, and I'm wet and tired. If you planned on visiting, perhaps another time would be better."

"I planned on us having a conversation," the Reverend said. "And I think the sooner, the better—Lola."

Terry took a deep breath. It was what he had feared.

"You'd better come in, then," he said, his mind racing. He would have to think of some way to convince the Reverend to keep what he knew to himself—though just at the moment, he had no idea how he was going to do that. The Reverend seemed to have no interest in money, and there was nothing else Terry could think of that he had to offer him.

Inside, Terry went straight to the table at the far side of the cabin and lit a lamp, its flame dancing wildly in the drafts that gusted about the room. Stalling for time, he yawned ostentatiously.

"I'm really tired," he said. "Why don't you say what you have to say, and get it over with?"

"Must be plenty exhausting, I reckon," the Reverend said, "getting all those men excited every night. Filling them with sinful thoughts."

"I never think about that," Terry said. "What they've got in their heads is their business, as I see it."

"You never even think about it?" Davidson sounded disbelieving. "Kind of hard to credit, you being the kind of fellow you are."

"What kind of fellow is that, Reverend?" Terry asked in a cool voice.

"A sinner," the Reverend said, his voice rising the way it did for his Sunday sermons. "The worst kind of sinner."

"I don't think dancing is a sin," Terry said. "Not even putting on a dress, it doesn't seem like to me."

Davidson's eyes flashed like the lightning outside. "Don't mock me, you demon. Do you think I don't know what you've been up to all this time? I've stood outside this very cabin and listened to you and your brother, rutting like animals, night after night. Your own brother."

"You—you've listened to us?" Terry gasped, hardly able to believe what he'd heard. He would never in a million years have imagined...

"And that other one, that Simmons boy, I saw what you did with him, too, out there in them woods."

Terry was speechless. His face burned crimson. All this time, this odious creature had been spying on him. It was horrible to contemplate. "It was you. You've been following me around, watching me. I thought there was someone..."

"Fornication," Davidson said, practically shouting. "Incest. Whoring. Taking a man in ways that even a woman would be ashamed of, ways that are an abomination in a man. You have much to pray over, seems to me. I am here to save your soul from eternal damnation, before God strikes you dead."

As if to punctuate his words, a bolt of lightning lit up the windows, and at the same moment, a mighty gust of wind blew the door open, bringing sheets of rain with it. Grateful for the distraction, Terry hurried across the cabin and struggled the door closed again. He glanced out into the night, almost wishing he would see Willis there. Right now he'd welcome any rescue he could get; but there was no one.

When he turned back to the room, he was startled to see the Reverend had followed him, was so close behind him that Terry actually bumped into him in turning.

"I saw," the Reverend said, dropping his voice to a sibilant whisper that could barely be heard above the noise of the storm. "Saw and heard it all, what you did, pleasuring that boy in the woods. Wicked things. Things I had never seen or heard of before, never even imagined two men doing together. Putting him in your mouth like that."

His nearness alarmed Terry, and there was something else, too, something different in the eyes with which Davidson stared down at him from his awesome height.

"Reverend," Terry said, trying to step around him, but the Reverend took hold of him in his giant hands.

"In your mouth. I couldn't even imagine what that must feel like," he muttered, more as if he was talking to himself than to Terry, and there was a different note in his voice, almost a pleading sound, "having someone's mouth on you like that, down there, doing what you was doing, sucking at it like it was a teat. It keeps going around and around in my head, it won't let me be. Wondering what does that feel like when you do it to a man? I can't help wanting to know, it's been preying at me ever since, like a cancer growing inside me."

He paused and when he looked down at Terry, his eyes were so intense they actually seemed to burn with flames. "Until I come to think, if you was to do that to me, just one time, what you did to him…if you was to suck that sin right out of me, drain the poison…"

"No," Terry said, sickened by the suggestion. He struggled free of Davidson's grip and would have run out the door, but the Reverend was too quick, with his long arms he reached past Terry and held the door fast.

"Just once," he said, his voice cracking with emotion, "once is all. I have to know, I won't have any peace till you've done it to me—and then, when you've got it all out of me, why, then, we'll pray together, the two of us on our knees, pray to God for forgiveness. He'll forgive us, I know he will, I am his humble servant. All I ask is just once, to heal me of it, and then we will pray."

Terry stumbled away from him, but there was nowhere to go in the little room. He bumped into the big wooden table.

"Get out," he said, but even he could hear the fear in his voice.

"You're just saying that to tease me." Davidson gave a funny kind of laugh, as if he were choking on something. "Playing hard to get. Just like a woman. I swear. You don't just look like one when you get all dolled up. You practically are a woman, ain't you, a fallen one, a whore, but a woman just the same. And even though I am a servant of God, I am a man, too. And you have got the man of me excited beyond reason."

He took another step in Terry's direction. Terry tried to dart around him, but Davidson was quicker, and in a minute, he had seized Terry in a firm embrace, dragged him close. Terry felt one of Davidson's enormous hands pawing at his bottom. To his horror, pressed against Davidson's body as he was, he could feel Davidson's erection between them. He thought of Martin Van Arndst…just like this…his head swam.

"Let me go," Terry said, his voice little more than a croak.

He got a hand into his pocket and managed to get his fingers on the Derringer, and pulling it free, he raised it between them and pushed it against Davidson's chest.

"I'm warning you," he said, but Davidson was beyond reason, he seemed entirely unaware of the gun.

There was a clap of thunder, deafeningly loud. Terry was not aware that he had even pulled the trigger, but he must have done so. Davidson gave a little grunt. His expression was more one of puzzlement than of pain. He took a step back, looked down. Already a crimson rose was unfolding in his chest.

Surprised, he looked wide-eyed at Terry, and reached for the gun.

Terry fired again. This time the shot rang loud in the silence between the crashes of thunder.

Davidson staggered backward and put a hand up to his chest, where two wounds now bled profusely. His wide eyes, staring at

Terry, seemed to be asking some question. He sank to his knees, made a funny gurgling sound in his throat, and pitched face forward onto the dirt floor.

Terry stood, swaying, breathing heavily, and stared down at him, waiting for him to move again. "Reverend?" he said in a small, frightened voice. There was no answer.

Terry took the oil lamp from the table, set it on the floor next to the Reverend, and knelt, rolling him unto his back. Davidson's black eyes were wide, staring without seeing. A trickle of blood seeped out one corner of his mouth.

"He's dead," Terry said in a whisper. "I've killed him."

A cannon went off with a violent explosion. Terry squealed aloud and looked toward the door, half expecting to see the Vigilance Committee already there, come to string him up. In the flicker of lightning that followed the thunder's boom, a frightened mouse darted across the room. The flour-sack curtains billowed inward in a sudden gust of wind, bringing a spatter of rain with it.

The door was still closed. There was no one there.

Terry jumped to his feet and ran panting to the door and flung it open. The angry rain spat into his face. In the distance a dog had begun to bark and to howl. No doubt he was only frightened by the storm, but at the moment he sounded to Terry like the hounds of hell.

He reached for his slicker on the peg by the door and as he lifted his eyes, they fell upon the crucifix that hung at the lintel. He paused, and then snatched it down and, going across the room again, knelt again and laid it on Davidson's chest.

Something glittered between the fingers of Davidson's clenched fist. Terry pried his fingers open. It was the little gold cross the Reverend normally wore at his throat. He must have grabbed it as he fell and yanked the chain loose.

Terry started to reach for his crucifix where it lay on Davidson's chest, but his hand paused in mid-reach. The crucifix was the only souvenir he had of the parents he couldn't remember and he had never been parted from it—but, some dread held him back from snatching it off the dead man's body. He half feared that to do so would open a rent in Davidson's chest, from which his accusing spirit might emerge.

He looked at the Reverend's chain instead and raised it to his lips and kissed it and said a silent prayer for the just departed soul and shoved the chain and the cross inside his shirt, the metal cold against his feverish skin.

He lifted the chimney from the lamp and in an instant the wind had blown out the trembling flame. The little cabin plunged into darkness. The open door was a pale rectangle across the room.

Terry scrambled to his feet and ran to it. Snatching his slicker, he threw it about his shoulders and dashed into the stormy night.

PART III

BUTTE

Chapter Eleven

Joshua and Brian had barely arrived in Butte when an early winter set in. They were just able to get a crude cabin up and get some supplies in before a major blizzard struck. It snowed without stopping for a full week, stopped for a day, and began to snow again, the sheets of white blown about in a strenuous wind that roared down from the mountains. Gray wolves drifted into town like wisps of smoke, and sometimes got bold enough to scratch at cabin doors.

In no time, Joshua and Brian were snowed in. For several weeks they went outside no more than was essential, and sat instead for hours before their stove, so close that sometimes their boots got scorched.

"Of all the rotten luck," Brian grumbled, pacing the floor like a caged mountain lion. He, at least, could pace; the cabin's roof was too low for the taller Joshua even to stand up without ducking his head. "We might be stuck in here till spring, the way it's snowing out there."

"Not much we can do about it, the way I see it," Joshua said. "We've got plenty of whisky, haven't we, and food enough if we're careful, and as soon as the snow lets up, I'm going to cut some more wood. Doesn't look like we'll be doing much mining, but we'll get by all right."

"That's easy for you to say."

"What's that supposed to mean?" Joshua asked him, puzzled. "Looks to me like we're in the same boat at this point."

Brian had been thinking about Terry, and now he was going to be stuck in a cabin for weeks, maybe for months, with Joshua, who he doubted was a likely candidate to take Terry's place.

It had never occurred to him that he might miss his brother in that way, but it hadn't taken him long to begin to miss his steady diet of sex. And the longer he went without, the better his memories of how good it had felt.

He couldn't very well say that to Joshua, however. "Nothing," he said instead. "I'm just riled, is all. All this damn snow. Might have been better to stay where we was."

"Too late to be thinking of that," Joshua said.

Brian grunted and went to throw some more wood in the stove. Joshua watched him and thought about what Terry had said, about him and Brian. Nothing like that had come up between them. At first, when Brian had suggested Joshua come with him, Joshua had wondered if Brian had any inkling of what had happened with him and Terry, like maybe Terry had told his brother. For the first day or so, he'd been alert for any untoward movement on Brian's part, half expecting to turn and find Brian's gun trained on him.

Nothing of the sort had happened, though, and Brian had said and done nothing in all this time to indicate that he had any idea of that business, and Joshua had decided after all that he had no suspicions and began to breathe easier.

They almost never talked about Terry at all, and then only obliquely. Brian asked one evening, out of the blue, "That dancer that came to the Gulch just before we headed out," and paused. "To The Dollar. Remember?"

"Lola Valdez?" Joshua asked, surprised to have that brought up.

"Was that her name? Well, what did you think of her?"

Joshua took a moment to consider anew what Brian might or might not know.

"What do you mean, what did I think of her?" he asked cautiously. "She was a pretty thing, wasn't she? Had most of those miners standing on three legs, seemed like to me. What is it you're wondering about?"

Brian gave him a long look. "Nothing," he said with a shrug. "I was just wondering, is all. What you thought of her."

"She was just a dancer, was all," Joshua said. "Pretty enough, I guess. If you like dancers."

Brian seemed content to leave it at that.

Supplies quickly began to run low. There was a little general store, with a table for poker, run by a bear of a man named Angelo, but he was no better prepared for the unexpectedly early winter than the hundred or so miners in the camp, and soon enough salt and flour grew scarce, and most everything else not long after.

Luckily, almost the first thing Brian and Joshua had done when they got there was to stock up. Many of the miners had little in their pockets by the time they arrived at the crude camp, expecting with the prospector's optimism to find enough gold dust right off to provide for themselves, and quickly chagrined to find out how misguided the expectations had been, but Brian and Joshua were luckier than most. Brian had the money he had taken from Terry, although he did not mention its source to his partner, and Joshua had brought with him the rest of the stake his father had given him when he sent him west.

As a result, they at least faced the winter with plenty of coffee and plenty of whisky, and enough beans to tide them over. They had killed a deer shortly after arriving, and the venison hung in the rear of their cabin, along with a big side of questionable beef they had purchased from Angelo, much of which had been made into jerky, the rest of it gradually growing its own overcoat of mold. By now, they were so used to it they never even noticed the smell.

Even so, by Christmas they'd had to reduce their three meals a day to two, as a precaution, and then to one, and they pretended they didn't hear their bellies complain, and kept a close eye out in case anyone started envying their provisions.

"You think this is bad," Brian said, "Christ, this is a damn picnic, I tell you. Back in the States, in the Five Points, people lived two and three families together, sometimes a hog, too, or chickens, in rooms so dark you couldn't see your hand in front of your face, and a man could never say for sure whether he'd fucked another man's wife or his own, or one of his kids, even, and didn't much care which, either, and women would lay drunk all day long in the shit piles they called their back yards. This ain't nothing, I tell you."

"What is it you came for, anyway, Brian?" Joshua asked him one day. "Was it just the money, is all?"

They were sitting by the stove, the toes of their boots beginning to scorch, and Brian was so long answering, Joshua thought maybe he hadn't heard the question, or didn't mean to answer it at all.

"I don't exactly know," he said finally. "I used to think it was the money, but maybe it was just getting out of there, as much as anything, getting away from, well, The Bowery, or something, anyway. Only, it don't seem like I've got yet wherever it is I was going." He looked around, at the dirt floor and the empty tin cans scattered on it, and the jerky hanging in the corner. "Sure as hell, this ain't it. I don't know where is, though."

As bad as things were getting, though, there were others in the camp far worse off than they were, and desperate men could resort to desperate measures.

"Best we keep our guns by our beds," Brian said one evening. "And sleep with one eye open, to be safe."

Even living in Alder Gulch, Joshua was no gunman, but on the trip here, Brian had taught Joshua how to handle a gun, a fact for which Joshua soon enough had reason to be grateful. He was awakened one night from a deep sleep by a hard kick from Brian, in the bed next to him.

"What," Joshua mumbled, barely awake, but he became immediately aware that Brian was struggling with someone. Even as that realization sprang into his mind, Brian swore in a strangled voice, "Son of bitch!"

Joshua immediately snatched up the gun by his side. In the faint light from the window, he could see someone bending over the bed. Without pausing to think, Joshua fired. There was a groan and somebody toppled to the floor. Beside him, Brian moaned.

"Carson?" someone asked from the dark and another shadow passed before the window. There was the click of a gun's hammer being cocked.

Joshua fired again. Another gun went off, and something nicked the wall over Joshua's head. He aimed lower and fired once more, and this time there was another groan and a gasp, and someone else fell to the floor.

"Brian?" Joshua whispered into the darkness.

"There's two of them, I think," Brian said. "Bastards caught me asleep, stuck a knife in me, one of 'em did."

"You okay?"

"I'll live. What about them two?"

Joshua crouched on the bed, gun held in front of him, waiting and listening. The silence felt weighted.

"I think I got them," he said.

"Light the lamp," Brian said. His gun clicked. "I got you covered."

Joshua slipped out of the bed, almost stumbled over the body lying next to it. Stepping carefully, he followed the moonlight to the table, managed to get a match struck with trembling hands, and lit the lamp.

There were two of them on the floor, both dead. The one nearest the bed still held a bloody knife in his hand. Brian had been stabbed twice, in the side and in the shoulder, but though both wounds bled profusely, neither of them seemed deep enough to have done any mortal damage.

Between them, they got the wounds washed with snow from outside, and bandaged with an old, dirty shirt Joshua tore into strips. Afterward, Brian gritting his teeth and swearing under his breath, they dragged the two dead men outside and left them lying among the trees.

"Won't take the wolves long to find them," Brian said.

The story quickly circulated among the miners, that Joshua had killed both the intruders, a couple of grizzled outcasts who had intimidated most of the others around the camp.

Brian looked sullen whenever the tale was told, since Joshua got the credit for the heroics and Brian's only contribution had been the scars he wore afterward, but at least he got to say, "I told you so." When he had early on taught a somewhat reluctant Joshua to use a gun, he had said, more than once: "The West ain't no place for a man can't look after himself."

When he said it, Joshua found himself unaccountably thinking of Terry and wondering how that slight boy—it was impossible for him to think of Terry as a man—could possibly look after himself.

"I should have stayed, to protect him," he thought, and then was angry with himself for thinking it. But the image of Terry continued to haunt him. He seemed to see Terry's wide, frightened eyes pleading with him from the cabin's dark corners, and sometimes he could almost hear Terry's voice whispering to him in the wind howling outside the cabin.

And, night after night, he woke from sleep convinced that Terry's lips were down there, on his cock. His cock that would not be satisfied then until he'd taken it in fist and pounded it into submission.

When finally they began to venture from the cabin, wrapped in their buffalo robes and buckskins so greasy they were black, to join the other miners at a game of cards at Angelo's, the men exchanged worried looks with each violent gust of wind that buffeted the little shack, and were afraid to voice their fears to one another. It wasn't all that far to Helena, and there was every reason to think things were better there, but there was little hope now of making the journey. They had, all of them, begun to worry that they would die here, buried under the snow, the wolves feeding on their carcasses.

One of the men actually tried to break for Helena, but he gave it up after a day in which he had gotten no more than a mile or so, and struggled back to the camp. His feet had gotten badly frostbitten in the attempt and without medical attention, gangrene developed in them rapidly. The others discussed whether or not they should cut off his feet, but the man begged them to let him die with both his feet attached.

They had, and he did. The snow was ten and twelve feet deep now and seemed nightly to grow deeper. It was impossible to bury anyone under that thick blanket. The best they could do was nail him in a hastily contrived pine box, and leave that outside, because nobody was willing to put up with its presence in their cabin, to remind them of the danger that stalked them.

They all knew, when they set the box atop a snowdrift among the trees, that it would be no time at all till the animals got to him. There was nothing they could do about that either, and when they had left him there, as if by some silent agreement, no further mention of him was made and none of them afterward even so much as looked in that direction, not wanting to confirm what they already were sure of.

In a strange way, though, as the winter progressed and the situation grew more dire, Joshua found himself taking a peculiar sort of satisfaction in it. In Philadelphia, after that incident with Winslow, he had begun to entertain doubts about his manhood, and when he had succumbed to Terry's seduction back at The Gulch, and found himself enjoying it so completely, so unbelievably, it had only fueled his doubts.

Maybe there was something wrong with him, he thought morosely, that attracted that kind of person to him. That was two of them, wasn't it, that had thought he looked ripe for the plucking, and something must have given them the idea. Maybe when something like that happened once, it naturally fostered another incident of it, the way a dirty pond breeds mosquitoes.

And at first, after it had happened, he'd had the uncanny sensation that everyone knew, that they had only to look at him to know what had happened—that everyone was laughing at him behind the placid masks they wore.

Now, though, here he was, sitting in a room where the smoke was so thick you could barely see the card player across the table, with men as fierce and manly as could be found anywhere in the world, any one of whom would have cut the throat of another in a twinkling, and he knew that he looked as ferocious as any of them, and now that the story of the two intruders he'd killed was commonly known, he was treated by all with a wary respect. He was convinced finally that he was just as much a man as anyone there.

After that, his memories of Terry began to trouble him less. They did not come less often. He still woke just as regularly in the night, his rigid dick remembering the dreams from which he had just awakened, and demanding to be relieved.

Knowing now with certainty that he wasn't queer, though, meant that he could savor the memories without any guilt or shame. It was Terry, after all, who had taken advantage, in a way. He had found Joshua with a boner, whacking it, which was just one of those things a man did. Had probably, now that Joshua thought about it rationally, stalked him for days watching for just such an opportunity, waiting to catch him in the act.

As for Joshua's part in what had happened, well, shit, you couldn't expect a man to refuse to be pleasured when it was practically forced upon him, could you, and especially not once he discovered how pleasurable it was?

That second time had become blurred in his mind so that, then, too, he remembered that it had been Terry who had come to him, had pursued his desires, and that he, Joshua, had only acquiesced in them. Besides, that time he had been drunk. Everybody knew a drunk dick had no conscience, once it was standing. Once it was hard, there wasn't anything for it but to get it soft again. The way Joshua saw it now, it didn't matter a lot at that point how that was done.

As the days and the weeks went by, however, and he and Brian were necessarily more and more together, Joshua began to notice that, ugly as he was, Brian nevertheless looked like Terry. Enough like him, at least, that you could tell they were brothers. It was like their features had been modeled just the same from clay, but someone had mucked the clay about on Brian's face, making the nose squatter, the ears beaten out of shape, the brow scarred.

The wide eyes, though, were surprisingly alike, although where Terry's looked mostly frightened, Brian's looked threats at you; and, now that Joshua took notice of it, when Brian spoke, his deep baritone managed somehow to sound much like Terry's alto. There were many words that they said alike, differently from the way other men said them. "Bird," for instance, came out more like "boyd," and when Joshua heard Brian say them, the words, too, recalled Terry to him.

Despite the ways in which Brian reminded him of Terry, though, and despite Joshua's almost endless memories of those fleeting experiences with Terry, Joshua never consciously thought about any kind of sexual connection between himself and Brian.

Moreover, if such a thought ever had occurred to him, he would have scoffed at it, Brian being the man he was, as tough as he was. Even here, in a town full of men hard as the rocks that dotted the hills, Joshua saw that the others gave Brian a wide berth at all times. Which meant, by extension, they gave him a wide berth, too, and for that he was grateful.

Afterward, though, he did realize that probably he had been primed for it to happen. He just hadn't consciously anticipated it.

Half asleep, he heard Brian get up to take a piss. The pallet shifted a little as Brian got back into bed, and Josh was just about drifting off to sleep again when, to his surprise, Brian edged cautiously across the distance that separated them, got right up behind Josh. For a long time, nothing happened, and Joshua feigned sleep to see what Brian had on his mind, though he already had a suspicion. Behind him, Brian breathed noisily, raggedly, clearly nervous.

After a while, tentative fingers touched Josh's backside. Hesitated, as if judging the reaction. Apparently, Josh's continued steady breathing satisfied Brian. Josh felt the trapdoor on his long johns fumbled with, and a cold draft on his bare ass, and a minute later, Brian was probing between his butt checks with the head of his dick.

Josh's first impulse was to tell him to forget what he was up to, and he actually opened his mouth to say something, and then, more on a whim than out of any conscious desire, changed his mind. They'd been snowed in now for nearly three months, and there wasn't a single woman in the camp. Josh jacked himself off most nights, and just about as often heard Brian doing the same on his side of the bed.

He'd heard a sly reference or two that made him think some of the other miners were making do with what was at hand. He hadn't been particularly curious about it, but now, suddenly, he was. He remembered what Terry had told him, about Brian fucking him. What was that all about, anyway, he wondered, guys fucking one another in the butt? He lay without moving or saying anything, let Brian work his way in.

It hurt at first, but no worse, really, than sometimes dropping a rock on his foot while he was panning back in the Gulch, or the time he'd cut his arm open on a thorn bush. He could think of lots of things that hurt more, and he hadn't cried over them, had he? He stifled a grunt and sent his muscles an order to yield, and after a minute, they did, and the pain got less, and by the time Brian was all the way in and had slid to and fro a few times, it hardly hurt at all. And, though he didn't have much experience of the matter, it didn't seem to him that Brian was all that big. It wasn't much of a stretch to accommodate him once he got used to it.

He couldn't say that it was much of a pleasure to him, either, but it was doing *something* inside him, that unfamiliar friction, because his own prick got as stiff as a poker and it half way felt like it was going to start shooting off any minute, although it didn't.

Even though this was unfamiliar territory to him, he knew well enough when Brian was getting close, and when he shoved it home hard, Josh felt the new and never before imagined sensation of a man coming up his ass.

He waited until Brian had finished, had slipped out, and pulled away, and then Josh turned around and, without saying anything, took hold of Brian and turned him over on his side, and quickly opened the back door of his woolies.

"I never done that," Brian said, but he offered no resistance.

"I hadn't either," Josh replied. "I took it like a man. Seems to me like you can too."

Brian didn't reply, just laid there stiffly while Josh found his spot and began to work it in, and then, "Goddamn," and, "Take it easy, why don't you?" Brian hissed, but he made no move to struggle or to pull away. If he had, Joshua would have stopped. They were stuck here together in this cabin, almost certainly until spring. The last thing he wanted was to be on the wrong side of Brian's volatile temper. It didn't seem, though, as if Brian were actually angry about what Joshua was doing, despite his hoarse oaths, so Joshua continued to do it.

He took it easy, but he didn't take it out either, and he didn't stop, he just worked it in nice and slow, pausing with each thrust to let Brian get used to it, and then the next time going a bit deeper, following his instinct—this wasn't something that needed much instruction to make it happen, as he quickly discovered—reading Brian's reactions as he progressed, until soon enough he was all the way in, clear up to his balls and way deeper than Brian had been able to travel, he thought with a prideful note of self congratulations, and he began, slowly at first, to fuck him.

To his surprise, it felt far better than he would have imagined. Tighter than any woman he'd fucked in the past, but there hadn't been all that many of them, and most had been whores and the couple who hadn't were married women, so no virgins then, and nothing as reluctant to yield to his advance as Brian's still-resisting tunnel.

What surprised him even more, though, was that it was quickly evident, as he began to fuck more energetically, that Brian was enjoying it, a little at first, and them more heartily. The initial curses and groans had become moans and whimpers that were unmistakable signals of pleasure, and he began to move in rhythm with Josh and twist his ass about and shove it back to take Josh all the way, which encouraged Josh heartily and added to his own pleasure.

Josh had his arms about Brian and all of a sudden, his hand, on Brian's belly, was wet, and he realized with a shock that Brian had shot off a load without a hand being put to his prick, and that discovery was so exciting to Josh that he let fly only a second or two later, what felt like the biggest load he'd ever fired, and the longest lasting.

It seemed like an eternity later before he stopped squirting and got his breath back and when he did, he was still stiff as a rock—and still buried to the balls in Brian's ass, and Brian showing no inclination to pull away.

Josh began to fuck him all over again, and this time, Brian took hold of Josh's hand and put it on his rock hard dick, and Josh jerked him obligingly while he fucked.

That was how they spent the rest of the winter. Josh fucked Brian nightly, and Brian just seemed to love it more and more each time. It was like he couldn't get enough of it, was Joshua's impression, and Joshua was happy enough to give it to him. It beat jacking off, that was for certain.

Sometimes Brian wanted to play turnabout, and Josh figured it was only fair, and let him have his way whenever he wanted it, though he'd quickly determined that was one of those things he could take or leave. Luckily, that idea didn't occur to Brian very often.

Somewhere in the back of his mind, Josh had a notion that maybe with the right fellow, he would find having a pecker up his ass as thrilling as Brian obviously did. It wasn't that he didn't like Brian well enough, and he enjoyed buttfucking him all right, sometimes almost as much for the reaction that he produced in his partner as for his own enjoyment. It gave him an odd sense of power that he'd never felt before, to know that he could drive someone into a near delirium with just the magic of his prick.

He'd actually never thought much about his prick before except just to pull it regularly. Now, though, it began to seem to him like it was some kind of magic wand that he had down there, some special gift with which to make others happy.

Gradually he found himself thinking about Terry while he was doing it, and about how happy his prick had made Terry in that other way. And began to wonder if maybe that was why he'd fucked Brian in the first place, and what accounted for most of the pleasure he took in it: because Brian was a homely version, with a battered face, of his little brother.

And the more he thought about Terry, the more Joshua felt that it was Terry whom he wanted to make happy with his magic wand.

Damnation, he thought while he plowed Brian steadily, *what a fool I was, not to see what was right there before my eyes. That I could have had whenever I wanted, just waiting for me to make use of.*

Would he ever see Terry again? And, far, far more important, would Terry still feel the way he had before. Would he ever again hear Terry say, "I love you." Which, now that he thought of it from this distance, was a pleasure in its own way. Why wouldn't a man like knowing that, hearing it said?

It was something he wanted to experience again. It was a good thing, wasn't it, knowing that someone loved you, found you unbearably desirable as a man? It remained inexplicable to him, though, a man loving another man that way. How could that be? The truth was, he didn't think he had ever loved anyone, man or woman. Or anything, either—except his cock. He loved that, and could easily see why others would too, the more practice he got with it. Could see, really, why others would love him. So, maybe that was someone he loved - himself. So, why wouldn't others? In that sense, it didn't matter much, did it, if it was a man or a woman?

The best of it with Terry, however, had been that Terry was happy to pleasure him without expecting anything in return, as Brian sometimes did. He felt now that this was how he would like things to be, but he half feared he'd come to this truth too late.

In the meantime, there was Brian, in the same bed with him every night, it took no more than scooting a few inches closer… but for all their similarities, Brian wasn't Terry. Even Joshua's cock knew the difference.

Sometimes when he was fucking Brian, savoring Brian's excitement, he found himself wondering if maybe Brian loved him, too, the way Terry had. He thought about how nice it would be to hear Brian say it, how much he loved it when someone said, "I love you," and sometimes he thought Brian was about to say it—but, disappointingly, he never did. He felt it, though, Josh was sure of it.

It was near spring. A mighty Chinook had swept down from the mountaintop, scattering woodpiles, overturning privies and turning banks of snow into rivers of mud that still froze over from time to time or got covered with new snow.

Brian came home later than usual from a game of poker at Angelo's. Bored and restless with waiting for spring to arrive, Joshua had passed on going with him this particular occasion, and had spent the afternoon trying to make some order out of the mess that was their cabin. Months of close confinement had meant piles of unwashed clothes, dishes and pots that had been used and, never washed, used again, until they were crusted over with remnants of previous meals.

"There's an Indian squaw in town," Brian said when he'd shed his buffalo robe. He got himself a glass of whiskey and came to warm himself in front of the fire. "Got in yesterday, with a couple of miners from Helena."

"Is that so?" Josh said, more interested than not. There hadn't been any newcomers in the camp since the fall, before the snows had come so heavy.

"Calls herself Happy Rabbit," Brian said. "Seems like mostly what keeps her happy is selling her pussy." He chuckled. "She was sure one happy injun last night, I'd say. Reckon half the boys in town took their turn."

"I guess you were helping keep her happy?" Josh grinned.

"I did my share." Brian grinned back at him. "Been a while since anybody around here got any tail. Any real tail, I mean to say. Thing is, she's about the ugliest woman I ever seen, and I don't expect she's had a bath since last summer. But it's not a bad piece of ass if you keep your eyes closed the whole time and don't breathe too deep. You ought to give her a poke. Might make you happy too. Sure did me."

Joshua gave him a wry smile. "I think I'll just take your word for that," he said.

Brian gave him a long, hard look. "How long's it been, anyway, since you fucked a woman?"

Josh shrugged. "I haven't been counting. Long enough, I suppose."

"Well, then? What's wrong with fucking this one?"

"Brian, I'm happy—well, no, make that contented—with what I got. Seems to me like it works good enough. For the time being anyway."

"So, what is it then that you think you got, that makes you so contented?" Brian asked, and there was a note of challenge in his voice.

Josh looked hard back at him. They had never actually talked about what they had been doing together for many weeks, but even so, he thought by now they were both surely past pretending it didn't happen. Besides, he was tired of waiting for Brian to say what he wanted to hear. Maybe Brian needed a little push.

"This," he said aloud, "If you didn't know," and in a sudden quick movement, he crossed the room to where Brian was standing, took him by the shoulders, and, to his surprise at least as much as Brian's, kissed him, tenderly.

For all the fucking they had done throughout the winter, it was the first time their mouths had ever come together. At first, Brian stood frozen, unresponsive. Josh might have been kissing one of those Indian totem poles. And, really, he wasn't even sure why he had done it, except that they never had, and it seemed funny not to after everything else they had done together, after six months of fucking one another nightly, and some afternoons too. It wasn't like there was a lot else to do to pass the time when you were snowed in.

Then, as if of their own accord, Brian's arms came around him, and Brian began to kiss him back, not at all gently, the way Josh had kissed him, but hard, fiercely, and Josh, initially surprised in turn, soon returned it in kind, mouths and teeth grinding together and tongues searching frantically, their bodies writhing against one another, so close they might have been a single entity, and trying to get closer yet.

They parted just long enough to shed clothes, each pausing in his own disrobing to take some piece of clothing off the other, neither of them able to get naked fast enough to suit either themselves or one another. Both as hot as if this were their first time and they were just now discovering the other's body.

They didn't even wait to make it to the bed, but dropped to the dirt floor, again clinging and wrestling. Brian opened his legs for Josh to kneel between them, taking it for granted that Josh was going to fuck him, but Josh had another idea.

He held Brian's short, stout cock tightly in his hand and looked down at it, stroking it for him, and looked at his own cock. He took that in his other hand and for a moment jerked on both of them simultaneously.

He had a memory, though, of what Terry had done to him, and what it had felt like and, hardly thinking about what he was doing, certainly with no thought of asking permission, he climbed up over Brian, bringing his cock up close to Brian's face. He put a hand on Brian's head and urged him forward, toward it.

Brian looked at the cock in front of his face. He reached and took hold of it and stroked it for a minute or two, and looked up at Joshua.

"I ain't never," he started to say, and then he looked at the cock again, right before his eyes, and said, "Oh, well, fuck it," and put his mouth on it.

It was a far different experience for Joshua from what it had been with Terry. It was evident that Brian hadn't done this before. He gagged and had to take it out of his mouth, and Joshua thought the experiment was probably over, but a minute later, he put it in his mouth again and kind of jacked it and slid up and down on it at the same time, trying to figure out how it was done. His teeth scraped the shaft often enough and badly enough that Joshua seriously considered whether this might have been a mistake and whether he wanted to continue with it or not.

Brian very quickly got better, though. He apparently felt Joshua wince, and began to take more care of his teeth, and to use his tongue more, and suck rather than chew, and Joshua found shortly that, if it wasn't the unbridled pleasure that Terry had given him, he nevertheless liked this better than the alternative.

He looked down between them, really noticing for the first time how hairy Bryan's body was, how different it was from his own smooth skin, just that bush at his crotch and the patches under his arms. He watched his hard dick slide in and out of Brian's thick lips, the sight adding to his pleasure. Again, he had that sense of what a beautiful thing his prick was, and the happiness he could give others with it, at the same time he had his own pleasure, and the sense of power that it gave him made him feel all the more a man. His appreciation of his own cock had grown over the last few months. He thought it entirely right that Brian should love it too.

He looked over his shoulder and down, and saw that Brian was whacking himself heartily. Looking at it now with renewed interest, he saw that Brian's dick, too, was different from his own, smaller, and with the knob only showing in intermittent glimpses from the long foreskin. Joshua made no move to help him, only watched while he fucked Brian's mouth, focusing entirely upon pleasing himself, which was what it was all about for him, why his partner was there, the way he saw it—to give him pleasure. Which, surely, was a pleasure for Brian, too, wasn't it?

As if to prove that point, Brian came suddenly, his dick erupting, a stream of jism spouting upward for two feet or more into the air and cascading back down over his hand and his belly. The sight was enough to bring Joshua to his own climax, but however much Brian had learned about the business of sucking cock, he clearly was not ready yet for that part of it. He gagged and choked and pulled away, and got most of Joshua's load on his face and in his beard, but he continued to pump Joshua's cock obligingly with his fist until it had stopped shooting and, at the end, he held it in his fingers and stared at it as if he didn't know what it was for.

Josh flopped down heavily on top of Brian with a satisfied grunt and kissed him, lightly at first and then more searchingly, discovering the unfamiliar taste of his own come on Brian's lips, and needing a moment or two to decide that, all in all, he kind of liked that too. It was himself that he was tasting, after all. His magic elixir, that made everyone so happy.

He lifted his face and looked, smiling, into Brian's eyes. Brian's answering smile was tentative, unsure, as if he were confused about what had just happened. He swallowed hard and wiped the back of his hand across his mouth.

"That was great," Joshua said, wanting to reassure him. "Really. You never did that before?"

"No," Brian said. "I never did. Nor had it done, either, if you was wanting…"

"I'll do it for you one of these times," Joshua said quickly. "Just so you can see what it's like." He looked down at himself. He was still as hard as ever. "Would you want…well, shit, you can see for yourself, I've got plenty more where that came from."

"I don't know if I can…" Brian stammered, looking away, embarrassed. "Not just now. Maybe some other time."

"That's okay," Josh said, and kissed him again. He scooted down, back between Brian's legs, pushed them further apart with his knees. This was a new position for them, face to face, one that had just popped into Josh's head, but as soon as he thought of it, he knew this was how he wanted it. Always before they'd done it one behind the other, in the dark. Fucking Brian's mouth, though, Josh had discovered that he liked doing it in the light, where he could see himself while he was at it.

Having just shot a load, Brian was really not of a mind at that particular moment to be fucked, but that idea seemed not to occur to Joshua. He spit on his hand and wet his dick and guided it to Brian's hole.

Brian sucked in his breath hard and started to object when Josh entered him, and then changed his mind.

Shit, he thought, that's what this is all about, ain't it, not queer stuff like with Terry, just a couple of guys helping one another out when they got hot nuts? Wasn't like it would kill him, was it?

Only, the position wasn't as easy as it had seemed when Josh had first thought of it. He could get it in, but not much more than the head. He looked down at Brian's hairy legs, spread wide, and on a hunch, lifted them up and rested them on his shoulders.

That was better, he could go in easier now. Plus, he had a better view, too. He knew he was big. He had measured himself often, since he was a boy, when it had been smaller. It was nine inches now and usually he took his time putting it in Brian, giving him time to get used to it, but the view between them excited him beyond restraint, and he drove it home in one long, powerful thrust, up to the balls, ignoring Brian's loud grunt, not even seeing his grimace of pain. He took hold of Brian's legs and lifted them into the air, and now he could see even better, could even see Brian's little hole yield to him, clinging as he pulled back.

He was conscious now of nothing but his own pleasure, the sight of his big prick plowing furiously in and out between Brian's cheeks. He made no effort to be careful or gentle, either. Brian closed his eyes, and lay unmoving while Josh fucked him with ever increasing violence. Soon—all too soon as it seemed to Josh, though to Brian soon wasn't soon enough—Josh got another load off, bending down to kiss Brian's mouth roughly while he pumped Brian's butt full of sperm.

Despite his discomfort at being fucked so roughly, so soon after he had shot off, Brian nevertheless welcomed Josh's mouth, had discovered that he liked that part of it, anyway, liked it a lot, kissed him back enthusiastically, tongue working eagerly— would, in fact, have continued kissing long after Joshua had lost interest in it, if Joshua hadn't taken his mouth away.

Later, they drank some whisky, passing the bottle back and forth, lying naked together on the floor. They didn't speak much. It didn't seem to Josh that much needed saying. Brian surprised him, though, when he did finally speak.

"Do you think this makes us queer?" He asked.

"What you did?" Josh countered. "What do you think?"

Brian thought for a moment before he answered. "Well, I think—don't take no offense now, but, buttfucking, well, shit, there's a lot of guys do that, whether they'll say they do or not. Half the guys in this camp have been doing the same thing all winter, you take my word for it. Shit, I've done it before myself, if you want to know the truth. Not taking it up the ass, like I told you that first time you did it, I hadn't ever done it that way, but I done the fucking part of it plenty of times before, never saw anything wrong with it. It's just a hole, ain't it, a place to stick your pecker if you ain't got nothing better available." He hesitated for a long pause before he added, "But, I got to say, now, sucking cock—well, that's got to be queer, ain't it? If anything is?"

"I reckon you're right," Josh said after a moment's consideration. This was the first they had ever said anything aloud about what they had been doing the whole winter. In a way, he felt relieved to have it out in the open between them. "It ain't like I hated it, either, when you were doing it. Truth is, I liked it just fine. To be honest, I was kind of figuring that was how we'd do it in the future. Some of the time, anyway. Seemed to me like you were enjoying it well enough, too. There's others have found sucking my dick plenty enjoyable in the past. It's a nice one, that's for sure, isn't it?"

He raised himself on one elbow and looked searchingly at Brian. "So, are you saying you didn't like it, sucking it? You think it makes us queer, doing it that way?"

"I don't know," Brian said, He sighed wearily and took the bottle from Josh's hand and swallowed noisily from it. "It's one thing, being snowed in all winter, and no women around. A guy's got to do something, don't he? But now, seeing as there's pussy to be had…I just don't know…" His voice trailed off.

Josh didn't think it made him queer, not at all. On the other hand, it wasn't him who had sucked a cock. But, he didn't think it wise at the moment to point that out to Brian, especially not as he was looking forward hopefully to more of the same in the future.

"So, then, did you like fucking that squaw better than what we just did?" Josh asked instead. "Or what we've been doing? You know, that other stuff."

"I don't know," Brian said again, and wouldn't look square at him.

"Well, I'll tell you what," Joshua said, rolling over on his back, "I sure don't feel like I'm queer, just because we had us some fun. That's just how I see it. And I don't think it makes you queer, either."

"Course, I was the one sucking cock," Brian said, echoing Joshua's own sentiments.

Which, Joshua thought, probably did make Brian queer, didn't it? It made him wonder, too, about all the times Brian had talked about queers, about how he hated them. Could a man be queer, Joshua wondered, and still hate them? And still love him?

That wasn't something he wanted to ask Brian, however. And, really, what did he care if what he had done meant Brian was queer, so long as he knew that he wasn't. He just liked having his cock sucked, was all, and if Brian was agreeable to doing it for him, and he was as sure as anything that, having once had a taste, Brian would come back to the well, so to speak, well, then…

"Well, shit, then," he said aloud, to mollify him, "one of these times, I'll try that on you, too, if it'll make you feel better," but, even to his own ears, the promise sounded false.

He doubted that Brian believed it either. If that was something you were going to do, you'd do it then and there, in the heat of the moment, wouldn't you, when you could see at a glance that Brian had a hard on at the ready, and not some time in the unstated future? It wasn't much of a reach to take hold of Brian's dick, wouldn't have taken much moving around to get a mouth down to it.

He didn't, though. Wasn't about to, either, though he wasn't going to say that. He didn't mind taking Brian up his ass from time to time, to keep him happy, but he was no cocksucker. Brian was right, you wouldn't do that for anything if you weren't queer.

Laying there side by side, neither one of them saying anything more about it, both of them were conscious of what hadn't been said, or done. And though Brian looked steadily at him for a long moment, Joshua kept his eyes carefully on the ceiling.

When Josh got up the next morning, the first thing he saw was that Brian was gone.

The second thing was he'd taken all their money with him.

Chapter Thirteen

It was early summer by the time Joshua made it back to Alder Gulch. He'd managed to make some money in Butte, but not much more than what it had taken him to return.

"There's money to be made there, though" he told his uncles when they questioned him, welcoming him back heartily. "More in copper or silver, I'd say, than gold. It could be done, but it would take some serious doing, some real investment of capital."

"You still got your claim there?" Pete Simmons wanted to know, and when Joshua nodded, he said, looking at his brother, Matt, "We've done all right here. Better than all right, to tell the truth. You have, too, by the way. That little claim of yours has been paying off nicely. But we've been thinking about branching out. There's several of us talking about new directions to go. Maybe Butte wants looking into."

"Could be," Joshua agreed, and nodded when his Uncle Matt offered a fresh drink from the whisky bottle.

"Too bad about Murphy taking off with your money, though," Matt said. "I never did trust the fellow. Had mean eyes. Always looked like he'd just as soon cut your throat as talk to you. I'm surprised you got along with him as well as you did, as long as you did."

"We got along okay," Joshua said. "Got along pretty well, really, up until he lit out like that, with no warning. I guess he didn't head back this way?"

Both brothers shook their heads. "Never saw hide nor hair of him since the night you two headed out for Butte."

Victor J. Banis

"Well, good riddance, I guess," Joshua said. "There wasn't a lot of money anyway, by the time he went. And if what you say is true, I'm probably richer now than I was then."

"I wouldn't say you're powerful rich," Pete said, "but you're a long way from poor, too. Of course, we've had to pay someone to work your claim, and there's been some other expenses. But even so, when we get settled up, you'll be all right."

"Glad to hear it," Joshua said. There was a moment of silence, the uncles and their nephew contemplating their own well-being and their sagacity.

"Say," Joshua said as casually as he could, "speaking of Murphy, whatever happened to his little brother, anyway, what was his name? Jerry? Barry? Something like that."

"Terry," Walt said and he gave Joshua a glance that said maybe he knew there was more to Joshua's question than Joshua had let on. Joshua quickly avoided his gaze. "He took off."

"Really?" Joshua said, surprised out of his feigned nonchalance.

"Say," Pete added, apparently oblivious to any undercurrents of meaning that had passed between the other two, "that cabin of theirs is still empty, come to think of it."

Since Joshua had left The Gulch, Pete's family had arrived from Philadelphia. Just now the women were down by the creek washing clothes and the children playing outside, no one but the three men inside the cabin, but even so it was clear that there wouldn't be room for Joshua to stay there. They had not until now broached that subject but it was on all their minds, and Pete's most especially.

"You ought to move in there," Pete said, looking pleased that the idea had occurred to him.

"I'm surprised it's stayed empty," Joshua said. "The way the Gulch has grown in one year, houses going up everywhere. I'd have thought someone would have moved in there right off."

The two older men exchanged glances. "Miners can be a superstitious bunch," Pete said, somewhat mysteriously.

"Superstitious about what?" Joshua asked.

It was a moment before either of the uncles answered him.

"Reverend Davidson was found dead there," Matt said finally.

"At least, a good part of him was. He'd been there a while and the door was standing open. The animals had been at him."

"Dead? Davidson? How'd he die?" Joshua asked.

"He'd been shot," Pete said.

Joshua took a minute to consider that. "Did Murphy shoot him? Is that what you're saying?"

"The kid?" Walt asked. "Doesn't seem likely, does it? He wasn't the shooting kind, I wouldn't have thought."

"But he did disappear the same time," Pete said. "Makes you wonder, kind of."

Walt shrugged. "Nobody knows what really happened. They found Davidson dead, at Murphy's cabin. He'd been shot, twice. And Murphy was nowhere to be found. That was all anybody talked about for a while, but when no trace of him ever showed up, well, people just kind of forgot all about it. Belle says maybe whoever shot the Reverend shot the Murphy kid too, or carried him off. She says probably his bones are rotting somewhere between here and there. I expect probably she's right."

He looked pointedly away from his nephew. "He was a pretty little thing, the kid, in a funny way. Almost like a girl, I always thought. I wasn't the only one, either. There's men around town that noticed him, it wasn't hard to see that. Someone might have carried him off. Miners can get pretty horny. And there's some that have different tastes. And, afterwards, somebody might have been afraid the kid would tell about it, and decided to see that he didn't. I'm not saying that's what happened, but it wouldn't surprise me any."

Joshua didn't know what to say. He sat staring into the distance, absorbing the news his uncles had given him.

But, then, something occurred to him. "Speaking of horny miners," he said, "whatever happened to that entertainer Willis had at The Dollar, that Lola Valdez? Is she still around?"

"She was, for a while," Matt said. "Just about the time that Davidson got shot, there was a fire at the Dollar. Wasn't much of a fire, the saloon was still standing when it was put out. As it happened, Willis had some buckets of water close at hand and they got it doused pretty quick. It destroyed the stage though, and according to Willis, Lola had been staying in that little room over it, and that got scorched bad too, so for a time, she stayed with Belle Blessings."

"Whoring?" Joshua asked, surprised.

"There was plenty of men had hopes of that," Matt said, "and there were some stories about incredible sums of money that were offered to persuade her, but so far as I know, nobody ever did. And then, just like that, she wasn't there anymore. Some sort of woman's spat, I reckon. Belle wouldn't talk about her, said, maybe she had gone to Frisco."

"That makes sense," Joshua said. Walt gave him a questioning look. "Well, she was beautiful as all get out, wasn't she? Why would a woman like that want to hang around a place like Alder Gulch, when she could surely do a whole lot better for herself in the big city?"

"Yep. She was a pretty little thing."

It wasn't until later that Joshua realized, Walt had used the very same words to describe Terry Murphy.

By then, stories had begun to reach Alder Gulch from other mining camps scattered through the western mountains—stories of the beautiful dancer, Lola Valdez, the miner's sweetheart. The gold dust queen.

Lola, the rose of the mining camps.

Part IV

The Barbary Coast

Chapter Fourteen

A jangle of sound spilled from the open doors of the Golden Crescent Saloon. Lola tapped her foot impatiently and waited for her companion to pay the cab driver. She ignored the clouds of cigar smoke that wafted out the doors, the stench of too-seldom-washed bodies packed too closely together, the babble of voices. Inside, a soprano warbled off key, glasses clinked, cards were slapped down on table tops.

"Full house," someone gloated loudly, and another said, in an angry voice, "Who shuffled these damn cards, anyway?" A woman squealed, sounding less indignant than titillated.

As with the other saloons up and down the street, the crowd here had overflowed noisily onto the sidewalk outside. It was evident that the Barbary Coast was booming. A drunk lurched against Lola and with a mumbled apology staggered away—a sure candidate, she found herself thinking, to be shanghaied. That, she had heard, was an ever present danger for any male wandering these streets alone—to be cudgeled or drugged, and find himself in the morning on a boat to China as an involuntary member of the ill-used crew. Two years before the mast, and only the hardiest returned to tell the tale.

None of the hurly-burly dampened her excitement. It was like a tonic to her after the years in the mine camps. She'd almost lost track of how long it had been, traveling from one camp to another, entertaining in a string of saloons that in time had become all but indistinguishable, staying at each one until the nightly take had begun to dwindle, as it inevitably did. Never much, but it had only to slacken for a night or two, and she was on her way to richer claims.

Somewhere along the way she had begun to sing as well as dance, her voice a clear, sweet alto. She stood by the ubiquitous piano—it was funny, wasn't it, a mining camp might be without nearly all the amenities of civilization but it was rare there wasn't a saloon with its upright piano, and someone to play it—and warbled *Oh, Susanna*, a favorite of the miners, and *Home Sweet Home*, which never failed to bring many of them to tears and even open sobs. By now, the singing was a regular part of her act, but she could not have said in which town the idea had first occurred to her.

For all that her memory of the individual mining camps might have blurred, however, she hadn't forgotten a single moment of that night when she had killed the Reverend Davidson, nor of her terrified flight to the sanctuary of Belle Blessings' whorehouse.

"You'd best go to Redville," Belle said as soon as she had heard what happened. "Only, not like that. Not as Terry Murphy, I mean."

"Travel as Lola? Isn't that dangerous, a woman traveling alone?"

"I'll send Wonkle with you. He'll see you get there safely."

"And when I do? What'll I do there?" Terry asked.

"Same as you've done here," Belle said, "dance for the miners. There's a man I know there, he has a saloon. I'll send a note with you. Have no fears, he'll be glad to have Lola Valdez dancing for him. That's far enough away, too, no one will have heard what happened to Davidson, or by the time they do, it'll be old news."

Willis had tried to make trouble. He had found them in Lola's dressing room, packing dresses into a couple of bags.

"You get any idea of leaving straight out of your head," Willis said, seeing in a glance what they were up to. "You try that and I'll see you lynched."

"He wouldn't be the only one swinging on that branch," Belle said. "Don't be a bigger fool than you are, Willis. You know damn well the miners would burn this place to the ground and string you up for fooling them the way you have."

Willis looked petulant, but it was obvious that he recognized the wisdom of Belle's words. "What the Sam Hill am I supposed to do, then? They'll burn the place down anyway if Lola ain't there to dance for them tomorrow night."

They were all three of them thoughtful for a moment. "What if I couldn't dance?" Lola said.

"Like, you broke your leg, or something?" Willis said. He actually glanced at her ankles, as if contemplating making the suggestion a reality.

"I was thinking more like, if the stage wasn't available. You said they would burn down the saloon. What if you burned it yourself? Not the whole place, but the stage part of it. Fires happen all the time in these camps. No one would think much of one happening here, and it would take some time to fix it, wouldn't it, even if it was only a little fire? And by then, who would be surprised if Lola had moved on?"

Willis didn't look happy with the way things had developed, but they could see he was considering Lola's suggestion. They left it at that. Really, what alternative did he have? Belle was right, and they all knew it. Terry felt no guilt, either, in leaving. Even in the brief time Lola had danced at the Lucky Dollar, Willis had made more than he could expect to make in a year's time, maybe two. He had no reason to complain.

Lola would have left for Redville that same night, but Belle said it was better if she lingered for a few days.

"Men get shot in these camps all the time. A few weeks, probably people will have forgotten about it. If they're looking for anybody, it'll be Terry Murphy. But if Terry and Lola both disappear at the same time, it might give folks ideas. I think it's best if Terry disappears right off, let them make what they will of that, but it's probably better if Lola was still around, at least for a few days. Sort of separate the two in people's minds, if you get my idea."

"But, sooner or later, Terry's got to reemerge."

"Does he?" Belle gave her a shrewd look. "Nobody in Redville knows Terry Murphy. If nobody ever sees him, ever makes his acquaintance, they won't recognize him, will they, when they see Lola dance?"

"Live as Lola, you mean? Full time?" It was something she had never contemplated.

"That's always been the risk here, hasn't it? If Davidson hadn't had his eye on Terry, he'd never have known who Lola was. I think for a time, anyway, you had best become Lola, and not just when you're dancing."

Which was what she had done. It must be five years now, or the better part of that, and Terry Murphy had scarcely existed in all that time. He had lived as Lola, not just in the flesh but in his mind as well, so fully that Lola almost never thought of that other person she had once been. When she thought now, she thought of herself as Lola, and Terry was like an old acquaintance from the past, someone she had known, but never saw anymore.

"Real beauty is a gift, but it can be a curse, too," Belle had told her years before. "It intimidates women, and even as it draws them, men fear it. Let no one get too close, is best. Lovely and lonely are only one letter different."

Lola had followed her advice. At first, it had been a strain to live full time as Lola. All the time on guard, keeping herself apart from everyone and yet always in fear that someone would discover the deception, realize the truth.

But no one had. Belle had been right; if no one had ever seen Terry Murphy, there was no one for them to compare Lola to. Everywhere she had gone, the men accepted her for who she was, cheered her, paid tribute to her, loved her, in a way no one else ever had. And, in her own way, she loved them back. It mattered to her little if they were only grubby little miners, unwashed and unschooled. They had been good to her.

Certainly they had made her a rich woman, too—rich enough, finally, that she had decided to give them up and try her luck in Frisco.

Jake had settled with the driver. Lola pushed her way inside, Jake following respectfully a step or two behind. The Golden Crescent was brighter inside than out. Gilt-edged mirrors lined the walls and reflected the flickering light of scores of gas lamps. At the far end of the room was a makeshift stage festooned with gold and crimson drapes, and dominating one corner, a splendid mahogany staircase, carpeted in more red, curved upward, to the galleries above.

She made her way through the crowds, eclipsing every woman there and looking hardly less regal than the elegant swells in sables and silks who made up much of the crowd—slumming was a popular pastime for the high hats who lived in the mansions of Rincon Hill and Nob Hill.

In the years since the birth of Lola, she had only grown more beautiful, and she was, without conceit, aware of it. She had always been good with hair and she had mastered the art of using rouleaux and chignons and Japanese bark to imitate the most elaborate styles she saw in the women's magazines. Tonight, her hair was twisted into a fantastic swirl, with one blood red rose in its center, and mere wisps of curls falling at the sides of her face as if some man's eager fingers had loosed them from their proper perch.

She had learned to touch up the inside of her nostrils with pink and use kohl to emphasize her eyes and lashes. Of necessity, she steered clear of the severe décolletage favored by many women today, but she had, through much trial and error, designed a bodice that pulled the flesh of her chest together to create a slight cleavage. It was uncomfortable at first, but she wore it regardless, until she soon got so used to it that she no longer noticed the discomfort. Her necklines were often cut low enough to reveal just an inch, no more, of that, and on the exposed skin she used a blue pencil to sketch ever so faintly the veins that could be seen on real breasts, to further the illusion.

The cheap dresses she had inherited from Lizette in Alder Gulch had long since been replaced by better ones that she made herself. Most of them were in the quasi-Spanish style she had first acquired and she eschewed the brighter colors that loose women throughout the camps favored, because she did not want to advertise herself as a prostitute and, more particularly, because she knew the somber colors better set off her pale coloration, her raven curls and her enormous dark eyes.

Wherever she had traveled she had paid highly for the latest in women's publications and for the best fabrics and accessories to be had, often brought in from the city expressly for her. From town to town, camp to camp, she had badgered and coaxed and shamelessly charmed shopkeepers and peddlers to satisfy her demands.

In the dress she wore now, an iridescent purple so deep that in a dimmer light it would have appeared black, with the black lace stole that had come all the way from Spain and cost her a fortune tossed carelessly about her bare shoulders, she was as stylish as any woman present, and knew it. Several of the men took appreciative note of her as she made her way through, and one or two of the women gave her an envious once over. Lola ignored them all.

The truth was, she hardly saw them. She had gotten used to going without Terry's glasses most of the time, except when there was something she had to read, or especially when she counted her money. In a way, she found she liked the world better seeing it a bit out of focus and indistinct. It seemed to soften many of the rough edges, and she had thought once or twice that a starry sky was far lovelier with the twinkle of lights blurred together.

"They're so cold, when you see them distinctly," she had told herself one night, looking through her spectacles at them, and afterward had been content most of the time to leave the glasses neatly folded atop her dresser.

Lola made her way to an empty table, the crowds parting as if by magic before her unhurried progress. Jake held the chair for her and sat opposite, glancing cautiously around.

He was her bodyguard, had been with her the entire time since Wonkle had handed her over to him in Redville years before. Despite the time they had spent together, often in almost intimate proximity, she knew practically nothing about him, except that he was devoted to Wonkle and to Belle and, since she'd been entrusted to his care, to Lola.

She wondered sometimes if maybe Jake didn't suspect the truth about Lola, or if Wonkle hadn't actually told him the truth when he entrusted Lola to Jake's care. If he had, if Jake knew, he showed no sign of it. He seemed to have no life apart from accompanying her, might not even have existed before the night Wonkle had introduced them, saying to her, "Jake'll see no harm comes to you."

None had, either. Jake was a giant of a man, towering a head or more over most others and so beefy, his beard so enormous and his chest, where his shirt lay open, so thickly covered with black-brown hair, thicker even than Brian's had been, that he might almost have been a grizzly bear dressed up like a man.

She knew from witnessing it that he was fearless, and as quick with a gun as he was with his fists, though in fact he rarely had to use either. His appearance alone was enough to put fear into most men. There'd been no more than a time or two when some man in one or the other of the camps, generally after a bit more whisky than he could safely handle, had become so taken with Lola as to overstep the boundaries she kept firmly established about herself. It took only a look from her, and Jake saw that the would-be suitor quickly learned the error of his ways.

She paid him generously, of course, though it often seemed to her as if that were of no consequence to him, and she couldn't imagine what he spent it on, since he was almost never out of her company.

She even wondered sometimes if he were in love with her himself, but if so, he kept that private as well, and she had long since ceased wondering and just took his protection for granted.

They made for an odd couple, she knew, and you could hardly have said they were friends, but she was at ease and comfortable in his presence in a way she never had been with anyone else, and she was as grateful for that as she was for the sense of safety he provided—maybe more grateful, truth to tell. In many ways, her life since Alder Gulch had been a successful one—but it was a lonely one, as Belle had predicted.

A waiter came to the table, looking Lola up and down appreciatively. He glanced once in Jake's direction, saw Jake's fierce scowl, and lost the smarmy smile with which he'd first approached.

"A glass of wine for me, something French," Lola said. "And a beer for him." She nodded her head in Jake's direction.

The wine came with a dingy glass that she wiped off with a delicate French handkerchief before pouring the wine into it.

Nothing could daunt her spirits, though. She was too delighted to be in the city of the golden gate after that long sojourn in the camps, and she took in the scene around her hungrily. The off-key soprano had given way to a juggler who was struggling to keep a half dozen or so apples moving through the air. From time to time one of the fruits fell into the audience, from whence it was returned violently, to the audience's roaring approval.

"I'd heard the Barbary Coast was a dangerous place," Lola said, to which Jake only grunted, as much conversation as she usually got out of him, but she saw that his eyes continued to rove about the room endlessly, looking for any danger that might arise before it got close enough to threaten his charge.

As if to belie Lola's remark, a fight suddenly erupted at a nearby table where some men had been playing cards. "That's one ace too many, you shifty-eyed bastard," one of them shouted, leaping to his feet and brandishing a gun.

With the swiftness of well-choreographed practice a bevy of waiters converged on the spot, one of them quickly breaking a chair over the head of the man with the gun, the result of which was that a window was shot out when the gun went off anyway, but no one was hurt. The unconscious man was carried to the front door and unceremoniously tossed into the street outside. The passersby stepped over him with hardly any notice.

Jake had tensed up when the incident began, but now he let out his breath and relaxed a bit.

"Looks like they know how to handle things, anyway," Lola said.

"Sounds to me like that was a compliment for the establishment," a man's voice said from behind her chair.

Lola looked over her shoulder at the tall stranger standing there and squinted near-sightedly as she tried to identify him. He was dressed in pristine white trousers and an elegant fawn frock coat with a diamond stickpin in his cravat, and a gold watch fob at his pocket. Obviously a man of means, then, and if not exactly handsome, he was distinguished looking, with red-gold hair and a neatly trimmed moustache to match, and kelly green eyes that twinkled now with a gleam that she recognized all too quickly. If she didn't know the man, she knew that gleam. Over the years, a great many men had looked at Lola Valdez in that same hungry way.

She couldn't quite put her finger on it, but there was something familiar about him, though. Someone she'd run into, maybe, in one of those camps? There had been a lot of men... though, no one, since Joshua, with whom she'd had any kind of involvement.

"Say, don't I know you?" the stranger asked, narrowing his eyes.

"It's funny, I was just thinking the same thing," Lola said. She looked up at him. For a minute, his appearance didn't register. The copper colored hair was like Joshua's, and the green eyes, too, though these were a more vivid green than Joshua's had been and where Joshua's could be hard, this man's twinkled like gemstones. He grinned at her inspection. In her experience, most men smiled—Joshua did—but this man grinned, which was not quite the same thing.

Red hair...green eyes...something stirred in her memory. The neatly trimmed little moustache was different, though. She tried to imagine the face without it.

"Heavens above," she exclaimed suddenly, gasping in surprise. "Why, it's Tom, isn't it? Tom Finnegan!"

"Yes, Finnegan it once was, but I ain't heard that name in many a year, not since I left the Bowery behind, and some coppers looking to throw Tom Finnegan in jail," he said with a laugh. "They call me Tom Fetters now, at your service." He made a little bow from the waist. "But you got the best of me, I don't think..."

Suddenly his eyes went wide and his mouth dropped open. "Why, it can't be...surely it isn't..." he stammered. "Is it little...?"

She lifted a finger to her lips in a quick, silencing gesture. "It's Lola," she said. "Lola Valdez. They call me the rose of the mining camps."

Tom laughed with surprise and delight. "I heard of you, of course, Miss Valdez," he said with a mischievous grin. "Who ain't?

I heard you was a great beauty, too, but that don't begin to do you justice. But, say, then, what brings you to my humble establishment? It's a little off your usual route, ain't it?"

"I'm thinking about branching out a bit, is all," Lola said. "And—oh, wait, you said your establishment. You mean you own this saloon?"

"Don't say that too loud," he said in a mock whisper. "Some of the customers ain't shy about letting their dissatisfaction be known, as you just saw. Okay if I sit down?" He asked this of Jake.

It was Lola who answered him. "Please do. This is Jake. He's my bodyguard."

"Well, I'd say that's a smart idea, for a beautiful creature like yourself, especially here on the Barbary Coast. And I don't imagine too many men make trouble." He grinned in Jake's direction. Jake's lips moved ever so slightly in what might have been a returning smile.

"No. Just the sight of Jake seems to settle most of them down," Lola agreed.

"Can I buy you a round?" Tom asked.

Lola cocked an eyebrow in Jake's direction but he shook his head. He'd barely touched his beer. He rarely did.

"I'm having wine," she said, "Though I confess, it's none too delicious."

He scoffed and signaled for a waiter. "That stuff? It's bilge, but it's good enough for most of the customers. A bottle of champagne," he told the waiter. "My private stock, tell Eddie to get it from the back, and no topping it off, either, if he wants to keep his ass in one piece."

It gave Lola time to study him more closely. It had been so long ago, that brief time together in his little basement room. What a child she had been then—or, Terry had been, at least. Over the years, she hadn't altogether forgotten that boy, no more than that himself at the time, if a more seasoned one than Terry had been, but she had long ago relegated him to one of the attic rooms of her consciousness, sure that she would never see him again.

Certainly he was a boy no longer, but a man, and a very self assured one, it seemed. She remembered his dream of becoming a card sharp and wondered if he had realized it since then. It gave her a momentary start, to remember that her own dream had been to be a dancer, or maybe a singer, and now she was both. Funny, how things worked out sometimes, and not in the way you had expected.

Tom was using the brief conversation with the waiter to recover from his own shock, of seeing Terry Murphy again—only, not Terry Murphy, he reminded himself, Lola. The legendary Lola Valdez. Everyone had heard of her. Miners flowed into the city after their lucky strikes, and to a man, they sang the praises of the beautiful dancer who won the heart, it seemed, of every man who saw her. He could certainly see why, too.

Who would ever have imagined that "the rose of the mining camps" was really that little wide-eyed boy from the Bowery with whom young Tom Finnegan had been so smitten, whom he had desired so intensely, about whom so many of his sexual fantasies had been filled over the intervening years.

And yet, the discovery wasn't nearly as shocking, or as surprising to him, as he supposed it ought to be. There had always been something about Terry, not so much sissyish, as they had accused him then, but inherently feminine, that he fully suspected had appealed not to him alone but to most of those other street hooligans he'd hung about with then, for all their professed disdain for "the little fag."

That young Terry had worn an air of vulnerability that had made Tom want to take him in his arms and comfort him. He'd wanted so often to kiss him, had dreamed of kissing him, in the same way he had dreamed of kissing girls, and yet not the same, either.

Over the years, he'd grown more convinced that Terry had affected those other young toughs in the same way, although they had been unable to admit their desire to themselves, and had expressed it instead in the scorn they had displayed for the benefit of their companions, and themselves.

Since then, Tom had kissed many women, but never a man, had never even desired to kiss another man. He'd had relations with men from time to time, always assuming the passive role, but as for kissing any of them, that was something that, inexplicably, he had felt for Terry alone—and now, here was Terry, both man and woman, it appeared and, despite her veneer of toughness, still radiating that air of vulnerability, that appeal to a man's protective nature.

And, as before, the old urge came over Tom. He wanted to take Terry—or Lola, it didn't matter which—into his arms and kiss her the way he'd dreamed of doing so many times.

He didn't try to do that, though, and not only because of that enormous grizzly of a man sitting at the table with her. He didn't do it for the same reason he hadn't done it all those years ago, when they had been alone together in that dingy basement he'd called home—because he was afraid she might not welcome it. For all that he had grown up over the years since, and despite his many sexual experiences, seeing Terry brought Tom's shyness forth like nothing had since then.

The champagne came. Lola took a decorous sip and smiled approvingly. "Very nice," she said. "Thank you."

"Not at all. You look like a woman as appreciates a good bottle of pop. Quite a change from the last time we met, aint it?"

"It is indeed," Lola agreed with a smile, fleetingly remembering that shabby little room. "But, speaking of changes, you've changed yourself, quite a bit, I'd say. This is a far cry from where you used to live. Back then you didn't have a pot to pee in."

"I've got a gold plated one now," Tom said, laughing, "and plenty of windows to throw it out of."

"How on earth…?"

"I had some luck with cards, if you want to know. Got into a bit of trouble back in the Bowery, though. I was still learning the tricks, and someone caught on to me, tried to put me in the hoosegow, so I had to light out. I worked for a while on a Mississippi riverboat, did very well, but when I heard about the fortunes being made out west, I decided to try my luck.

"I got as far as Frisco, meaning to visit some of the camps, but I needed to make some traveling money first, and I got into a few games. Next thing I knew, I had won this place in a poker game. And, when I saw how much money was to be made running my own tables instead of cheating at someone else's, I just stuck around."

"So this," Lola waved her hand at the saloon around them, "is all luck, is what you're saying."

"In a manner of speaking. Somebody said to me once, it was when I was on that riverboat, that a successful man was one who has the good luck to run into someone stupid at the important times in his life. I thought about that, and I started looking out for the fellows was dumber than me to play cards with, and it was true, I saw soon enough when I found them that they mostly made my luck for me."

Lola laughed. She had never thought Tom was dumb, for all that he might have lacked sophistication. And, looking at him now, she could understand how things had worked so well for him. He was still kind of homely, but in a pleasant way that was unlikely to put other men off, the way a truly handsome face could, and he had a warm, open look about him that made you feel you could trust him. Just the thing, surely, for a good card sharp.

There was an awkward moment of silence. Tom broke it to ask, "You still have that dream of yours? The one you told me about?"

For a moment Lola misunderstood. "Of dancing, you mean?"

"No, that other one, the walled city and all."

"The walled city," Lola said, looking into the distance with a wistful expression. "Yes, from time to time still, now that you ask. Me rushing along the road, going to something, to someone, but I don't know what." She looked directly at Tom then. "But I hadn't even recalled telling you about that. Imagine your remembering it after all this time."

"I reckon I remember pretty much everything," Tom said, the look he gave Lola intense and searching.

Lola looked away from it, around the saloon. "Looks like you're doing well," she said.

"We do plenty well, thank you. I try to run a clean place,

by Barbary Coast standards. We get some of the uptown set. Of course, they get charged twice as much as the regulars do." He hesitated slightly and lowered his eyes. "Then there's my other businesses."

"All of them saloons?" Lola asked, cocking an eyebrow.

His grin was a bit sheepish. "Not all of them, no," he said.

"Let me guess—you're running a bordello."

"Two of them, though I prefer to call them fancy houses. They're a little dressier than most. And one peg house. Same thing, only the girls are boys."

"Does that do well?"

"Matter of fact, it does. Some weeks it's the biggest paying of the lot. Why? Do you...uh, do you know anyone who might be interested? As a customer or—well, I'm always looking for the right entertainers."

"I'll bet," Lola said dryly. "No, that's not my cup of tea. But, now, speaking of entertainers..."

It took him a moment to catch the innuendo. "You mean, the great Lola Valdez is looking for a stage?"

"She might be. The right stage."

"She couldn't do better than the Golden Crescent," Tom said, all excited. "What an idea! Imagine that, the two of us hitched up after all these years. And, what a team we'd make, too. Why, I'll put up posters all over the Coast, uptown, too. The Legendary Lola Valdez dances at the Golden Crescent. We'll have the swells fighting to get inside. Course," he glanced around the saloon, "we'll have to clean things up some, redo the stage, that one ain't good enough, we need something way grander for you, and I'll..."

"Whoa, slow down there," Lola said, laughing. "I haven't said yet I was willing to dance here."

"But you couldn't do better anywhere in Frisco, and...oh, the money, you mean?"

"That's part of it, yes. And I'd want to know what else was included in the deal."

"What else?" For a moment Tom looked blank. "Oh," he

said then. "You mean, was I expecting, well, something more personal? Is that it?" Lola nodded.

Tom grinned. "I don't mind telling you, Lola, I always was hot for you, even back when you was...well, not the same as now. I used to go half crazy, wanting to...oh, you know."

He grew sober. "Hell, I thought you knew then what I wanted, why I was hanging around, following you everywhere the way I was. I thought you turned me down because I wasn't, I don't know, because I was just an ignorant mick, or I just didn't appeal to you, or, hell, I don't know what. I'm not the handsomest guy around, I know that. Never was."

"I never thought you weren't good enough for me, Tom," Lola said. She allowed herself the slightest trace of a smile. "And I wouldn't say you didn't appeal to me in your own way. Truth is, you appealed to me a lot."

His grin came back in force, brighter than the gaslights above. "Well, then," he said. "Unless..." He glanced in Jake's direction. Jake's expression was utterly impassive. He might not even have heard their conversation.

"Oh, there's nothing like that with Jake and me," Lola said, but she grew serious. "I may as well be honest with you, though, there is someone else. Someone I love."

"But, he's not with you?"

Lola sighed. "No. Not in the flesh, at least. But I'd be lying if I said he wasn't always in my head. Anyhow, I'm the same as any other woman in that respect. I want something more than just a wrestling match. I want to be with a man I love."

Tom sat back in his chair with his own sigh. "Well, since he ain't around," he said after a moment, brightening a bit, "what's to say you couldn't settle for a man who loved you?"

"And you're saying that you do?"

He gave her a long solemn look. "I'll be honest with you, too, Lola, I'm not real sure that I know much about this love business. I know I've wanted you since clear back there, in the Bowery. Wanted you something fierce, old Tom Finnegan did. But, love? I ain't completely clear what that is, even, and that's the God's truth." He grinned again, and added, quickly, "I think I might love you, though, if you was willing to give me a chance, let me try it on, so to speak."

"And in the meantime," she said, "I suppose you'd settle for that wrestling match?"

"I'd be lying if I said I didn't truly love a good wrestling match." He gave her a naughty smile. "I've got my own apartment upstairs," he said, with a nod in the direction of the wide curving staircase. "If you'd like to come have a look at it."

Lola hesitated. But when she looked at Tom again, looked into his face, she saw not the predatory look she saw too often in men's eyes, but something tender and hopeful. His eyes seemed to plead with her, urgently. All of a sudden, he looked very like the boy he had been when last they had met. She felt something melt a little bit in her heart.

"Can't hurt to have a look," she said with a coquettish smile.

He looked again in Jake's direction. "Tell me something— does he go everywhere with you?"

"Not everywhere, no," Lola said.

Chapter Fifteen

Tom's apartment, at the head of that curving staircase, was even more elegant than the room downstairs—the floor was covered with an obviously expensive Turkey rug, the walls were rosewood panels hung with dark paintings and more gilt-framed mirrors and gas lights, and gilt framed furniture uphol-stered in horsehair.

When they were actually inside the apartment, though, with Jake sitting on the floor just outside the door, seeming-ly oblivious to what the two of them were about, both Tom and Lola found themselves shy and uncertain about how to proceed.

"And I didn't say I was going to make love to you," Lola said as Tom opened the door and ushered her inside.

"Well, like you said," he said, looking altogether like a little boy told he cannot play on the swing, "it can't hurt to have a look, can it?"

"Oh, well," she said, relenting in the face of his chagrin, "I didn't say I wouldn't, either."

Which brightened him considerably. They paused, several feet apart, looking at one another hesitantly.

"Uh, how exactly do you manage in all that get up?" he asked after an awkward silence.

"Are you saying you've never been with a woman?"

"Well, things are bound to be a little different, ain't they? Anyway, generally, they get out of all that somewhere else. By the time I see them, there's a lot less to rassle with."

Lola glanced down at her finery. "To be honest," she said, "I don't exactly know to manage in all this, either. I've never...well, Lola has never..." She paused.

"Never?" Tom said, gaping disbelievingly.

She shook her head, and smiled. "But I expect we can work it all out."

He looked her up and down. "You know," he said, "Lola is beautiful, and I think one of these days I would like to see if we can figure that out, I expect it would be kind of interesting, but, to tell you the truth—see, I've been carrying around this picture in my head for years, of Terry Murphy. Carrying a torch for him, I guess is how you'd put it. Every since that day in my little basement room, I've wanted...well, if it's all the same to you, I'd kind of like if it was him this first time."

"With Terry?"

Tom nodded. "I'd like that, yes," he said. "If that was okay with you, that is?"

Lola was surprised. She'd gotten used to the fact that men found her beautiful, but so far as she had known, no one had ever been smitten by Terry. Van Arndst's drunken lust hardly counted and even with Brian, all those times, it had always been more a matter of need, his need. As for Joshua...

She frowned at the thought of Joshua. She had a fleeting sense that she was being unfaithful to him, to his memory at least. But Joshua wasn't here, hadn't been anywhere nearby for years. And Tom was right in front of her. And, if you wanted to be honest, Tom had come first, hadn't he? He was the first man she had ever been conscious of wanting. She still did want him, she realized.

"Yes," Terry surprised her by saying out of the blue. "I think I'd like that, too."

There was a washstand against one wall, with a ewer and basin atop it. She went to it and quickly wiped the makeup from her face, and let her hair down, setting the rose aside, and turned back to a waiting Tom.

"Is there somewhere I can get out of all this?" she asked, indicating her costume.

"What's wrong with right here?"

"Here?"

"I want to watch you undress." He actually giggled like a schoolboy, happy, but nervous too.

For a moment, Lola hesitated. She had always undressed in well-guarded privacy. No one, not since Martin Van Arndst, had ever seen her naked.

"Please," Tom said in a soft, coaxing voice.

"Well, what about you?" she asked.

"Me?"

"If you're going to watch, why shouldn't I?"

Tom said, reddening. "I've never…well, women don't usually want to look at man that way, is my experience. When he's naked, I mean. Or even while he's getting that way."

"You may have noticed," Lola said, smiling, "I'm not your typical woman."

Tom hesitated a moment longer and, blushing, he said with a laugh, "Well, shit, what the hell," and began to shed his clothes—and Terry began the transformation from Lola Valdez to Terry Murphy.

It had been a long time since she'd allowed anyone to look upon Terry Murphy. Now, though, it was such a relief, for once not to have to keep up her guard, to be unafraid of being found out. And, she found it oddly exciting to let Tom see her for what she was underneath the makeup and the skirts.

Just as oddly, Terry found it exciting, too. Lola was delighted with Tom's evident desire—but Terry wanted to be loved for himself. Maybe Lola had been all this time, in her own way, loved by all those adoring miners, but that love had been for Lola alone. It was something Terry was still looking for.

As they undressed, they watched one another. Terry was glad he had insisted. He had long dreamed of what young Tom Finnegan might look like in the raw, and he was not disappointed with the more adult Tom Fetters. The body being hastily revealed was every bit as splendid as he had imagined—tall and long-legged, broad of shoulder and narrow of hip.

And, yes, when he slid his drawers down and stepped out of them, both shy and proud all at the same time, he was splendid indeed to behold. Already full erect, he jutted out in front of himself to a considerable distance, long and thick, with a pair of enormous globes hanging beneath, and with a deep thicket of wiry gold. Terry hadn't seen any man aroused like this since Joshua, and he had to admit, Tom was Joshua's match, maybe even his better. Plus, he was getting to see Tom in the altogether, a pleasure that his experiences with Joshua hadn't afforded him. He found that he liked the view.

Tom tossed the last of his garments aside and paused, still red, but smiling too. "Well?" he asked. "Will I do?"

"You'll do," Terry said. "Very nicely." He was down to his own drawers now. He swallowed nervously and caught his thumbs in the waistband and slid them quickly, decisively down, and stepped out of them. For a moment more, they stood naked, just drinking one another in. Incredibly, Tom's erection seemed to stiffen and lengthen even further. It was Terry's turn to redden.

Tom laughed. "Now, that is a sight to see," he said. "I used to love it when you blushed that way. I got me a hard-on every time, had all kinds of the devil trying to keep the other boys from noticing when you'd go by."

"I don't blush so much anymore," Terry said. He stepped backward and lay down upon the bed.

"Maybe we can bring them back, then, them blushes," Tom said, and quickly crossed to the bed and sprawled atop him. He took Terry in his arms and kissed him, gently at first and them more demandingly.

Terry thrilled at the touch of his lips, full lips for a man and incredibly soft, kissing him just the way he had dreamed so often. Unlike in his dreams, though, they did not fade away at the last minute.

It was the first time in his life he had ever been kissed, as Terry, anyway. Joshua had once kissed Lola, but that had been different, and not just because he had been a different person then. There had been something desperate, something angry, in

Joshua's kiss—and something guilty, too, that he had been immediately ashamed of afterward.

Nothing in his experience nor in his imagination had prepared him for how wonderful it felt, to lie in a man's arms like this, a man obviously consumed with desire for him, and to have those lips crushed against his.

It was a long time before their mouths parted. Tom lifted his head just enough to look down into Terry's eyes.

"I never kissed a man," Tom said, and did it again, even better than before.

This time, when they came up for air, Terry asked, "Do you want me to turn over?"

Tom looked briefly puzzled. "Oh," he said, comprehending. "Well, sure, I was sort of thinking of trying out a bit of everything while we're at it. But, I had some other ideas about how to start, to tell the truth."

Terry, who just supposed that most men shared the same taste that Brian had exhibited, said, "Such as?"

"Such as this," Tom said, and rose up and scooted down on the bed, and to Terry's complete astonishment, took hold of Terry's member. He too was stiff—but he had never had anyone take hold of him there and he was so electrified by the touch of Tom's hand that he nearly went off in the instant.

Tom looked up with a surprisingly timid expression, and said, "I never done this either."

"You don't have to," Terry said.

"Well, I know that. Fuck, I didn't say I didn't want to, I just said I never done it. There was never anybody that I cared enough about that I wanted to do it for them—until now. I've had it done some, though," he added quickly, "I reckon I can figure it out, if you was just to be a little patient with me, is all I was trying to say."

"Oh, sure," a bewildered Terry said. "Take your time. I wouldn't know, really. I've never had it done either."

"No?" Again, Tom looked surprised. Terry shook his head. "Well, damn, that's great, isn't it, first time for both of us? And, together. It's like we was saving it all this time for one another. That makes it kind of special, don't it?"

"Tom," Terry said, and hesitated. He wasn't sure exactly what he wanted to say. That he was grateful. More than grateful, that he was deeply touched. That he'd had sexual relations with other men, but nobody before had wanted to satisfy him. That was what was so new to him, so special. Not the prospect of being sucked, though that prospect was far more exciting than he would have expected, considering that he had never even contemplated the possibility before, but the fact of Tom's wanting him that way. But, he couldn't quite find the words to share these feelings with Tom.

At the moment, though, Tom wasn't interested in hearing them. "You know, Terry," he said, "we could just lay here all night and talk. Or we could, well…" He brought his head down, and took Terry tentatively into his mouth, just the head of it. Terry gasped aloud with the intensity of the sensations that alone produced in him. He had never imagined…

"Whew," Tom said, taking it out of his mouth for a minute. "That's like, shit, I don't know, like nothing I ever tried before. Nothing like I even thought it would be, to tell the truth."

"If you don't want to go on," Terry started to say, disappointed, but not altogether surprised, either.

"Don't want to?" Tom glanced up at him and laughed. "Just try and stop me, you little tease." With that, he took it again, this time all the way down, held it there for what seemed an eternity, and slowly eased up on it, his lips sliding up the length of the column, until he held just the head in his mouth again, and paused to suck vigorously on that.

Just like that, Terry came, his legs jerking, his whole body convulsing. He had shot off plenty of loads in his life, but always just using his hand. He would have supposed, if he'd ever considered it, that this would feel much the same, but it wasn't, good lord, no, it wasn't anything like that. The intensity was almost unbearable. He wanted to scream—wasn't altogether sure, afterward, that he hadn't.

Tom kept hold of him and rode the jerking, spewing cock until it was finished, and a minute or so longer. Finally he took his mouth from it, ran his tongue over his lips, and took a deep breath.

"Say, now, that was kind of sudden like, wasn't it?" he asked.

"I'm sorry," Terry said, embarrassed. "I didn't know, well…"

"Sorry?" Tom laughed and scooted up the bed and took him in a fervent embrace, and kissed him long and hard.

"I just, well, I didn't know what I was missing. All those other times, those men…" Terry said when Tom finally relinquished his mouth.

"I'd say you weren't the only one didn't know what he was missing," Tom said, and kissed him again. "Hey," he said, pulling away once more, "I hope that little pistol of yours isn't just a one shot-er. I was only about getting warmed up, you know. Am I going to get some more practice?"

"I think so," Terry said. "I need to get my breath back, first, is all."

"I can be patient," Tom said, hugging him close. "Hell, I waited all this time for you, didn't I? What's a few more minutes?"

"Oh, we don't have to just lie here and wait," Terry said. He reached down between them and took hold of Tom. Now there was a real handful, he thought, and was shocked at himself for thinking it. *Hussy*, he told himself. "I've got an idea how we could occupy ourselves in the meantime."

Even taking Tom inside him, though, which was how they tried it next, Tom lifting Terry's legs atop his shoulders, as if this, at least, he'd had some experience of. Even this was an entirely different business from what it had been with Brian. To his surprise, Terry found himself enjoying it, too—not just the pleasure that he was all too obviously giving Tom, but finding his own real pleasure in it.

At first, he couldn't understand. It was the same act, wasn't it? A man, thrusting inside him—thrusting, in fact, far more deeply inside him than Brian could ever have managed. So why did having Tom do it have him feeling like he had never done it before, like he was soaring upward into a bright golden light, higher and higher…

Until Tom kissed him, and he remembered that he had fantasized about that long ago, when he had been with Brian, of Tom's kissing him while he had him—and then he understood.

"I love you," Tom whispered, so faintly he could barely be heard. "Always have."

That, of course, was the difference. Brian had fucked him. Tom was making love.

Chapter Sixteen

It was the beginning of a new era in Terry's life. Lola was used to the desire she inspired in men, but Terry had never before had the luxury of basking in anyone's adulation, and with each day that passed, he savored it more fully. Always shy, and never wanting anyone to see him naked, he found now that he reveled in displaying himself for Tom's eager enjoyment.

"I don't know why you was shy about that," Tom said, staring unabashedly at him.

"Were shy," Terry corrected him, and far from being offended at being corrected, Tom only looked all the more pleased.

"I swear, Lola," he said, "you'll make a gentleman out of me yet.

"I'm not Lola just now," Terry said. "I'm Terry Murphy."

Tom chuckled. "Shit, it's like being married to two different people," he said.

"We're not married, either," Terry said.

Tom thought for a minute. He sat up on the bed and looked up and down Terry's naked body, and smiled into his face.

"We could be, though," he said. "Well, not us two, but me and Lola Valdez. What's to stop Lola from marrying me?"

"You're talking crazy," Terry said. "If anyone found out…"

"Who's to find out? No, I mean it," he said when Terry started to object further. "Think about it. I'm making lots of money. We don't have to live down here on the coast. We could build ourselves a mansion. Not on Rincon Hill, I reckon that's for the blue bloods, ain't it?"

"Isn't it," Terry said, automatically.

"Isn't it. But Nob Hill, there's lots of new money building up there these days. Plenty of it Barbary Coast money, too, if they do try to pretend otherwise."

"What would we want with a mansion on Nob Hill?" Terry asked.

"Why, we could have our own little love nest, just you and me. I could take care of you, too. I told you a long time ago, back in the Bowery, I wanted to. Hell, I guess I wanted to marry you then, if I never thought about it just that way. But that's what I really wanted, not just fucking around with you. Well, sure, I wanted that too, but more than that, I wanted to take care of you. I'd have moved you in with me right then if you'd been willing, lived with you, shared my life with you. What is that, then, but being married?"

"Two men can't get married," Terry said. "It's against the law, for one thing." He didn't really know that, but he thought it was a safe bet.

"Hell, everything we've been doing is against the law, if you want to tell the truth. We been together now almost six weeks, ain't we? What's any different about our getting married? That's still what I want, too, more now than ever. And you'd never have to work again if you didn't want to."

"I like what I do," Terry said. "In case you hadn't noticed."

"Okay. I like it too, like it a lot, the sight of you up there spinning and prancing, getting all those men excited, and I'm sitting there thinking, dream all you want, boys, but I'm the one's going to be sharing her bed before the night's over," Tom said. "But, that doesn't mean we can't get married. You could go right on dancing, I got no quarrel with that." He grinned broadly. "Fuck. I like the idea. Mister and Missus Tom Finnegan. Damned if that don't sound great. I'll even change my name back."

"Doesn't. And why not Mister and Missus Lola Valdez?"

"Because it don't—doesn't—work that way, is why. But, you could still use your name when you was performing. Were performing?" Terry nodded. "I kind of like the idea of having me a famous wife, too. Take a look, if you don't believe me. I've got a hard-on just thinking about it."

"You've got a hard-on most of the time," Terry said.

"Just when you're around. Anyway, if we were married, I could have them up on Nob Hill. I'll bet we'd be the first two fellows up there to be doing it regular."

"Maybe not," Lola said. "You'd be surprised about some of those society types. I see them in here, I watch their eyes sometimes. They're with women, they're pretending to be the same as everybody else, but their eyes get different when one of the good looking young waiters passes by."

"Shit, don't tell me you've been making eyes at my waiters?"

"No, I haven't looked at any man since you and I got together, not that way. But, they are a good looking bunch, that's for sure."

"Course they are. I handpicked 'em myself. I was thinking about them tickling the women's fancy, but I confess, I never thought about the men. I guess that's cause, except for you, I never really thought about any man that way. Not about their being good looking, I mean. Things happened sometimes, I told you that already, but it wasn't 'cause a guy tickled my fancy, especially, it was just, well, something that happened. I just let it happen, I guess is what I'm saying."

"Anyway," Lola said, "I don't know that I have any particular yen to be up on Nob Hill."

"Well, where then?" Tom asked. "Hell, I'll take you anywhere you want to go. You just say the word, sweetie. You know I'd do anything to make you happy."

"You have, Tom. You do."

Tom kissed him gratefully, but came right back to the subject. "So, then, where?"

"Maybe the mountains." Terry surprised even himself by saying that. It hadn't so much as occurred to him until the words were out of his mouth.

"The mountains?" Tom was surprised too. "I thought you always said you hated the mining camps?"

"I guess I did," Terry said. "The camps, anyway. But, there's something about the mountains, now that I'm gone from them. There's like a song they sing. All that air, that space, and the sky so blue. And the pine trees, they have a scent like nothing else, and the sound of a mountain stream, it's like ghosts chuckling. There's eagles, too, you see them flying against the sun. Have you ever seen an eagle? There's nothing more majestic, I swear it, they look so noble, and so free when they fly. I feel free, then, too. I don't know how to say it, exactly. Bigger, maybe."

"Well, shit, if you like the mountains so much, we'll go to the mountains. We'll get married here, and live out in the woods. I guess I can learn to chop firewood and hunt bears, stuff like that."

Terry looked past Tom for a moment, staring up at the crystal chandelier above their bed, thinking of Tom's proposal.

Married. Just the way he had once thought of him and Brian, but this would be different. More like the way he had always dreamed it would someday be with Joshua...

He frowned then, thinking of Joshua. He had hardly thought of him of late. Joshua and Tom had gotten all mixed up together in his mind across the years. Tom had come first, back when they were just kids and for a long time, it was of Tom that he had dreamed his romantic dreams. Maybe Tom had even primed him for Joshua. They sort of looked alike. There were alike in lots of ways. Sometimes, when he was down there, with Tom in his mouth, and he saw that golden bush, he remembered fleetingly, that spun gold that had so fascinated him with Joshua.

But, there it was: it was Joshua he had fallen in love with. It was Joshua he had vowed to love forever. Nothing could change that. You couldn't just forget a vow, surely, not that kind of vow. So, how could he be in love with Tom? You couldn't love two men that way, could you?

Only, really, what did he know about love? He never had understood it. When he was with Brian, when he was submitting to Brian's desires, he'd thought that was love, a kind of love, anyway, just to be used for someone else's pleasure. And, when he began to perform as Lola, and the miners cheered and shouted and showered him with their tributes, that, too, he'd taken for love—until he'd found himself with Joshua, and that had surpassed all the rest of it. But, was that love?

Or, was love what he shared now with Tom, which was yet again something else? That sweetness, the peace he felt in Tom's arms. It was more than sex, certainly, far more. Tom made him laugh. It didn't seem to him now, looking back, that he'd known how to do that before, or maybe he just hadn't had much to laugh about. He had never laughed with Brian, or with Joshua. But, laughing wasn't love, was it?

Tom made him sing, too. Not that he hadn't sung before, but now, it seemed to come from some place deep inside himself, some place that, even if it was in him, was Tom's place nonetheless. He sang *Drink To Me Only With Thine Eyes* almost every night, because it was Tom's favorite.

He was more beautiful, too, than ever before—or anyway, he felt more beautiful, basking in Tom's adulation.

Was that love? How did one know?

"No, it wouldn't work," he said aloud, giving his head a shake.

"Why not, then?"

Terry looked directly into Tom's face. "Because there's someone else," he said. "I told you, back at the beginning, I can't get him out of my mind."

"Well, where is he, then? I don't see him hanging around," Tom said, half angry.

"That doesn't matter. It doesn't change anything. I promised myself years ago I was married to him. How could I marry somebody else if I'm already married?"

"So, what about me?" Tom asked in an aggrieved voice. "You're saying you don't love me? Not at all?"

Which was a question for which Terry had no answer. He thought he did. He nearly said so, and knew that hearing it would make Tom happier than anything else in the world.

He couldn't get Joshua out of his thoughts, though. He was still there, between them. He rolled over and put a hand down to take hold of Tom's erection. "I love this well enough, if that makes you feel any better," he said, and that much, certainly, was the truth. He scooted down on the bed for it.

Which ended the argument. For the moment, anyway.

It was liberating, to be able to live, at least part time, as Terry again, and especially in such a happy way.

That, however, was only within the walls of their apartment over the Golden Crescent, and almost exclusively for Tom's benefit.

"I can't help it," Tom would say, "I love Lola just fine, too, but it was Terry that I fell head over heels for. I guess he will always be the one for me."

Tom's wizened Chinese servant, Lu Chen, who took care of the apartment and cooked for them, obviously was aware of Terry, but on that score, Tom was fully confident.

"You don't have to worry about him," Tom said. "He won't say anything. Hell, he almost never talks at all except to ask me what I want for supper."

"Dinner," Terry corrected him, and quickly concluded that Tom was right about his servant. Lu Chen was an excellent cook, and he could serve them an entire dinner, splendidly prepared— terrapin soup and roasted pheasant and ices and cakes—and not say more than two words the whole time, although it seemed to Terry that he looked appreciative of the hefty appetite his food obviously aroused in Terry.

"I don't know how you can put away so much and keep your figure the way you do," Tom said, picking at his own food.

"Dancing is hard work," Terry said. "Not to mention all that fooling around with you in bed, that works up an appetite."

"Works mine up," Tom said with a lewd grin, "but it ain't for this stuff."

"Isn't," Terry said, and went back to the pheasant. In the camps, you learned to make do with rancid bacon and eggs fried in old grease and bread turned green with mold. He'd never in his life eaten so splendidly, and he took to it with a vengeance, which only inspired Lu Chen to greater culinary heights.

Apart from Tom himself, however, and the Chinese servant, the only other person who saw Terry was Jake. Clearly, Jake was aware of the change from Lola to Terry, but if the discovery surprised him at all—and Terry wasn't quite sure that it did—he kept that to himself as stolidly as he did everything else. He rarely came into the apartment, and only when invited, but elsewhere, he was still Lola's constant guard.

And, from the moment she stepped out the door of the apartment, always in full regalia, Lola was Lola, and Terry left behind. Because as much as Terry enjoyed his new life, Lola continued to love hers. It seemed to her, in fact, that with Terry no longer a prisoner of her subterfuge but now set free in a sense, and so happy with Tom, that Lola was even more free as well to be herself. She became more utterly Lola Valdez than she had ever been, even when she was off stage, and when she was on it, she seemed to sing and dance with a new fervor.

She was no less a sensation here on the Barbary Coast than she had been in the mining camps. True to his word, Tom had plastered not just the Barbary Coast, but the entire city with posters trumpeting her engagement at the Crescent, and had even taken out an advertisement in *The Bulletin*, the first such newspaper ad for any event on the Coast. Lola Dances, it proclaimed, and by now, everyone knew exactly what those two words meant.

Even without the ads and the posters, though, Lola's success was virtually guaranteed. Her reputation had preceded her, and from the night of her first appearance on Tom's hastily redesigned stage, the audiences had roared their approval of the now legendary entertainer, The Rose of the Mining Camps.

Audiences that were, she found herself thinking, not so much different. There were more women here than in the mining camps, but most of them fell into two categories: the proper socialites who only rarely ventured down to the Barbary Coast and always safely in the company of male companions, and the prostitutes that worked the houses and plied their trade in many of the saloons, though not at the Golden Crescent.

The city's population was disproportionately male and those men were little different from the men she had entertained in the mountains and the woods, if they dressed a bit more grandly. Many of them, indeed, were the same men, who had made their fortunes and left the camps behind for the city by the Golden Gate. Sometimes, with their gold and their coins, they tossed her little notes, saying that they had seen her in Confederateville or Willow Run or one of scores of other camps where Lola had danced.

And while Terry confined himself to the little apartment above the saloon, Lola knew no such restriction. She did not limit herself to the stage or even the Golden Crescent, but went out day and night, sometimes for hours at a time, to explore the city—always with Jake a step or two behind her.

She was quickly known to everyone in the limited world of the Barbary Coast, and in no time she was as beloved there as she had been in the mining camps, maybe even more so.

At first, she had been the source of much speculation. Men, of course, had made tentative advances, quickly warded off by Jake, and the fact that she was soon established as Tom Fetter's woman discouraged the rest. Tom was greatly respected on the coast, and just as greatly feared. It was known that he was a man generous with friends and implacable with enemies, and the two qualities set him apart from the run of the mill Barbary businessman.

Lola was much respected in her own right, however, and the esteem in which she was soon held was its own form of protection. It was already known that Tom ran the cleanest and most honest saloons and bordellos in the neighborhood, and with Lola as his partner, their reputation was enhanced even further.

She visited all of the houses and each of the saloons regularly, to see that standards were maintained, and at each of them, she quickly befriended both the madams and the workers. When anyone took sick, she saw that they got the best medical treatment and were paid while they convalesced.

"That's for our good as well as theirs," she said when Tom had originally questioned the extra expense.

Some of the women in the houses and the entertainers at the saloons had children, and Lola provided for their care, too, and education for the older ones. She established a home for the younger children and though the mothers were required to visit them regularly, Lola saw to it that the children were raised without any Barbary Coast stigma attached to them. Many of them, indeed, grew up ignorant of their mothers' professions.

"It'll be easier on them when they get older," was how she expressed it.

Though she always carried her little Derringer in her bag, and Jake was never more than a few feet away from her, Lola was perhaps the only woman who could walk through the streets of the Barbary Coast without fear. Everyone knew her, and when Tom suggested once, as they were riding in their carriage, that maybe she ought to have more than one bodyguard, she said, "I have scores of them," and indicated with a sweeping gesture the crowds thronging the streets, many of them grinning and waving or shouting "Hello, Lola," as she rode by.

Chapter Seventeen

Joshua was amazed, every time he walked Alder Gulch's main street, at the changes that had been wrought in the years since he had first come here. It seemed like every stroll, he saw a new city. Houses were going up everywhere, the hammering and the sawing seemed never to lessen, and not the crude cabins of the old days, either, but real houses, with false fronts and front porches, the kind of houses people lived in back in the States.

Traffic was hopelessly snarled, too—drays and oxcarts, their wheels squeaking, and elegant buggies careened around one another and sometimes collided in the often muddy street. Horsemen rode, alone or in groups, and sometimes one of them would larrup up his steed and go at a gallop, people dashing out of his way as if blown in a wind, and there was nearly always a parade of foot traffic on the newly constructed wooden sidewalks.

Willis' Lucky Dollar had been replaced by a much bigger and gaudier, though no less raucous, saloon, The Silver Dollar, and though hers was still the most popular and generally considered the safest, Belle Blessings' whorehouse had been supplanted by two others—a sure sign of progress, as Walt liked to say wryly.

There were other businesses, too. The meager supply store that had served the camp in the old days was gone. In its stead was a large general Emporium that would not have looked out of place back east, although the wares were a bit different from what might have been offered in Philadelphia or Chicago.

There was a ladies' milliner, and a stable, where one could rent not only horses, but a buggy or a wagon as well. There was a Baptist church, and of course there was the Simmons bank, considered by many the crowning evidence of their attainment of real civilization.

Mostly, the difference was in the number of people. Some said, perhaps a bit optimistically, ten thousand of them, but even the most pessimistic among them agreed that it was more than five. Not just the miners, either, though a steady trickle of them still arrived weekly, hoping even at this late juncture to make their fortune. Most of them were white, but there was an occasional Indian or a Chinaman, and now and then a Mexican.

The biggest change of all, to Joshua's way of thinking, was the number of women you saw. Not just the prostitutes either, though there were plenty of them, the decent women averting their eyes when the whores drove along the street. There were wives aplenty too, now, and children. Matt's family had arrived not long after Pete's, and both families lived in their own splendid houses just at the edge of town, the biggest, most affluent houses around, which most thought appropriate to the town's richest and most influential citizens.

Joshua was rich, too, in the eyes of many of the town's citizens. Rich enough, anyway, that he didn't have to work fifteen and sixteen hours a day in the gravel, as others still did. Since the first strike, the prospectors had taken more than thirty million dollars in gold out of Alder Gulch, and he'd gotten his share of it and then some. He worked as a collector for his uncle's creditors, for which he had twice been shot at from ambush, but whoever it was who fired at him, they did not linger to take a second shot, and he took that as a sign that they were more afraid of him than he was of them.

His reputation had followed him from Butte, and the fact that he had survived that arduous winter there, to which not a few had succumbed, and singlehandedly killed a pack of desperadoes to boot—that story had gotten enhanced over time and he said nothing to correct it—meant that he was admired by the men as well, who said of him that he was a man with the bark on, which was to say, a tough customer

He'd followed his uncles' advice, too, and invested in different enterprises with them, and mostly those had done well for them, so that his account in their bank grew steadily over time.

Joshua had begun to notice his cousin Luanne, an orphan who had come west with Matt's family. Back east, that might have been considered too close a relationship for marriage, but here, things weren't so rigid. A man didn't have so many prospects to choose from if he was considering marriage, and by this time, Joshua was.

He was already, in fact, past the age when most men considered getting wed, although the idea had never occurred to him until recently, when Pete's wife had made a remark about his "extended bachelorhood." After that, it had seemed to Joshua that people had begun to look at him a little funny, as if they wondered if there might be something peculiar about him. So, he had decided that he would marry, and looking around, Luanne seemed to be the best of the prospects.

Up till now, he had made do with the occasional visit to one or the other of the whorehouses. It seemed to him that he was less troubled by that urge than some men, and for the most part, he was content with solitary pleasures and his memories, but he went from time to time, as much out of a consciousness of a certain male approval among his companions as out of real desire.

He was entirely aware, however, that he was considered "a catch." It remained only for him to "pop the question" when he judged the time ripe. That Luanne would agree to his proposal, he had no doubts. As would, he knew well enough, most of the town's young ladies. You didn't see them on the street, of course, but whenever he went to a party, and there were few to which he wasn't invited by simpering mothers, he saw them there, and there were some among them who were prettier, certainly, or better versed in the art of charming a man. Luanne was plain and quiet to the point of dullness.

Far from deterring him, her passivity suited him just fine. What he wanted in a wife was someone compliant, someone to keep house and cook, and he already knew that she was a good cook.

He gave little thought to the sexual business. He had been content all this time with satisfying himself and those occasional visits to Belle's, and he saw no reason why that should change much when he was married.

He had observed, moreover, that once they got married, the pretty young women like the ones who were so obviously paraded before him for his inspection seemed to change into something else overnight, as if they had just enough energy or spirit to convince a man that he wanted to marry them, and as soon as that was accomplished, they began all too quickly to fade, so that after three or four or, at most, five years, there was hardly a trace to be seen of that charm with which they had tricked a man into thinking he could not live happily without them. So far as he could see in observing those acquaintances of his who had married, and taking notice of those once spirited wives, he thought that, to a woman, they had lost any interest they might have had in the poor fellow they'd snared, other than to bedevil him for this or that or whatever for their houses or their personal use.

Luanne's chief recommendation, in fact, was the one that pleased him most—she adored him. When she looked at him, her eyes brimming with her love for him, he was convinced that she would be content with that, and would require very little of him in return. What he wanted was someone who could put aside her own wishes and concentrate solely on his. That was, after all, what Terry had done, in the long ago past. And it was, it seemed to him, a perfect basis for marriage, if marry one must.

He reached the edge of town. He had his own cabin now, nothing as grand as his uncles' houses, and not far from theirs. Not far, either, from the cabin in which Brian and Terry Murphy had once lived. It had long since been occupied by miners, a changing parade of the pilgrims, as they were known, who took up residence and, when they could, built themselves better houses and left the cabin for the next one.

Joshua passed by it on the way to his own place. Most of the time, he didn't think of Terry, except when he was pleasuring himself. Sometimes, he wasn't sure why, he did that at the rock where he'd first met Terry.

He remembered then, their experiences and, less heartily, the ones with Brian during that winter in Butte. Sometimes he wished there were someone with whom he could repeat them, and a time or two he thought he had spotted a likely looking candidate, but he never did anything to encourage them. Too close to home, he told himself, and when these thoughts got too insistent to be assuaged with just his hand, he would pay a visit to a whorehouse.

He supposed that the girls there would probably be willing to do what Terry had done, but he was afraid to suggest it, afraid they would think he was queer and, once a rumor like that got started about him, it would be all over town in no time. Best to savor it in memory and use his hand.

He let himself in the front door of his cabin. Night was quickly descending, and the interior of the cabin was in deep shadow. He had actually taken his gunbelt off and hung it on its peg by the door, and was halfway across to start a fire in the stove, before he realized that there was someone sitting at the table in the far corner.

"Who's there?" he asked into the gloom, stopping and wondering if he could safely get back to the peg and his belt and holster.

"Whyn't you light a lamp and see," a voice said.

At first, Joshua didn't recognize the voice. It had been a long time since he'd heard it. When he did, he said with a chuckle, "Well, I'll be a son of a bitch."

He did as suggested and struck a match and lighted one of the lamps by the stove, and held it up, to reveal Brian Murphy sitting at his table. Brian had been eating. There were a couple of cans of beans, empty now, in front of him and the tail end of a piece of beef jerky. He held a fork in one hand, and a six shooter in the other, balanced on the table-top, and aimed at Joshua.

Lola Dances

"That doesn't look too friendly," Joshua said, nodding in the direction of the gun.

"Wasn't sure what kind of reception I'd get," Brian said, grinning. But the gun stayed where it was.

"So," Joshua said, not moving from where he stood, too well aware that Brian was a crack shot, "what brings you to Alder Gulch? Hard to imagine you've come just to pay me a visit."

"Maybe. Who's to say I wouldn't? We was friends wasn't we, seems like. Special friends, you might say." Brian's eyes narrowed and his grin faded. "You haven't told folks what kind of friends, I hope."

"Don't be ridiculous," Joshua said. "Why would I tell anybody about that? That was pretty private, seems like to me."

"Just so it's stayed that way," Brian said.

"Is that what brought you? Just to ask me about that?" Joshua asked.

"Plus, I was looking for my brother," Brian said.

"Terry?"

"The only brother I got."

"He's not here."

"I know that much," Brian said. "I been sniffing around, careful like."

"Hasn't been here for years. Left, so I heard, not long after we did."

"Where'd he go?

Joshua hesitated. Over the years, he'd heard often of Lola Valdez, entertaining at this mining camp or the other; but, so far as he could say, Brian didn't know that he knew that Terry and Lola were one and the same, and he thought it best not to tell him that now. Anyway, he didn't feel like he owed Brian any favors.

He shrugged. "Can't really say," he said, "It isn't like he and I were friends, or anything. I've heard he went to Frisco, but I don't know how much truth there is in that."

Brian continued to look at him for a moment. Then, he pushed back his chair and got up. Joshua took a step toward him, but Brian waved him away with the gun.

"I don't need no hugs, if that's what you were thinking of doing," he said. "Nor nothing else, either. It was one thing when we were snowed in that whole winter and letting you talk me into that stuff like you did, but that was a long time ago. Where do you keep your stash?"

Joshua almost laughed—robbed, by the same man twice? But, Brian did not look like he'd take kindly to being laughed at.

"The tin box under the bed," he said. It didn't matter greatly. There wasn't more than a few dollars in the box. He had uncles for bankers, and most of his money went there regularly.

Brian got down on one knee, keeping the gun trained on Joshua while he felt under the bed and found the box. He pulled it out, tucking it under his arm, stood up, and sidled in the direction of the door.

"You leaving? I got time to spare," Joshua said. "If you were inclined to, well, you know. For old time's sake." To his surprise, he felt a stirring in his trousers, remembering their last time together. He wouldn't have thought a man could still get to him like that.

"Nice seeing you again," Brian said. At the door, he paused to look back and said, like an afterthought, "If I was ever to hear that you was telling anybody about that other shit…" He let his words trail off, nodded, and disappeared out the door.

Joshua crossed to the door in three long strides, snatched his gun out of his holster, and stepped outside, in time to hear a clatter of hoof beats quickly vanishing into the darkness.

"Well, that was sure something," he said to himself, laughing. He went back inside, and closed the cabin door and took time to drop the latch, though it was a bit late to be thinking of that.

He thought of Terry. He didn't exactly know where he was at the moment, but someone was bound to know where Lola Valdez was dancing. Belle Blessings probably knew. Although she had never admitted to it, he had always believed she knew more about Terry's disappearance than she let on. No doubt his whereabouts, too.

If he were to tell her that Brian was back, and looking for Terry…but, what the hell, he thought, dismissing the idea. It was none of his affair, was it? Best if he keep his nose out of it.

Chapter Eighteen

It seemed to Tom as if he had the world by the tail these days. His business was booming, the money rolling in faster than he could spend it. He was known and respected throughout the Barbary Coast, and in the wider city as well, as a man who ruled his private world the way a man should, who dispensed favors generously at his own inclination, or withheld them when he chose.

Happily, he had the boy—a man now—of whom he had dreamed for years. Even in his dreams, however, he had never imagined how happy Terry Murphy could make him. When he lay in bed in the afterglow of sex, holding Terry's slim little body in his arms, with the smell of sweat and semen teasing his nose, her lingering perfume the only reminder of Lola, he thought that life was as good as it could get.

As if that weren't enough, though, he had Lola, too. He'd refurnished the apartment for her soon after she had moved in, replacing the horsehair sofas with ones covered in flowered brocades of blue and gold, and midnight blue draperies hanging in velvet swags at the windows. Rosewood tables with tops of marble stood against the walls and on one of them was the present he had given Terry for their first Christmas together, a glass dome containing a bouquet of wax roses, that had been shipped from back east at incredible expense.

"For the rose of the mining camps," he said, when he whipped off the cloth with which it was covered until unveiling time, and the delight on Terry's face when he saw it had been worth every penny that Tom had spent. Lola never left the apartment, either, without pausing first to touch the glass dome, as if for luck.

He could sit happily, fascinated to watch Terry transform himself. Tom, who had lived all his life as a bachelor, delighted in the rows and rows of dresses, petticoats and stoles and high-heel shoes. Most of one wall had been taken over by an elaborate dressing table, its surface covered with tortoise shell combs and brushes backed with gold, china jars, little hand-held mirrors and crystal flagons of perfume.

"Costs more than my champagne," he said, sniffing at one of the stoppers.

"Gets a man drunk faster, too," was Lola's reply.

And, finally, when Lola was satisfied with her art, when Tom came down the grand staircase of The Golden Crescent with Lola on his arm, he knew that he was the envy of every man present. And, as much as he loved Terry, he loved Lola too, in a different way. When she was dolled up, her hair piled high, her petticoats swishing with every step, he forgot the same as she did that Terry Murphy was there under the costume and the makeup. It was, in some mysterious way, as if she had truly become a woman, and when he saw her, when he thought of her, it was as Lola, and not as a dressed up Terry. For him, too, they were two different people, and he loved them both, in different ways.

Certainly Lola was beautiful. He'd never seen a more beautiful woman. Oddly, he didn't think Terry was beautiful, at least not in the same sense. At his persuasion, Terry had started wearing his glasses again when it was just the two of them in the apartment, but their thick lenses only made his enormous dark eyes look all the more owl-like. Where Lola was saucy, Terry remained shy and mostly retiring, and despite the years, his body still had a little boy's gawkiness, which somehow mysteriously vanished when he became Lola.

All of which, in fact, only endeared him all the more to Tom. When he saw Lola, he felt the kind of attraction a man felt for a woman, but he could not look at Terry without feeling the same instincts that Terry had aroused in him all those years ago, a desire to shelter and protect him, to cherish and, as he said often, "squeeze you to death." Which, he was finally convinced, was love, plain and simple.

In his heart, he was convinced that Terry loved him, too, if he hadn't yet faced up to that fact himself. Yes, Lola continued to insist that she loved this other fellow, Joshua Somebody-Or-Other. In Tom's mind, this was just another way in which, when she put on those skirts, she became utterly and completely a woman, and this Joshua fellow was just the one she had decided to cherish as her long lost love, without which he had come to believe no woman considered herself complete.

Which troubled him hardly at all. Terry was with him, wasn't he, and so was Lola, and whoever this Joshua was, he was nothing more than a phantom from her distant past. Why should that bother him? He was sure in time Terry would say to him the words he wanted to hear—"I love you, Tom."

The day would come. He could wait. He could afford to, couldn't he, while his days were filled with Lola and his nights with Terry? What man had ever had it so good?

Lola was waiting for him when he came downstairs. She was seated at the long mahogany bar, sipping a glass of champagne and chatting with a man instantly recognizable as a city slicker from back east. She introduced him to Tom as Homer Fletcher.

"Mister Fletcher," she added, "is with one of the newspapers back east. Which one was it, now?"

"*The Tribune. The New York Tribune*," Fletcher said, smiling to reveal a row of teeth glittering with gold. "I was just telling Miss Valdez, I've come west to write a series of articles for my paper. Folks back there love reading about the wild west."

Tom looked around the saloon, noisy and as dense with smoke as usual on a Saturday night. "The Barbary Coast is wild enough, I guess," he said. "Though it seems to me that you would get a different view if you was," he saw Lola's quick frown and corrected himself at once, "if you were to venture into the mountains."

"Oh, I expect I will, in time," Fletcher said. "But Miss Valdez has told me so much about her sojourns there, I feel as if I've already been. And, anyway, I think my readers would especially enjoy reading about 'the rose of the mining camps.' She's more or less typical of the western woman, I'd say."

"I don't think I'd say Lola was typical," Tom said, and Lola gave a little laugh. Fletcher grinned with them, but he looked a little vague, as if he didn't quite get what had so amused them.

"Well, people don't always want to read the unvarnished truth, they like their imaginations sparked," Fletcher said. "You know, more and more of them are making the journey west, and not just for the gold fields anymore. I traveled here with a real society figure from New York City, one of the Fifth Avenue crowd. Martin Van Arndst."

He could hardly have missed the quick glances Lola and Tom exchanged.

"Do you know him?" he asked, his curiosity piqued.

"You might say we're old friends," Lola said dryly. "What on earth brings him to San Francisco, I wonder?"

Fletcher gave her a confidential wink. "He says it's just a desire to see the wild west but, to tell you the truth—I'm a newspaper reporter, remember—things had gotten a little hot for him. He favors the boys, you know…but, wait, he's a friend of yours, did you say? Maybe I'm talking out of turn."

"It's nothing we didn't already know," Tom said. "And Lola was just having a joke. He's no friend of ours. Go on, what's the rest of it?"

Fletcher looked a little uncertain, but as they both continued to stare at him expectantly, he cleared his throat. "Well, there was a story about someone dying. The rumor is, Van Arndst likes to play a bit rough with them, the boys, that is, and there were whispers about things getting out of hand. Anyway, his family thought he should leave the city for a while, so it's said."

"I thought his usual game was to sail for the continent," Lola said.

Fletcher smiled knowingly. "I heard there were places there where he wasn't exactly welcome, either. Frisco is just as far away, and nobody knows him here. Except for you two, it seems."

For a moment the three of them were silent, contemplating one another and their own thoughts.

Tom signaled for the bartender. "Another bottle of champagne," he said, and to Fletcher, "Well, then, why don't you bring Mister Van Arndst down to the Golden Crescent one night?"

"Why, there's no need to," Fletcher said, looking past him. "There he is now."

Tom and Lola looked. Sure enough, there was Martin Van Arndst just coming in the door with a group of Nob Hill swells. Lola's heart contracted at the sight of him, and for an instant she felt again the old fear that Van Arndst had once roused in Terry Murphy.

Things were different, now, though. This was her domain. Martin Van Arndst had walked into her parlor as unsuspecting as a fly landing on a spider's web. She'd have to think how properly to welcome him.

"I guess I'll go say hello to him," Fletcher said. "Oh, don't worry, I won't repeat our conversation to him." He emptied his champagne glass and, wiping the back of his hand across his mouth, and bobbing his head at both of them, he scurried across the room to the table where Van Arndst and his friends had been seated.

"A bag of gold dust says he's already telling the varmint about us," Lola said.

"Let him," Tom said.

She looked directly at Tom. "Tom, I can't perform tonight. What if he recognizes me?"

"Go on," Tom scoffed. "Your own mother wouldn't recognize you, Lola. Besides, it's been years. Anyway, what if he did? He can't get you arrested here. He's no threat to us."

"The skunk," Lola said, glowering in Van Arndst's direction again. "To think of all the trouble he caused me, and it seems I'm not the only one, and there he sits, sipping champagne and looking like he owns the world."

"You want me to put some rat poison in his food?"

Their eyes met. Despite the fact that Tom was smiling, she could see that he was serious. He'd do just what he said. She had only to nod her head. Van Arndst would be dead before he set foot outside the Golden Crescent.

After a moment, though, Lola smiled. "No. I've got a better idea," she said, sweetly returning the smiles Fletcher and Martin Van Arndst flashed in her direction. "You're acquainted with the Brady brothers, aren't you?"

Tom's eyes widened. "The Bradys? Why, those boys would shanghai their own mother for a dollar," he said. Lola continued to look at him steadily. Tom laughed. "Remind me never to get on your wrong side, my darling," he said. He leaned close to give her cheek a peck.

"Careful of my makeup," she said, and laughed with him. "I've got a show to do. I think tonight I'll sing 'I'm Going to Get You.'" It was one of her bawdier numbers, and popular with the audiences.

Martin Van Arndst was asleep that night in the apartment he had rented on Van Ness, when the door was suddenly and violently thrown open. He sat up in bed, bleary eyed, and stared mouth agape at the two big thugs who burst into the room.

"What…" he started to say, but one of them grabbed trousers from a chair and threw them at Van Arndst.

"Get dressed," he said curtly. "You're going on a trip."

"A trip? What kind of trip?" Van Arndst asked, trembling.

"A sea voyage," the other said, and the two men roared with laughter. "Compliments of an old friend of yours. I'm to tell you your accommo…" he stumbled over the word and tried again, "your accommodations are compliments of Terry Murphy."

Van Arndst dropped his head into his hands and groaned.

Chapter Nineteen

It was the dream again: the crowded road, and everyone hurrying toward a walled city in the distance, and Terry was rushing along with them, practically running, but he didn't know why, or who or what he was running to.

He sat up suddenly in bed, awake in an instant. Beside him, Tom stirred.

"What?" Tom asked in a voice thick with sleep.

"I thought I heard someone try the windows," Terry said.

"They're locked, ain't they?"

"Aren't they. They're supposed to be," Terry said. He slipped out of bed and went to the windows and tested them, but they were all locked securely. He held the curtains aside and looked at the landing outside and the narrow, wooden staircase that ascended the back of the building, but there was nothing to be seen.

He imagined that he smelled a strange, rank scent, and recognized it for what it was—the long ago smell of Brian when he had been assaulting him in the dark, sweat and semen and sour breath, unwashed hair and the wind he sometimes broke, blending together, assailing his nostrils, choking him.

It was nothing, only the assault of memory. It wasn't the first time he had smelled it in his memory. And Brian was far away, still in Butte as far as he knew. Belle would have written him if Brian had returned to Alder Gulch—they still sent notes back and forth from time to time.

The clock on the mantle struck. It was nearly dawn, late even for the Coast. In the distance, male voices hailed one another, and a carriage went by on the street, wheels clattering, the horses' hooves beating a steady rhythm. Everything was ordinary, as it should be.

"Someone walking on my grave, I guess," he said. He took a deep breath and that odd smell was gone, as mysteriously as it had come. He went back to bed. Tom had already drifted back to sleep. Terry lay beside him, staring up at the pattern the moonlight made on the ceiling. He'd had a funny sense, lately, as if someone were trailing him, watching him. Yet, no matter how often he looked around, or how carefully, he saw nothing untoward.

He was inclined to dismiss it as just his imagination—but he could not altogether forget that the last time he'd had that sensation, Reverend Davidson had indeed been stalking him. And look where that had led.

He gave his pillow a good thump and settled on his side, moving up close to Tom. Still asleep, Tom turned toward him and put a protective arm over him. Terry sighed contentedly and snuggled into his embrace. Really, he was so lucky. Tom was a wonderful man, and so good to him. More than once, he had thought of Tom's proposal that they get married. He knew that Tom wanted it still, but he was careful not to badger Terry on that point.

And it wasn't as if he didn't love Tom. He did, in a way he had never dreamed of loving anybody.

Yes, there was Joshua. But Joshua was long gone to him. Chances were they would never meet again. And it would be so easy to make Tom happy. Why didn't he, then?

He had no answer himself for that question. It was like Joshua existed in some sacred, inviolate part of him. He tried often to compare the two men, but even he knew that put Tom at a disadvantage. The distance, as he had said in the past about his dancing, lent enchantment, while Tom was here, in the flesh and blood, with the failings that a man couldn't help having. Safe in his enchanted niche, Joshua was free to be perfect.

Even as he recognized this, though, Terry could not help being enthralled by that mythical perfection. Joshua was a part of his past, the first man who had ever fully awakened the desire that had only stirred vaguely in him before; the first man with whom he had ever done it "that way."

Oddly, though, when he tried to remember, exactly what it had been like when he had done that to Joshua, the memory no longer came. Whatever else Tom had failed to do, his eager loins had managed to drive that clear out of Terry's memory.

Even if Tom was better in that sense, though, even if Tom were better, as he suspected he was, in every possible way, he couldn't just forget the past and what it had been like for him then, the thrill of just seeing Joshua that first time, of loving him. He had tried to dislodge Joshua from that niche where he resided, but so far, he had just refused to budge.

A shadow crossed over the ceiling. Terry's eyes darted again to the windows, but there was nothing there.

It was a long while though, morning just making the windows pearlescent, before he gave up watching them and drifted, finally, to sleep.

It was only a day or two after that night when Lola came in from her show feeling in a strangely apprehensive mood, and with no idea why. Tom was downstairs, keeping an eye on a dozen tables packed with gamblers, one or two of whom, as he told Lola with a wink, were dirty rotten card sharps. "You never know when one of the suckers might catch on, though," he had added. "Best I keep an eye on things for a bit."

Jake, as usual, had seen Lola to her door and left here there to go to his own small room they'd furnished for him right next door.

At the dressing table, she toweled off her makeup, and let her hair down. When she stood, slipping out of her dress and her petticoats, she changed as she did each night now, from Lola back to Terry.

He was naked except for his drawers when he felt a cold draft of air blow through the room, chilling his bare skin.

He looked in the mirror and saw the curtains at one of the windows billow inward—but the window should have been closed. At almost the same moment he became aware of someone standing in the shadows in the far corner.

When he saw that Terry had spotted him, Brian stepped into the lamplight.

"You?" Terry couldn't have been more astonished. "How on earth did you find me?"

Brian laughed, one of those mean little laughs he had sometimes given in the past, a signal that he was about to get violent.

"Now, that wasn't hard to do," he said. "Shit, you're the talk of the town. Them posters all over the place—Lola Valdez, The Miner's Sweetheart. Rose of the Mining Camps. Made me right proud of you, little brother."

Terry looked at him coldly. "You weren't so proud at one time, as I recall," he said.

"Back then? Hell, that was different. I thought for sure you were going to get us both killed. I was trying to protect you, is all. That's all I ever did, wasn't it, look after my kid brother. Shit, I sacrificed my own life, didn't I, trying to take care of you? Hadn't been for you, I'd still be back in the Bowery. I would've been somebody important by now, you can bet on it. Instead of a penniless drifter. Which is how things turned out."

"That's not my fault," Terry said. "You could have stayed in Alder Gulch. I told you, the night you left, I'd take care of you for a change. I was making plenty of money. You could've been somebody there."

"In Alder Gulch? What did I care about that one horse town?"

"You're the one brought me there."

Brian's eyes narrowed and he smiled, but it was not an affectionate smile. "Speaking of all that money you make, I could use me some. I've been down on my luck so long, I forgot what up feels like."

"Is that what you're here for? Money?"

"I ain't got any. And you do. Seems to me like you owe me, little brother."

Terry regarded him steadily for a moment. Looking back, he could see that Brian had been the worst bully of his life. Brian had used and abused him in every way. It was the tenderness of Tom's love that had made him see that clearly.

Still, he supposed that, in a sense, he did owe Brian some thanks. He would almost certainly have gone to prison if Brian hadn't spirited him out of the Bowery when he did, never mind what motivations he might have had of his own. And if Brian hadn't taken him to Alder Gulch, he might never have discovered Lola.

Terry sighed. He went to the bookshelf along one wall, removed some books and brought out from behind them the wooden box in which he kept his ready cash. He brought that to Brian and handed it to him. Brian snatched the money from him greedily.

"That's all?" Brian asked, looking down at the cash in his hand.

"That's plenty," Terry said, bristling.

Brian grunted and shoved the money into his pocket, and glowered at Terry.

"Now I think you'd better go," Terry said.

"Not yet," Brian said. He grinned again, that same nasty grin. "Hell, Terry, this is kind of a reunion like, ain't it? We ain't seen one another in years. Seems to me we ought to be celebrating. Old time's sake, and shit like that."

"Brian, you got what you came for, I think…"

"Not all of it," Brian said.

Terry stiffened. He had forgotten that he was wearing nothing but his drawers. "All you're going to get," he said.

"Now, Terry," Brian said, and took a step toward him, "don't tell me you forgot how it used to be for us, all that fun we used to have together. You used to love me, seemed like. The way I made you happy. I ain't forgot, that's for certain. I ain't forgot how to do it, either. I can still make you happy. You going to try to pretend you wouldn't like some of that while I'm here—for old time's sake, is what I'm saying."

"I'm with someone else, now," Terry said. "Someone who loves me."

"Loves you?" Brian snorted disdainfully. "That tinhorn gambler? You can forget about him, now, Terry. I'm your man. I always was. We've got the same blood in us, seems to me that makes us special. You was mine long before you was his," he said, and after a pause, he added, in a cold voice, "and you'll be mine when he's dead."

"What do you mean?" Terry asked, alarmed.

"Just that," Brian said. He slipped a Bowie knife from the holster on his hip. "What time does he come upstairs, that boyfriend of yours? I think I'll prepare a little welcome for him."

Terry stared at him, his mind awhirl. He knew only too well how dangerous Brian could be. Not that Tom was any pantywaist, he wasn't—but, coming in the door, unsuspecting, Brian waiting for him with a knife, to take him by surprise—Tom could be dead before he knew what was happening.

"Brian," he said, forcing himself to speak reasonably, "what if I were to give you some more money, lots more? Would you leave then, and not come back?"

Brian's eyes narrowed. "How much more? Where is it?"

"I'll get it," Terry said. "Then I want you to go. Is that agreed?"

"Let's see the money," Brian said, ignoring the question.

Terry went to his dresser, pulled the drawer open. His little Derringer lay atop a pile of neatly folded stockings. He reached for it, got it in his hand, brought it out—but Brian was there in an instant, his fingers clamping about Terry's.

"Planning on plugging me, was you, like you did that damn fool Reverend Davidson?" Brian said. "Oh, yeah, I heard about that. Only, I ain't Reverend Davidson."

Terry struggled to get his hand free, to get the gun between them, but Brian was stronger. The gun went off, the bullet breaking one of the globes of the chandelier above them.

Brian wrenched the gun from Terry's hand. It clattered to the floor. "You little nancy," he hissed angrily, "Ain't you learned nothing yet? Looks like I've got to start your lessons all over again, brother." He spat the last word out on a note of loathing.

Terry struggled in his arms, but Brian was as strong as he had ever been, maybe stronger, and although the years had toughened him up somewhat, Terry was no match for him. Brian bent him backwards, pinning Terry's arms to his sides.

"Let me go, damn you," Terry cried aloud.

"Not till I've had what I want," Brian said with a chuckle. "What I been wanting since I had it the last time. I have to admit, that's one thing you were good for."

All of a sudden, Brian was gone. Terry had closed his eyes when Brian's lips touched his, not wanting even to be conscious of what was happening. Now, he blinked them open.

What he saw was Jake and Brian, wrapped in one another's arms, staggering about the room as if they were engaged in an energetic two-step. They bumped into a table, sent it crashing to the floor, and finally tripping over a big, tasseled hassock, they fell to the floor, Jake on top. He got his hands on Brian's throat, and began to choke him.

Suddenly Jake grunted, half rose up on his knees, and looked down at himself. Blood was gushing from a knife wound in his belly. Brian struggled to get out from under him, but the next moment, Jake had grabbed him again by the throat. Brian's eyes seemed to bug from his head, his mouth fell open, his tongue hanging out. He swung the Bowie knife wide but ineffectually, and it slipped from his fingers.

Brian gagged and grunted, but his struggles quickly began to weaken. Finally, the hands with which he had been clawing at Jake's fingers dropped to the floor. There was a rattle in his throat and his eyes rolled back in his head. He went limp.

Jake continued to squeeze his throat for a moment more, panting with his exertion. Finally, he let go and rolled off of him, on his back on the floor. When he did, Terry saw that he was covered with the blood that continued to flow from the wound in his belly.

"Jake, Jake," Terry cried and ran to him, falling on his knees beside him.

Jake looked up at him, his eyes already clouding over. "The bastard's dead," he said, "He won't bother you again."

"Oh, Jake, hang on," Terry said, "Let me get someone…"

"Too late for that," Jake whispered.

"It…it can't be. Lord, tell me what to do."

"I'd like it a lot if you was to…" Jake tried to say, but the words wouldn't come. His eyes closed.

"Terry," Tom shouted, rushing through the open door behind them, "I heard a gunshot. What…?"

Terry sobbed. He thought he knew, though, what Jake had tried to say. He leaned down and placed his lips on Jake's, and tasted blood.

When he lifted his head, Jake smiled up at him ever so faintly—and died.

Chapter Twenty

It seemed to Terry as if Brian's death had closed a door on his past. The Bowery was far behind him, he would never see that again. Van Arndst was gone. A profligate and a drunk, it was unlikely he would survive his two years before the mast.

Now Brian was gone too, spirited out of the Golden Crescent by a pair of Tom's cronies and left in an alley. Dead men weren't uncommon in the Barbary Coast. There was nothing on him to identify him, nothing to connect him with Terry or the Crescent. He was just another anonymous fool who had fallen victim to the dangerous streets of the Coast.

Terry mourned for him. He was his brother, and as children they had been close. But Terry thought that Brian, the one he had loved, the one who had sometimes seemed to live so that he could care for his younger brother, had died long ago. He wondered what or who had killed him, and worried that perhaps it had been he. But what could he have done differently from what he had? It seemed as if Life had come at him with all its winds blowing and he had only just managed to weather the storms the best he could. Was anyone ever really prepared for life, he wondered, did anyone really know what to expect of it, so that they could manage it efficiently and not be tossed about by it, as he had been?

He mourned Jake far more than Brian, truth to tell. They held a full-scale funeral service for Jake, saying only that he had died in an altercation. Even Terry and Tom were astonished at the turnout of mourners. It hardly seemed as if they would have known Jake, but everyone knew he had been Lola's faithful body-guard, and that had been enough, apparently, to earn the respect of the denizens of the Barbary Coast.

All that was left now of those olden days was Belle—and, of course, Joshua, but, really, both of them were nothing more than distant memories. Lola had exchanged occasional notes with Belle over the years, but hadn't written or heard from her since she had settled in with Tom, more than a year ago now. As for Joshua, well, she had long ago accepted that she would never see Joshua again. And, all in all, she thought that was probably just as well. She had a good life now, with Tom. Why trouble it with ghosts from a past that was dead and gone?

The last thing that Terry or Lola, either one, could possibly have expected was that Belle and Joshua both would reach out from that distant past to touch them now.

The note came first, from Belle: "I thought you might want to know that Joshua Simmons left this morning for San Francisco. He plans to stay, I'm told, at the Morgan Hotel on Pacific Street." Here, Belle had written something and then scribbled it out. "There's more as I could tell you, but I think it's best if you hear it from his lips, if you're interested."

Lola looked at the date on the letter. With the erratic mail delivery between the camps and the city, it had taken nearly two weeks for the letter to reach her. Which meant Josh was almost certainly already here, within the city, no more than a mile or two away from where she stood.

She read the note again. That cryptic final line puzzled her. "...It's best if you hear it from his lips..."

Which meant, certainly, that Joshua had something to tell her. Could Belle have been hinting that Josh was coming for her? Was that what Belle had hinted at, that he had come to real-ize that he loved her, and wanted to tell her so? Or loved Terry, maybe; it didn't matter which, did it? He had dreamed of such a possibility for so long—what if now it were true? A part of him had devoutly wished for many years that it might be so.

Only…did he still, really? What about Tom? The life they shared was so perfect in so many ways. What did those memories from the past mean, in comparison to that?

As if summoned by that thought, Tom startled him from his reverie, coming unheard into the apartment. "You look as if your best friend died," he said.

She looked at him, at this gentle man who had given her such happiness. At one time, she'd thought him homely, but somehow, over time, he had become handsome to her. How could she tell him…?

Tom came quickly across to where she stood and took her in his arms. "Lola, honey, what is it?" He asked, concern written across his face.

"It's Josh," she managed to say in a hoarse whisper. "He's here. In Frisco."

For a moment he didn't understand. "Josh? Josh who?" he asked, confused. Then something clicked in his mind. His expression went somber. "Oh. He's the one, ain't he?"

"Isn't he," she corrected him automatically.

He let her go, turned his back on her and went to the sideboard and poured himself a big glass of whisky. He rarely drank anything but the occasional glass of champagne because, as he said often, in his business, a man wanted his wits about him. Now, he downed the glass in one quick draft, and poured another.

"So, he's finally showed up, has he? Here in Frisco. What are you going to do?" he asked, still without turning.

"I…" Lola sighed wearily. She hated saying it, but it had to be said. "I have to see him, Tom. That's all there is to it. I have to. You'll have to understand that."

"I never have told you what you could or could not do, Lola," Tom said, with no more than a touch of bitterness in his voice.

"I know that," she said, feeling more miserable than she could ever remember feeling. How could she feel so desolated, when at last, over all these years, she was going to see Joshua again? Her first love. That ought to have been an occasion for great joy, for celebration.

Whatever she felt now, though, and she wasn't sure she could properly define it, it was certainly not joy. She was certain of only one thing: she had to see Joshua. Maybe then, her feelings would sort themselves out. If she didn't go, she'd be haunted forever, wouldn't she?

After much debating with herself, she went as Lola, rather than Terry—in large part because no one outside of their apartment had ever laid eyes on Terry, and she thought it best to keep things that way. And, surely, Josh would remember. He had told her she was the most beautiful woman he had ever seen, hadn't he? Lola had always cherished those words.

She pondered long, though, over what to wear. Not the Spanish dresses she favored for her shows. Something, she thought, more girlish, gayer. She settled on a green plaid taffeta dress she had not worn before, with a skirt shorter than was the style, so that as she walked or when she sat down and crossed her legs, it showed glimpses of the green and black stockings she wore under it. She carried a green parasol and a little hat topped with feathers, and wore too much rather than too little of tuberose perfume, though she had underdone her makeup. Still, even as she was preparing to leave the apartment, she scowled indecisively at herself in the mirror by the door. It seemed there was something left undone—but what, she had no inkling.

Tom did not see her out. He was at play at one of the gambling tables, something he rarely did himself. His back was to the stairs and if he saw her come down them he did not show it.

She hesitated at the foot of the stairs, thinking she should say something to him. What could she say, though, when she was on her way to meet with another man? There was a trio of fiddlers on the stage, sawing energetically, and the music seemed to carry her forward, as if she had no will of her own but was merely being swept along by some force of destiny. Which she fancied might well be true.

In the end, she left without speaking to Tom. He watched her in one of the mirrors as she vanished out the door.

"That was a dumb play, now," one of the gentlemen at the table said, bringing his attention back to the moment.

"Couldn't agree with you more," Tom said, reaching for a card.

The Morgan Hotel, taking up most of a full block on Pacific Street, was the city's newest hotel and the first one to cater to the new money pouring into San Francisco. An endless parade of stylishly dressed people descended from the carriages and broughams and hackneys that lined the curved driveway beneath the porte-cochere, and trailed down the street.

Partly to give herself time to calm her nerves, Lola had walked. She remembered, as she strolled, the day back in the Bowery when Terry had walked up Broadway for his meeting with Martin Van Arndst, the meeting that had set so many things in motion. That had been a cool autumn day as well, and he had sensed some strange force guiding his steps then, too. He felt the same, now, as though, finally, he were coming face to face with that future that had always lain before him, teasing him on, never making itself seen as more than a shadow. He had a conviction that, at last, he would know where everything led.

The Morgan's lobby was somberly elegant, with dark walls and marble columns and big wide stairs carpeted in green that led to the upper stories.

Lola paused inside the door, ignoring the glance of a concierge, and looked around, not quite sure what she should do. The lobby was just as busy and crowded as outside. Impatient women waited while elegantly garbed men stood in line at the carved oak desk to check in or out, and heavily breathing porters dashed up and down the staircase with enormous trunks on their back or countless bags precariously clutched under their arms.

Lola Valdez was known throughout San Francisco, and probably here as well—but, she reminded herself, she was known as a saloon performer. She remembered that Joshua had been raised a gentleman, notwithstanding the circumstances under which they had met. Would it embarrass him if she asked at the desk for him? Or, should she write him a note and pay one of those boys hovering near the desk to deliver it to him?

In the next moment, the question was solved for her. She glanced at the stairs and there, coming quickly down them and neatly sidestepping the hurrying porters, was Joshua himself, dressed as splendidly as any man in the place, and looking not at all like the rugged frontiersman she remembered.

He looked in her direction, but no more than the sort of passing glance most men gave a pretty woman. He stopped at a table lined with the daily newspapers and picked one of them up to scan the headlines.

Lola walked up to him and paused just behind him. "Joshua?" she said, suddenly very shy.

He turned and looked at her. For a moment his expression was puzzled. Then, suddenly, his eyes flew open.

"Terry?" he said.

"Lola," she quickly corrected him. "Lola Valdez. We met some years ago, if you remember."

He looked her up and down, his mouth hanging open. "Jesus," he said, "You're even more beautiful than I remembered. But, how in the name of Sam Hill did you find me here?"

She smiled. "A little birdie told me you were coming to town," she said.

"Belle Blessings," he said. "I chatted with her just before I left. I sort of hoped...she didn't say..." His words trailed off and he could only stare at her, speechless.

Lola smiled and nodded. "And, here we are," she said.

"Yes, we are." There was something apprehensive about the way his eyes quickly swept over the lobby. He looked at her again, like he was weighing something, and then seemed suddenly to come to a decision. "Here, come with me," he said. He took firm hold of her arm and piloted her quickly to the wide stairs leading up.

"Where," she started to ask, but he put a finger to his lips.

"Wait till we're inside," he said.

His answer, the speed and, yes, the furtiveness, brought back her sense of embarrassment. She had hoped that the fact that she was now famous and admired would have impressed him a bit, but if anything he seemed uncomfortable about being seen in public with her and eager to spirit her away to someplace more private.

"Inside" turned out to mean inside the sitting room of what was obviously the hotel's grandest suite. The door had barely closed behind them before Joshua seized her in his arms and kissed her frantically.

"Shit, you can't know how glad I am to see you," he said. He took a step back to look more carefully at her. It had been so long since he had seen Terry, and if he hadn't known, he would not in a million years have guessed that the woman standing before him was really a man.

His thoughts were all awhirl. He had remembered Terry not with any particular affection but for the pleasure Terry had given him, and not just sexually. He had not found anyone since who had so completely idolized him, who had made him feel so fully desirable, so utterly a man. Seeing Lola now, though, roused all kinds of feelings in him that he had never been aware of. He felt a warmth of longing that he had never felt for anyone—but, how could that be, knowing what he knew?

"I wanted to see you," Lola said, looking steadily at him now, as if she had never seen him—and, indeed, for all that she had recognized him in an instant, he nevertheless seemed to her like a stranger, someone she had never seen before. She had difficulty fitting the image of the man before her and the image of the one she remembered over one another. It seemed as if something didn't belong, but she didn't know what.

If anything, the years had only added to his appeal. His hair was still red-blonde, a bit yellower than Tom's, and his skin had leathered with the outdoors life, adding the faintest lines around the corners of his mouth and his eyes. But, really, physically, he had hardly changed at all. He was still the best looking man she had ever seen. Something was different, though.

For a moment, they regarded one another, as if each expected from the other the answer to some question that had not been spoken.

"Well, you can see for yourself, how glad I am you're here," Josh said with a laugh that sounded less confident than he had intended. He took Lola's hand and put it on the front of his trousers, where a big erection was already straining mightily against the fabric.

To his surprise, Lola took her hand away, quickly, as if it had been burned. She was suddenly disconcerted by the intensity of his desire, as much by what she saw in his eyes as by that crude gesture with his erection. But that was what she had remembered all these years with such longing, wasn't it, at least in part? So why should she now find it so distasteful, that he should make his interests so blatant? Tom had more than once done the same thing, if not so crudely, and she had never resented it from him.

He gave her an astonished look. "You want it, don't you? Isn't that what you're here for?"

"Yes, I suppose I must have had that in mind," she said, as much to herself as to him, but she made no move to put her hand back where he had placed it. She took a step back, instead, and smiled hesitantly up into Joshua's face.

"Well, then?" Joshua asked. He looked at her with a kind of hostile suspicion. He felt as if the boy he remembered held some sort of mortgage over him, as if Terry were now demanding payment for some long overdue debt, when surely, it was Terry who owed him. "Time's a-flying, isn't it, while we stand here and jaw." He made a crude gesture in the direction of the undiminished swelling in his trousers, as if getting that done would settle everything.

"But I was hoping for more than that, to be honest."

"What more could you be thinking of?" he asked, and the angry edge to his voice had become unmistakable. "That's what we did before, isn't it? That's what you told me then you wanted, all you wanted, to do that for me."

"Yes, of course it was. But, I told you I loved you, too. Don't you remember my telling you that?"

"And I told you, I didn't love you back. I didn't then and I don't now. I can't," Joshua said, making a chopping motion with one hand, as if to sever some inconvenient chain that had grown between them. "I'm not queer, Terry. I thought you understood that. What we did, I never did that with anyone else." When he said that, it didn't even seem to him as if it were a lie. And, really, in a way, he hadn't really ever done anything with Brian. If you looked at it the right way, it had been Terry all the time. Brian had just been a convenient substitute. "I only let you, well—you were awfully eager, then, as I recall. So why don't you want it now?"

She sighed. "I guess I do. But that doesn't mean…well, I was thinking…now that we're both gone from Alder Gulch, and we don't have to worry about what anyone thinks…what if we could share something more than that, something more, more significant, I guess is what I'm trying to say."

"I don't know what that could be, Terry. More significant? Like, what?"

Lola took a deep breath. "Well, like, what if you and I were to, say, live together." *Like Tom and I*, she nearly said, but caught herself in time. "Something like that. A couple, say. Partners."

Joshua laughed and shook his head. "Shit, are you crazy, Terry? For starters, I haven't left Alder Gulch, except temporarily. I'm going back."

"I could go too, then," Lola said, but even as she said it, she knew that the conversation had gone too far in the wrong direction, had turned into something quite different from what she had imagined in her head over and over through the years since they had last met.

"So we could live together? Were you really serious? What do you suppose people would think, me living with someone like you? You don't think they would guess what we're up to? Two men, one of them a sissy, what kind of foolishness is that?" He snorted his disdain.

"It wouldn't have to be two men, so far as anyone would know. I could live as Lola. I have, for many years."

"Besides, I thought you knew, since you knew I was here, I just figured you knew the rest of it. I already have a wife. That's why I'm here, I'm on a honeymoon."

Lola stared at him, so surprised out of her thoughts by what he had just said that she could scarcely grasp its significance. "What do you mean, a wife? Where is she?"

"She's out doing some shopping. And, what I mean is, I'm a married man, Terry. That's what men do, they get themselves a wife, and they live together and make babies. That's what real men do."

Real men? Hadn't Brian, too, taunted him with those same words? Though it was still Lola standing in the room with Joshua, it was Terry who said, coldly, "Most of them don't bring another man up to their hotel rooms and get all excited like that." He gestured at the erection still tenting Joshua's trousers "Real men, I mean. While they are on their honeymoons."

"What are you saying?" Joshua asked, and his anger suddenly turned his handsome face ugly. It might have been a stranger that Lola was watching. "Are you saying you think I'm queer, just because I offered what we both know you want?"

"I'm saying, having a wife out shopping didn't seem to discourage your interest any."

Joshua laughed and his face relaxed into something more akin to its usual good looks. He took a step or two around the room, swaggering, almost, and seemed to be thinking things over.

"Well, look," he said finally, "it's not like I'm saying suck me off and goodbye. I'll be here for a month, maybe longer. We'll find ways to get together, maybe every day, even. If that'll make you happy, I'm willing. I can fuck you, too, if you like it that way. Shit, just because I don't love you, the way you want, doesn't mean I don't care about you. I always did. I'd like to make you happy, the way I did before. Luanne, that's my wife, she isn't all that enthusiastic about sex anyway. It would be handy for me to have someone else to take care of business for me. As far as that goes, maybe you *should* come back to the Gulch like you said. Not so we could live together, but we could do it all the time, on the sly. I'd like that, if you want to know the truth. It would kind of make it more exciting for me, to tell the truth, having a wife and a mistress, sort of, on the side."

"And what would I get out of that?" Lola asked. "Living by myself, in Alder Gulch, nothing to look forward to but a married man slipping away from his wife when he could?"

"I told you, it could be every day, just about. She doesn't care what I do. And you'd get yourself what you like so much, some good cock, a steady supply of it. That's all I got to give you, but it seems to me that ought to be enough to keep you happy. What more could you want?"

For a long moment they stood, looking at one another in the afternoon sunlight that poured through the window. *Just like Brian*, Lola found herself thinking out of the blue. Really, he was no different. It was all about him. That's all it had ever been. They had neither of them cared the slightest bit about her, or Terry either. Why had it taken her so long to realize it?

"You're not Joshua," she said.

He gave her a baffled look. "What do you mean?" His eyes narrowed. "Maybe you *are* crazy. Of course I'm Joshua, Joshua Simmons."

"Oh, Joshua Simmons, yes," she said. "Of course you are. I meant, you aren't my Joshua. The one I've carried around with me all these years."

"Well, then, what's so different about your Joshua, Terry? The one you've been carrying around?" He asked, looking genuinely baffled. "I haven't changed. That hasn't changed." He gestured down at the somewhat diminished swelling in his trousers. "I'm just the same as I always was."

"You know," Lola said finally, "I think you're absolutely right about that." She started for the door. "And for your information, it isn't Terry. It's Lola."

"Where are you going?" Joshua asked.

"Home," Lola said.

"Well, now, wait, damn it," and the tone of his voice was suddenly different, less belligerent, more worried, "if it means so hell fire much to you, I'll say it, then."

For a moment she actually didn't understand what he meant. "Say what?" she asked.

"I love you. There, does *that* make you happy? Now will you come back here and…?"

Lola paused at the door and looked back at him. "No."

"No? You mean you won't?"

"No. I mean you don't love me, Josh."

He gave an exasperated sigh. "Jesus, first you…I do, damn it. It was just hard for me to face up to, but I know it now, I…" He stopped as if he had just heard what she said. "Why would you say that? That I don't love you, when I just told you I do."

She smiled at him, but sadly. "I think maybe you hate me, really."

"Damnation, what more do you want?" He asked again, and he had a strange, almost desolate look on his face, as if any minute he might start to cry like a child. If she had been a vengeful person, it might have given her some satisfaction, but as it was, it only saddened her.

He looked away from her, around the room, as if seeing it for the first time—the flowered muslin of the curtains, flowers on the wallpaper, in the rugs. Flowers everywhere. Why did it feel so wintry, then? All at once he felt such despair that he thought surely this what was a man must feel when the doctor tells him it's all over.

"Oh, hell, okay," he said with a sigh, "I'll get you a house in the Gulch, I've got lots of money. I won't leave Luanne, I've got my reputation to think of, but when we're together, you can play at being my wife all you want, if that suits your fancy. You can wear your dresses—whatever you like. Look, I'm saying, I want you. I want you for mine. Mine alone. You're crazy, saying I hate you. You tell me how to make you happy and, if I can do it, I will. That's love, isn't it?"

Lola gave her head a shake. "You can't, Josh," she said. "You can't make me happy. You can't even make yourself happy. I just realized that. A little late, but I'm glad now I came, I'm glad we had this talk. It's made a lot of things clear to me that had me all muddled before."

"Maybe," he said, his wheedling tone changed in an instant to a spiteful one, "maybe it's you that hates me." Which seemed to him all at once the most reasonable explanation for her behavior. He had long ago observed that even the sweetest-natured woman could turn vengeful and cruel when her pride was bruised. Maybe, he thought, Terry was more a woman than he had realized.

"No, not you," she said. "Not even myself, really."

"Well, then, you're just saying this shit because you're angry."

"Not even that. I think I'm more ashamed than anything."

He breathed a sigh of relief, as if this at least was something he could grasp. "Oh, well," he said, grinning, "as long as nobody knows about it, I guess it's nothing to be ashamed of, dressing like a woman. You make a pretty one, that's for sure. I always did say that."

To his great surprise, she laughed aloud. "Goodbye, Josh," she said. "I think after all I may go back to the mountains, I talked about that not so long ago with someone. It just won't be with you, is all."

"Goddamn it, what am I supposed to do, then?" he asked, angry all over again.

"Go back to the Gulch. With your wife. Be a model citizen. Make people envy you. They will, of course they will. We're the only two who will ever pity you."

"Shit fire, dammit! You said you were in love, didn't you?"

"I was. I am. I just got things mixed up." But, really, it was Terry who said that and for once, for the first time in her life, Lola thought that she had made a fool of herself.

"Listen," Joshua started to say, but Lola didn't hear whatever it was he wanted to say. She went out quickly, closing the door firmly after herself, and all but ran down the hall, as if Joshua might come after her and try to force her back.

As she came down the stairs, she saw a woman coming up, her hands filled with packages. Some instinct told Lola that this was Joshua's wife. Luanne, wasn't that what he'd said her name was? She was plain, dowdy almost. In the past, Lola might have felt jealousy toward her but, now, oddly, she found herself thinking instead that in a minute or two, she would be on the street outside, and Luanne would be in that hotel room with Joshua. With a husband who assuredly didn't love her, who could never be for her what a real husband should be.

As they passed, Lola staring, the woman gave her a puzzled look, as if she thought she ought to know her, but Lola only smiled and nodded, and hurried on down the stairs.

She reached the lobby and then the sidewalk outside, walking fast down Pacific Street, driven now by an urgency to get to where she was going.

Suddenly, she found himself thinking of her dream, that dream she'd had all those years, of hurrying toward that walled city, toward something, someone, waiting for her, hidden within. It almost seemed as if she could see the city now even in the bright sunlight of San Francisco, see the ancient walls and the gate standing open.

Only, all at once, she knew who was waiting for her within that secret place, behind those concealing walls. Tears filled her eyes till she could hardly see. She began to run. Passersby stared at her, this beautiful woman racing down the sidewalk as if someone were after her, but she only ignored them and continued to run.

About the Author

Victor J. Banis is the critically acclaimed author ("The master's touch in storytelling" — Publisher's Weekly) of more than 200 published books and numerous shorter pieces. A native of Ohio and longtime Californian, he lives and writes now in West Virginia's beautful Blue Ridge.